Praise for *We All Begin As Strangers*

'A dazzling debut . . . Beautifully plotted, fantastically written and compellingly strange' *Daily Mail*

'Cummings is a brave, new talent. The world her characters inhabit is recognisable: it's a world where the most terrifying thing anyone can do is tell the truth about who they really are'
Sarah May, author of *The Internationals*

'A great summer read . . . Suspense, plot twists and drama makes this an exciting read to the very end' *The Pool*

'A thought-provoking mystery' *Amazon reviewer*

'Wonderful . . . Full of surprising twists, right up until the final revelations'
Caroline Lea, author of *When the Sky Fell Apart*

'I was reminded of William Golding's *The Lord of the Flies* . . . A book about community and how trusts can be so easily broken' *Writing.ie*

'A real page-turner' *Amazon reviewer*

'I so enjoyed *We All Begin As Strangers*. No "characters" in sight – just meticulous, tender, complex portraits of people'
Emylia Hall, author of *The Book of Summers*

'An enjoyable debut' *Amazon reviewer*

Harriet Cummings is a freelance writer with a background in history of art and gender studies. As a script writer, she has had work performed at The Edinburgh Fringe Festival, as well as independent venues around London. While studying at Faber Academy, Harriet threw herself into her first novel and hasn't looked back since. She lives in Leamington Spa with her husband and Springer Spaniel.

Follow Harriet on Twitter @HarrietWriter or find out more at www.harrietcummingsauthor.com

WE ALL BEGIN AS STRANGERS

HARRIET CUMMINGS

ORION

An Orion paperback

First published in Great Britain in 2017
by Orion
This paperback edition published in 2018
by Orion Books,
an imprint of The Orion Publishing Group Ltd
Carmelite House, 50 Victoria Embankment,
London EC4Y 0DZ

An Hachette UK company

1 3 5 7 9 10 8 6 4 2

A CIP catalogue record for this book
is available from the British Library.

ISBN 978 1 4091 6906 2

Typeset by Deltatype Ltd, Birkenhead, Merseyside

Printed in Great Britain by Clays Ltd, St Ives plc

MIX
Paper from
responsible sources
FSC
www.fsc.org   FSC® C104740

www.orionbooks.co.uk

For Richard

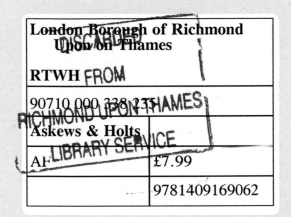

Acknowledgements

I'd like to thank: my agent Hellie Ogden for believing in me as a writer, plus all the lovely people at Janklow and Nesbit; the team at Orion including Ben Willis, Katie Seaman and Virginia Woolstencroft for making the experience so much fun.

My Faber and Woolpack writing groups also provided invaluable advice and encouragement.

But most of all, thank you to my parents and family for listening to me harp on about this novel, especially my husband Richard who has long supported my ambitions. You are pretty great.

Foreword

In the summer of 1984, residents of a number of villages across the Chilterns were alarmed to hear that an unknown intruder was breaking into people's homes.

What he wanted was unclear. Windows were found open, personal belongings moved, and back doors left blowing in the breeze – but nothing of value was taken. In some ways, this made the break-ins even more unsettling. No one quite understood what this person wanted, or what he planned to do.

The local newspapers quickly dubbed him 'the Fox', not only because he was skilled at slipping away unheard into the night, but because some residents later found dens he had made in their bedrooms.

Understandably it was a time of hysteria, of not wanting to open windows despite the sweltering heat. Of scrabbling together any sort of makeshift weapon in the hopes of defending a possible attack. These were villages where, until now, it wasn't uncommon for people to leave their back doors unlocked or hide keys beneath mats. Of course, that summer changed all this.

Suddenly people had rifles on their bedside tables, tripwires set up across lawns. Neighbours became suspicious of one another and started to question how well they really knew the people who'd lived next door for years.

This novel was inspired by the stories still told by villagers today.

Prologue

The Fox is almost silent. A soft step in the damp summer leaves ... She glances behind through the silver birches, their trunks pale as bone in the evening gloom.

He's like an animal, they say, but with hands to pick your locks. And shallow breaths to hide beneath your bed then wait for the first creak of mattress.

She begins to run. The path is narrowing and brambles catch at her skirt, her skin. Rain pricks at pools of water in the pocked earth, sliding under her ankles. Is that a face reflected in the dark surfaces? A snuffle in the bracken?

She charges onwards towards the stream, her heart lurching, big and bloody, as she pounds.

The Fox has escaped every police siren, has slipped unseen through the village.

If she can make the stream she might be all right, though. The flowing water, a stick sent home ...

But the Fox is behind, matching her every step like a shadow.

Fingers appear and wrap tight.

A scream, hot against palm.

PART ONE

1

Deloris stares. She is transfixed by the glowing lights inside the wood-lined television.

'*Oh J.R., how could you?*'

A blue-ish colour is cast across her face, the rest of her features lost to the dim of the living room. It flickers and rides around her wide eyes and her lips which she presses together.

'*After everything we've been through ... you've destroyed it all.*'

As Deloris's fingers curl inwards, shapes appear on the lacquer of her nails, faint trails in the velvet of the sofa arm below.

'*Come on, Sue Ellen, it was a mistake.*'

'*Get away from me! I never want to see you again.*'

As the music starts – a series of bold, brassy notes – the television set vibrates against the stand. Deloris always puts up the volume until the voices boom and crackle, the galloping hooves or engine of a Ford Mustang all around her. Now the character names slide up the screen. The show is over for another day and Deloris feels empty. A cliffhanger will do that to you. For a few minutes more she sits in the dark and replays the last scene: the break-up of one of *Dallas*'s most unpredictable love affairs. J.R. had always liked his women, but for a while he and Sue Ellen were drawn together and had apparently waltzed their way through the steps of love, dating, marriage ... It was all frothing champagne glasses and embraces under the huge Texan sky. Then Holly Harwood came along. Tanned athletic legs and a smile that flashed whenever J.R. entered the room. Deloris wonders if Sue Ellen will take him back and whether she should. Any conclusion evades her and then she's back in her own body, in a small English village, thousands of miles from the Lone Star State.

Deloris drags herself up. She should unpack the shopping – it's been out for over fifty minutes and the margarine will be softening against the wax paper. After opening the curtains, she crosses the living room and walks through the long hallway of undecorated walls. The kitchen is stuffy and smells of the new plastic floor. On the central island, the frozen prawns have thawed and left a puddle of water below. She puts her bare feet right up to it and uses her big toe to draw a pattern.

The washing-up she leaves for now. Harvey said they might get a dishwasher if he carries on doing well. She already has the Autumn Leaves tea service, a SodaStream and a microwave oven, though after three months she's only used it once: a roaring noise and spinning plate that was, like her mum said, unnatural. All in all, she reminds herself, it's a dream home like the kind shown in *Good Housekeeping*. Ceilings patterned in swishes that look like meringues if you stare long enough. And large wardrobes with empty wire hangers in a row that softly clang when she pushes them. At twenty-four she is married with almost everything a woman might want.

She smiles to remember how gobsmacked her mum and little sister had been the day they helped her move in. They'd prodded the waterbed in the spare room and said the television must be twice the size of their one back home. Sharon giggled that she didn't need posters to cover orange wallpaper any more, had put on a pretend serious voice to say she was 'all grown up', though as the two of them left after the last bag was unpacked, Deloris felt tears sting her eyes. 'You're a lucky girl,' her mum said stiffly after insisting they'd catch the bus to the train station rather than wait for Harvey to drive them. 'I am,' she told herself as they walked down the drive in their tatty jumpers, pointing out next-door's huge house, just like her own.

Lately, though, Deloris keeps noticing how much of her day is occupied by clearing away the daddy-long-legs and washing glasses, by straightening the net curtains that catch on the owl-shaped knick-knacks she arranges into lewd sexual positions. It's tempting to just vacuum around the furniture, which she does more and more, letting the machine suck up any dropped biros or stones into its cylinders. She rarely empties the bag, so that it bulges close to breaking point.

'It won't work like that,' Harvey told her a while ago.

She pretended to go and empty it, but instead stood on the landing imagining an explosion of silver dust covering his entire wardrobe full of suits, ties and golfing slacks. The only thing it wouldn't touch would be the patent stilettos he'd bought her, still unworn inside their box and now last summer's fashion.

Leaning against the worktop, Deloris sighs and opens the

cookery book she borrowed from Aylesbury library. A creak upstairs makes her frown, but she's not got time to get distracted. The evening ahead is important and she must make a good job of it. After wiping away someone else's crumb from the book's spine, she flicks to the page for prawn cocktails – the recipe looks pretty straightforward. Ten O levels and an offer from college should be enough brains to mix up some mayonnaise.

As she uses the electric whisk, the kitchen gets even hotter. It's tempting to open a window, but she promised Harvey she wouldn't. *I don't want you getting hurt,* he told her. *Not by some freak.* Deloris reminds herself not to be afraid of someone who hasn't stolen anything of value. Three reports to the police but no actual damage, just some doors left open, Elsie's missing postcard, and finger smudges on the outside of the Watkins' dining room window. Nothing to get worked up about, surely?

Deloris is from Croydon and is used to stories of robberies and break-ins. Not so long ago a traffic warden was beaten with a brick and all it prompted from her dad was a brief pause before he turned to the sports page. Still, there is something unnerving about living in this village enclosed by woods either side. The silver birch trees loom just beyond their patio in a line of ghostly white shapes. And behind that, endless thick trees are dark with spindly branches. Her eyes can't pick out anything more. Harvey tells her the countryside is what middle-class folk aspire to, the Buckinghamshire village prized for its protected woods, but to her there is something comforting about London's concrete, its car parks and blaring radios, shopkeepers who stand out on the street and whistle as you walk past. And crowds where you can be anyone. Here she is utterly alone, with just the quiet of her mind.

It *is* hard to ignore what the villagers are saying. Every huddled conversation is about footsteps across paving slabs, a dog suddenly barking in the night. And now this intruder even has a nickname she overheard in the post office three days ago.

Deloris had been reading the latest *Smash Hits* while Elsie stood beside her, rustling through the pages of the local *Gazette*. Their paths seemed to cross several times a week and the elderly woman would give a gummy smile but not bother to make conversation like she did with the other villagers.

As soon as Stan walked in, Elsie's eyes lit up.

'Another report,' she hissed.

'Really?' he said, stopping beside her. His freshly shaved skin looked pale against his supermarket uniform. Whenever Deloris saw him organising trolleys at the local Budgens or staring at rows of tinned soup she thought he looked out of place and wondered if he ever thought the same about her.

Putting on his tortoiseshell glasses, he peered at the article but let Elsie read to him.

'Apparently Elizabeth Robinson saw a figure over her bed a couple of nights ago. Says she "felt a shadow slip over her and heard breathing but was too shocked to wake up her husband."'

The two neighbours' eyes met for a moment and Deloris, forgetting the magazine article, leaned closer.

'It says here,' whispered Elsie. 'They had a purse by the front door and other valuables lying around but he didn't take anything. So what was he there for?'

Stan remained silent as the woman read on. 'They're calling him "The Fox". Folk reckon he's breaking in and *watching* people. And then disappearing as quickly as he came.'

'He'll just be some bored kid,' interrupted Deloris. 'Harmless.'

Elsie's mouth fell open. 'Excuse me?'

'Let's hope so,' Stan said quickly. 'Newspapers blow things out of proportion.' He waved a dismissive hand but looked doubtful and offered to walk them both home.

Since then Deloris has been arguing with herself over whether or not to lock all the windows; whether to fetch the spare key that lives underneath the bin in case she forgets her set. So far she has left everything unchanged – it isn't as if the police seem too worried.

Deloris now listens to the sounds of the house. Is that a clicking noise from above? A radiator, perhaps, though they haven't been on since March.

She goes upstairs and lets her feet bang against the floorboards. The bathroom door is open a crack; the towel she left drying over the bannisters is perfectly straight. She tramps her feet harder to break the spell. *Or to let them know she is coming.* In the bathroom a brown shoe points outwards from the door and her breath catches, warmth drains from her cheeks. But it's just her slipper, forgotten on the carpet, she realises with a laugh. The rest seems normal: the lines of toiletries along the bath, the peach doily splayed across the toilet.

She thinks it'd be awful to die now, having achieved so little. Still, at least she might be famous – her photograph in the paper. Which would they use? One from the final school party hopefully, not her wedding where she looks like someone else in those acres of white fabric and the bodice that dug into her ribs all afternoon. Deloris shakes her head and strides across the landing. One step, two steps, three. She is outside her bedroom door and with unsteady fingertips touches the outer edge of the frame and begins to push, the carpet brushing against the door and getting wider and wider. Nothing resists. She continues to push but the room is empty, the sheets slightly rippled where she couldn't get them straight, the wardrobe slats closed.

The only difference is the perfume bottle on her dresser; she sees it instantly. It's a spotted lilac bottle that once belonged to her grandmother, which her mum agreed she could have. Harvey calls it old-fashioned so she keeps it in the drawer and just looks at it from time to time. Now the squeezer ball is dented, as if fingers have pressed it inwards. Is that lavender in the air? A mist of droplets on the pine below?

Leaving the bottle, Deloris is lightheaded as she runs from the room, downstairs, and out the back door. The silver birch trees turn to a stream of luminescent white as she passes. Air fills her lungs, which become impossibly huge as if she might take to the sky like an eagle.

Only once she is out in the street does Deloris slow. Beyond her own gasps, it's quiet, with just a magpie ruffling feathers on the neighbour's roof, a silhouette of sharp beak against the sky.

Everything looks fine at first: the four redbrick houses include her own, the largest. Where once there was a view to the woods, its tall facade now stands, devoid of any ivy or bindweed as if placed there overnight like a toy home. Its patch of lawn and gravel driveway matches the other houses, which soon give way to the older bungalows and cottages painted white. The grass is damp with the last rainfall, a wet summer so far, the air filled with clouds of gnats that agitate wings against the colourless sky.

Deloris walks along, not sure what to do. Maybe she should warn the neighbours that someone might have been in her house – but who? It's only Cynthia at number three that she sees.

'Hullo.' Emerging from her bungalow, Cynthia gives a limp

smile before she stoops to collect the milk outside her front door. Despite it being early afternoon, she's still in her dressing gown, which has a pattern of small blue flowers and an ironed lace hem. Her hair is neatly permed, as always, an aura of talcum powder around her skin.

'Hi, Cynthia. How are you?' For a second, she's not sure the woman will reply. It still isn't clear whether she has forgiven Deloris for turning up at her door last month. Harvey had come home from the local parish meeting and laughed about his mum suggesting to Cynthia she might save up to buy her council house. Without hearing the rest, Deloris had marched around to number three. People were always telling her dad about the pride of having your own property, going on even as he dragged on his third cigarette and muttered he didn't feel it right. *Such arrogance,* Deloris thought as she drilled the bell to apologise on behalf of her mother-in-law. Then drilled again. Cynthia cracked open the door and, for a second, Deloris imagined the two of them complaining about the other neighbours over glasses of gin. Toasting to doing whatever the hell they liked as the alcohol slopped over the sides and made their fingers sticky. But the woman was gruff as she asked what Deloris wanted. In the living room behind, a man was crouched by the wall where rows of empty milk bottles were lined up, pieces of cardboard between them so they could stack high around the window. It must be her husband, Ralph, Deloris realised, remembering how people said he never left the house. Twelve years of them living in the village and they'd barely seen the man. Most likely he didn't feel comfortable with people turning up at his door at ten o'clock at night either.

'I'm all right,' Cynthia now says at last. She eyes Deloris and presses the milk to her breast as if it's a child. 'What 'bout you?'

Her brusque tone makes Deloris wonder what she thinks of her. Just the girl married into the rich family? Stuck up now she's one of them? But it's her feet that Cynthia is frowning at. 'You're not wearing any shoes.'

Anna doesn't open her front door after three raps of the speckled lion knocker and Deloris is now self-conscious, with grit pressed into the soft patches of her feet. She thinks about turning back but doesn't want to walk past Cynthia again. The side gate rattles as she pulls its circular handle.

'Who's there?' calls a voice.

'It's me. Deloris.'

'Oh hi.' After some scurrying sounds, Anna blushes as she opens the gate. 'I'm sorry,' she says breathlessly. Her floral dress doesn't sit quite right on her wide hips.

'What for?'

Anna frowns. 'I-I don't know.'

They both laugh awkwardly and Deloris follows her into the house.

The kitchen is the galley kind with a small round table at the end. Deloris has only been in the house once before – to borrow a chair for a party – and now regrets coming. The cottage, presumably older than all the other houses on the street, is like something from a hundred years ago. Teapots hang from hooks along the dresser and a dank smell drifts from the misshapen walls where framed embroideries protrude.

'What brings you here?' Anna asks shyly. Her eyes flicker to Deloris's bare feet but she says nothing.

Deloris considers telling her about the noises upstairs. Her running like some child through the back door, which – she now realises – she didn't think to lock.

'I just thought I'd pop in.'

'You did?' A smile expands, her cheeks dimpling either side. There's something so girlish about her though she's in her late twenties, a few years older than Deloris. 'That's so lovely. I'll make us some tea. No! Some *ice* tea, although I don't know how to do that. It must involve ice cubes, do you think?' Her words run away, tripping over themselves. She gasps and the buttons of her dress are pressed outwards beneath the flowers, swirls of orange in old-fashioned fabric.

The living room is even busier with items: bronze pans hang low from beams so Deloris must stoop to reach the end. Everything is covered in a mist of dust. Beneath glass, speckled brown with age, a photograph shows Anna with a woman who must be her mum. They are stiff side by side, like a portrait shot, and both have cream, dog-shaped brooches pinned to their lapels. Anna inherited the house when her mum died last summer – almost a year ago. Deloris is shocked to think she's been married to Harvey that long.

The first time he'd driven her to the village he said they could take a stroll through the woods, and when she said she'd prefer the pub, he laughed. She was surprised at how chatty the locals were as they sat in the yard. Hanging baskets dripped water on the concrete but the rest wasn't so different from the Nags Head back home: rounds brought out on plastic trays, folk stretching legs into the last patch of sunshine. It was only when someone mentioned they hadn't seen Ruth in a long time the atmosphere cooled. When Deloris later asked Harvey who she was, his forehead crinkled and he talked about something else.

Ruth's funeral was the day they got back from their honeymoon in Bermuda. As their taxi drove along the high street, they passed the hearse waiting outside the church. Pink and white carnations arranged on the panel of wood read, 'mother'.

'Who calls their mum "Mother"?' Deloris had asked, watching the villagers line up to get into the church. Everyone was there, it looked like, decked out in smart clothing with handkerchiefs folded into top pockets or giving a series of small nods, chins multiplying.

Harvey didn't seem to hear the question.

'She reached a fair age,' his mum Sandra said when Deloris mentioned it the next day. 'Died peacefully in her sleep.' The lines were like something from a pamphlet on death.

As Deloris's tan wore off, Anna's grief endured all summer long, then into autumn. Whenever Deloris saw Anna in the post office or street, she was hunched with bloated skin puffed around eyes that were always watery, big drops threatening to cascade on to her cheeks. By winter she had started to wear colours again but patterns, floral things with high necks and corduroy trims. Deloris thought she must still be grieving, though perhaps that was how she always dressed.

It wasn't until the Easter fair when they had their first proper conversation. Deloris was supposed to be helping Sandra with her cake stand but, after being shooed to the side, she found an empty seat by the back of the hall next to Anna who said she didn't like the crowds. Flat leather soles remained next to Deloris's own wedges, which she began to swing as she relaxed. Twenty minutes later Deloris realised she'd done all the talking and wondered if she was being rude, but Anna continued to ask about her little sister's hairdressing certificates, about the potato skins her mum cooked. Since then they always said hi if they passed each other in the street and Deloris meant to invite her over but wasn't sure they'd have much in common.

Now Anna calls from the kitchen. 'So, tea for two?'

'Actually, honey,' Deloris starts, 'I'd better go. I have this dinner party to organise tonight.'

'You do?' Anna appears in the doorway.

As Deloris walks back through the dim kitchen, she notes the table still has two chairs; a family-sized granary loaf is shrivelled around the edges.

'Are you going to be OK?' Deloris asks. There is a sour smell – possibly from the milk pan left on the hob with a tide of white thickening inside.

'Oh yes, thank you,' she breathes. 'Although I'd be happy to make us some tea?'

Deloris hesitates. 'You could help with my cooking?'

'Really?'

'And come to the dinner party, of course,' she quickly adds. 'We'll have loads of food.'

They return to the house like two schoolgirls bunking off. Anna stands back from the Magimix and island as if she's worried she might break something. She's tentative with the cookery book, turning the pages with gentle hands and beams at the offer of SodaStream lemonade.

Running up the stairs again, Deloris is almost giddy to think she was afraid before. How different things could feel from one hour to the next. She could easily have left the perfume bottle out herself. As for the dinner party, this might just be fun now Anna is coming. A new friend, she thinks, and hurries back to the kitchen.

'Hey, Anna?'

'Yes?' She uses a single finger to save the recipe page.

'What do you think will happen in *Dallas*?'

Anna raises her eyes and smiles. 'What's *Dallas*?'

18

The two stand side by side at the counter while Deloris explains the various characters, although Anna seems more concerned with the cooking. She cracks the eggs with one hand and asks what's her preferred technique for making blancmange. Deloris points out the pages in the book, then flicks through the radio stations to find a song she likes and settles for Dan Hartman's 'I Can Dream About You'. The crackling intensifies with the volume and breaks up the lines so she sings over the top. Anna doesn't join in. Even as Deloris spins away from the counter to pump out her elbows, she remains beating eggs, the fork tinkling against the bowl over and over.

'Good song, isn't it?'

Dancing alone, Deloris thinks of her friends back home – how they made fun of each other's dancing, nudging for more space at The Wag on a Friday night, but at least never left one girl dancing on her own. Hot with sweat, she jerks to a stand-still by the counter.

'Oh you shouldn't stop dancing halfway through a song,' Anna says, turning from her egg whites. 'It's unlucky.' She smiles and motions to Deloris who sighs, but then throws herself back across the lino, pleased to scream along in time for the chorus.

An hour later Deloris realises that Anna has made most of the food and insists she should prepare the beer and potatoes herself.

'Oh, OK,' Anna says. 'I suppose I should find something to wear for later. Not that I can compete with you, of course.'

'Don't be silly.' She notices how delicate Anna's hands are as she wipes them on her dress. 'In fact, I have something you might like.'

The purple lace gloves are ones she saw in a basket by the till in C&A, but on getting them home, realised they were too tight. She finds them in the back of her underwear drawer and brings them downstairs.

'Are you sure?' Anna gasps. 'You don't mind?'

'Course not. You'll look fabulous.'

Harvey comes home not long after five o'clock and goes straight upstairs for a shower. Deloris wipes down the work surfaces with too many bubbles that froth and burst as she slops about the J-cloth.

'Everything ready for tonight?' he says ten minutes later in the kitchen. A towel is wrapped around his middle and fat bulges over the muscles of his chest.

'Hi, honey.' She lands a kiss defiantly on his mouth – he usually likes a vodka and diet lemonade first.

'No disasters, I hope?'

'Actually, it's all gone smoothly.'

He goes to the fridge to inspect the blancmange, which wobbles but holds true to its pink form. 'I'm impressed.'

'And I . . .' She lifts her chin. 'I invited Anna from down the road.'

Harvey whips the fridge shut. 'You did?'

'Uh-huh.'

'It's nice you're making friends, but why her?'

Deloris isn't sure how to respond but it doesn't matter. Harvey is already making arrangements to even out the numbers, saying he'll have to pair Anna with Brian who he rings at the police station. *Decent grub if we're lucky,* he tells him. *Dolly's cooked, Christ help us.* Upstairs, Deloris rubs her make-up brush into the powder blue, then dabs her eyelids. It's probably too much but she enjoys the feel of it. She chooses a dress that gropes her at all angles with its material and has shoulder pads like sharp mountain ridges.

'Is that the new frock I bought you?' Vodka heats Harvey's breath as he kisses her neck. 'It does look nice. How are you doing your hair?'

Deloris turns to kiss him. 'Does it matter?'

They fall on to the bed and Deloris begins to peel herself free from the dress but Harvey says to keep it on, he needs to refill the ice cube tray.

His parents arrive early with Bucks Fizz which they both point out is from France – Sandra first as she presses it into Deloris's hands, then Michael with a slow scratch below his leather belt. They live on the high street, a few doors down from the post office and church, but Michael has driven them in case it rains and parked his Jaguar with one tyre on the grass as if claiming it. They did help with the house payments – more than Deloris's own parents were able to do. Now Sandra adjusts the knotted pearls that lie on the bones of her chest as she admires the kitchen floor even though she's already seen it. 'Quite the ticket, isn't it?' She's the only person who doesn't take her shoes off and Harvey never asks, so a trail of dents marks her passage to and from each counter.

Michael hangs behind and lets his eyes fall lazily on Deloris's dress. Grubby patches stain his shirt and he's no doubt come from his carpet factory where he stays until late most evenings. Apparently Sandra brings him dinner in a Tupperware dish and the two eat together at his desk. It's hard to imagine the neat, chaffinch-like woman among the clanging machines of the factory but she says it's the work of a marriage to spend time together. Meanwhile Harvey is long home and tells Deloris it's to see her, though he often goes straight upstairs to his office where editions of *GQ* and *Custom Car* are hidden in his old briefcase.

'What do you think of this Madonna business?' Michael now asks Deloris with a steady gaze, drawing a hand to his sturdy hip. It feels like a challenge, seeing as he's often playful in trying to provoke her.

'Her music video's pretty wild,' she says, determined not to blush.

'You look like her tonight.'

Sandra's delicate eyebrows shoot up. 'Rather tarty, don't you think?'

'Who?' Deloris asks, turning to face her mother-in-law. The two women have never spent much time together and Deloris colours to glance down at her own outfit, a stretch of bare thigh on display.

'Madonna, of course,' says Sandra with a smile. 'You are far prettier than she'll ever be.'

The dinner party is to celebrate the latest business contract Harvey has secured for the factory.

It's Michael's own friends – the Morgans – who make the guest list. Mrs Morgan stamps an orange kiss on each of Harvey's cheeks as he compliments her cashmere cardigan. Like most older women, she lingers in front of him, wrinkled hands wrapped in his before he politely excuses himself to make some gin and tonics. At this her husband behind perks up and then plops his small body in one of the armchairs.

Mr Morgan is vice president of the golf club and gets invited to all sorts of gatherings, as if he's some sort of politician everyone wants to keep happy. Deloris views the two crinkled guests and tries not to get too close as she serves the vol-au-vents. It reminds her of the waitressing job she had when she was sixteen in Mario's Pizzas by Croydon shopping centre: just the odd mutter of thanks as she busies around, but without the coins left on plates afterwards. Sandra offers to help but carries on standing beside the window that looks on to the street where rain is leaving shiny puddles.

Deloris is relieved when Anna arrives, excited with pink cheeks and a carton of tomato juice already opened. The lace gloves are already fraying at the ends but Anna seems happy enough. She takes them off to wash some glasses and delicately pulls them back on afterwards.

There's just about enough conversation to go around the guests but really, once they hear Brian is coming, they're all waiting for the doorbell. It gets to eight thirty and Michael is scraping the remains of the spinach dip and apologising to the Morgans who continue to sit with glazed expressions. Too old for any more talk about the golf club's upcoming ball, the difficulty finding staff despite all the youths needing jobs ...

At the long oval table, Deloris serves up the prawn cocktails in glass ramekins they got as a wedding present. She assumed they'd save them for a special occasion but now realises this is it. They all pick at the food and thirstily glug wine, which Harvey insists on pouring. Only Anna licks her spoon afterwards and says how wonderful they were. *Isn't Deloris a promising cook?* They all half-heartedly agree, apart from Harvey who is too busy listing carpet-finishing techniques to Mr Morgan; the old man angles an ear in his direction but fails to nod or murmur in the gaps left for a response. Deloris is all too familiar with the talk, the prices of different types of synthetic fabrics, supposedly easier to clean than wool. Draining the last of the wine, Michael rolls his eyes at the delicate strokes of Sandra who spears each carrot and thoroughly chews. The beef Wellington is over-cooked and the mashed potato lumpy. Anna's blancmange, however, is a triumph and cutlery clinks until all seven bowls are shiny and white again.

Brian turns up once Anna has cleared all the plates.

'Ah, sorry folks. I thought this was a casual thing.' He wipes his Reeboks several times on the hallway mat and gives a wave. He looks different out of uniform, Deloris thinks for the umpteenth time since they first met: less handsome but still cute. He's wearing the same striped shirt she noticed a while ago in the pub. That evening they'd laughed together at the jukebox, when he suggested they play Barbra Streisand. And, pleased to find herself chatting so easily with a neighbour, she poked him in the side. It was what she used to do with the boys from school she wound up about their hairstyles or the ties they put on back to front. But the surprised look on Brian's face made her edge away. Without another word she had returned to Harvey and his parents, assuring Michael that no, she wouldn't like another white wine.

Anna now hurries over with a glass of water. 'Here you go, Brian.'

'Oh, thanking you.'

They glance at each other and are both silent for a second.

'How's Beattie?' Anna asks. Deloris had forgotten about Brian's older brother who lives at home with him; according to Sandra, a carer visits twice a day in a van that carries a hoist.

'Not too shabby, he—'

'Glad you could make it,' interrupts Harvey before he swings an arm around Brian and guides him to the living room. All that is left of Anna is the fingerprints on Brian's glass.

'Any more news?' asks Sandra from the window.

'News?'

'On the Fox, of course,' says Michael, who's pouring his son's third vodka of the evening.

'Ah, the intruder. Yes.' Brian looks around for somewhere to sit and Deloris offers up her chair. 'Thanking you, very kind.'

'So? Any news?' Sandra repeats.

'I'm not meant to release any information,' Brian says with an apologetic shrug.

'Oh, come on, we won't say anything.' Michael grins as he thrusts a glass of whisky into Brian's hand. He sniffs it uncertainly and holds the brown liquid at a distance.

'We do live in this village, we have a right,' says Sandra.

They all nod, apart from Anna who hovers in the doorway. Her face is pale around lips sucked inwards.

'Property prices,' says Michael.

'And our own personal safety,' adds Sandra. She shakes her head at her husband though represses a smile as if proud he's always got a handle on the finances. 'I heard he's been roaming the village for weeks. Hiding in the woods and removing his shoes in houses so he doesn't leave footprints.'

'Ah. Yes. Well, newspapers have a tendency to exaggerate '

'So you've not been patrolling the high street?' says Sandra, her voice rising in pitch.

'No, no.'

'Why ever not?'

Brian speaks up. 'I've filled out the necessary reports but this character hasn't actually caused any damage.'

Sandra becomes shaky in her heels. 'We have no clue what

he wants, though. If he's not taking anything, not causing any damage then it must be *something* else.'

'I admit it's troubling, but—'

'A sexual pervert, I bet,' Sandra says with a point of her finger at Brian who shrinks lower into his seat.

'I saw a BBC programme about it,' she says, turning to find approval from her husband. 'The effects of pornography creating this need for voyeurism.' A silence paralyses everyone's lips, including those of Michael who sips his drink to avoid her eye. 'Disgusting,' mutters Sandra.

For a while longer no one says anything. It might usually be Michael's turn to speak but he is inspecting his whisky glass while Harvey broods about something by the fireplace. Deloris realises Brian hasn't eaten yet and makes a plateful for him, annoyed that it's somehow her duty.

Anna has started the washing-up in the kitchen, lace gloves draped on the window ledge. Deloris goes to tell her to leave the burnt pans but catches the end of Harvey's sentence.

'... seems like he's just watching people.'

'That's what I mean,' says Sandra, pleased to have confirmation. 'Looking in on our lives, our private affairs.' The Morgans nod vaguely from the armchairs.

'What's so wrong with that?' Deloris asks. 'It's not like he's hurt anyone.' She is out in the hallway and turns to come back in. The others look up too, even Mrs Morgan with a glass suspended by her lips.

Harvey almost laughs. 'It's deranged.'

She flares with heat, her voice unsteady. 'There are worse things people do.'

'We're not talking about watching soaps, here,' he says,

frowning into his glass. 'Although it might not hurt you to watch less of those.'

'Why?' She's not sure where her anger has come from. Her mind swims.

'Because you could be out making friends, becoming part of the village.' Harvey ignores his mum who gives him a frantic look not to argue in front of guests. He only speaks more insistently. 'Why do you love all those ridiculous shows anyway?'

Everyone waits for her reply.

'I don't know,' she says at last.

'Well then.' And with that he downs the rest of his drink.

In the bedroom mirror, Deloris sees her make-up smeared in blue streaks across her face. She leaves it on, like a sort of war paint, and sits on the bed. The evening light illuminates the curved shape of the perfume bottle. The squeezer isn't compressed this time. No fingers have been around it.

There's a faint knock at the door.

'I was worried about you,' Anna says softly from the hall.

'Come in.' Deloris goes to wipe her eyes clean but stops, thinking the smears are a kind of evidence, although of what she's not sure.

'Everything quite all right?'

'Not really.'

Anna puts a tentative, lace-gloved hand on her shoulder and Deloris sniffs. 'I'm being stupid, really,' she says, pulling Anna down to sit next to her. 'It's just that Harvey can be such a pig.'

Her eyes fixed on her knees, Anna goes quiet.

'Sometimes I don't know why I married him. Or him me.'

'Oh no, Deloris,' Anna says. 'You two are just perfect, everyone says so. He must love you.' Her eyes grow wet and shiny as she looks about. 'And you have this lovely home with all this room to grow.'

Now it's Deloris's turn to put her hand on Anna's arm, which hangs uneasily in her lap, her back arched.

'A family,' Anna blurts.

'Yeah, of course.' Deloris nods and has the familiar sense of déjà vu. Any conversation about Harvey seems to go this way. What a lucky woman she is. Doesn't she understand that? 'Well, ta for coming to see if I'm OK.'

Anna shakes her head and hurries up, not wanting to outstay her welcome. She goes to the door. 'Oh, your gloves.'

Deloris barely hears. She is looking at the perfume bottle. 'Keep them,' she says absently.

'Really? Are you sure?'

Deloris doesn't respond. She is holding the bottle up to the evening light and removing the glass top to smell the lavender.

2

Deloris lies across the sun lounger in her bikini. An ice-cream van is moving along the high street, a distance away so its jangling melody is faint like an echo from childhood. Her summer holidays used to drift on forever in a haze until September – homemade lollies made from orange cordial, trips to the newsagent and the sprinkler at Nanna's garden shooting diamonds across the sky. Now, it only being June, the summer stretches ahead but is buffered by nothing at the end. Housework, cooking blancmange, a week somewhere if she's lucky, and then home to piles of washing and prickly sunburnt skin in the shower. The ice-cream van song has faded and Deloris bends her knees so her thighs unstick from the plastic slats. Her hair crackles behind where she's squeezed lemon juice on it, though the sun's no longer out. Grey clouds are thickening over the sky, trapping the damp heat. There's something sad about this summer. She looked forward to it all through spring – and now it's here, time is draining away, her thighs bloating and creasing with wrinkles. Her hips seem wider, too, with silvery trails etched over bone.

Times like these she thinks about meeting Harvey, the man who came into the chip shop that Saturday afternoon. As soon as the doorbell tinkled she'd pulled off her hairnet and watched as he surveyed the chalkboard menu. Other customers might ask for the daily special or when the fish was cooked. Harvey already knew what he wanted: an un-battered fillet of their best cod, sprinkled with vinegar and *none of that cheap white pepper*. Between the jars of pickled eggs on the counter, Deloris had noted his tanned skin against his white shirt, its collar parted like the wings of a bird.

It'd all happened quickly between them. Her mum wasn't sure – did she really not want to go to her college interview? Not many girls had the chance, even in this day and age with Thatcher leading the country and *Superwoman* displayed in bookshops' windows. But Deloris didn't listen. Even college didn't seem too exciting, what with the textbooks and exams and smeared chalkboards that never got properly clean, just like in school. Wasn't life supposed to be about adventure? And love affairs? Finding a Darcy, a Heathcliff, a Rochester?

She put on her best halter-neck dress and a scarf round her neck for the car rides, just like in the films. The wind rippled through the fabric as they rode in his Audi Sport through Camden as the market sellers were clearing away and the streets filled with punks, skinheads, and men in blazers, all glancing across to see their car. When she eventually began to shiver Harvey insisted on winding up the windows and she'd sink back while he navigated the city's vast network of roads and tunnels, all cast a darkish blue as the evening set in.

He took her to places she'd never been before – West End restaurants where he was on first name terms with the owners and ordered wine without looking at the menu. They met his friends who, like him, were a few years older, so already part of a life in motion: bankers, executives, a woman who had been a debutante and was thinking of starting a record label.

When her friend Trish called up one afternoon to see if she wanted to go down the arcades, Deloris had plans for Soho's L'Escargot where media types were photographed eating from tiny plates. Even if Harvey never turned up that night, at least she'd got the chance to write the words in her diary in looping gold ink.

Better yet, Harvey claimed not to mind her background. The time he came round for dinner, they all sat crowded in the living room with the radio still on, talk of tennis over cod and mushy peas she'd brought home from work. She was embarrassed by her dad's hacking cough and apologised afterwards. *We'll never have to sit through that again*, Harvey had promised but as he said the words she felt a weird sensation fizz in her stomach. She pushed it down and let him whisk her away to this new life of shiny surfaces and rooms she danced in that first day. Around and around she spun, him smiling with a vodka in hand. *Diet lemonade*, he'd told her when she offered to make him one. *Fine, anything you like*, she said, and laughed as the *Fame* song played on a loop in her head.

But Deloris can't escape the present. It asserts itself at every point. Even in her dreams she is aware of the scratch of sheets, of Harvey's damp arm heavy beside hers. Now, sitting up as rain begins to fall, she is aware of the soreness between her legs from that morning.

At midday she watches *Dallas*. The opening credits show the usual rolling farmland, oil rigs, and the Texan landscape. It's the season finale and she wonders when the next one will be.

Just as Sue Ellen comes on to the screen, telling the bartender she wants '*A branch and ice. Make it snappy will ya,*' the doorbell goes. The high, drilling noise is intrusive and at first she ignores it. But it goes again and she scrabbles around to find the remote for the VCR. It was a wedding present they gave themselves, at Deloris's suggestion, and, she likes to think, the envy of the neighbours, though really, what does it matter?

Mrs Morgan is at the door. The same fusty cardigan as the evening before with its oval buttons too heavy for the fabric.

'I've come round to pay my thanks for last night.'

'You have?' Deloris grimaces to remember her argument with Harvey. She's not sure how obvious it was when she ran to the bedroom, pounding up the stairs two at a time.

'Yes, dear. It's what you're supposed to do, you know.'

'Right.'

Mrs Morgan peers down Deloris's body – the bikini, cut-off denim shorts open at the button.

'Well, ta for coming round.'

'You know ...' Mrs Morgan dithers with a finger in the air. 'You might be a little more careful with your appearance.'

Deloris presses each consonant like she used to with the teachers. 'I'm at home.' Surely she wasn't doing anything wrong?

'Indeed you are at home. However there are certain individuals who may be ... encouraged ... by such a sight.'

'Individuals?' Deloris looks over the head of the crinkled old woman to the street. A crow pecks at the empty pavement from where the smell of wet concrete wafts. 'You mean the Fox?'

'Indeed I do.'

'And what do you even know about him?' Deloris's voice is rising. She slings an arm below her hip like she's reaching for a gun holster. 'This supposed criminal who's gone into a couple of houses.'

'Three houses. *Homes*.' Mrs Morgan fidgets with a button, edging away.

'And what do you know about me? Saying I'm encouraging him?'

'Well—'

She looks out on to the street, like a hundred more people are listening.

Mrs Morgan shakes her head and a pin springs free from the tight bun. 'Anyway, dear, thank you for …' She shuffles away along the gravel.

Deloris doesn't know whether to carry on watching *Dallas*. She can hear the voices – J.R. and Ted arguing over some business deal – but thinks she should be strong and wait until the whole thing is recorded. With an arm over her eyes she goes to the controller and turns it off. Upstairs she sits on the bed. Everything is draining from her and her body sags forwards. It isn't like her to argue with people. As a schoolgirl she had her fair share of fights, mostly just slaps and scrambling on the playground, a handful of ponytail for good measure. One time she'd had a screaming match with a supply teacher over her algebra homework, miraculously doubled for a friend, but that was all years ago. Her mum always taught her good manners and she must remember these around the villagers. Besides, you can't rail against adults if you're supposed to be one yourself.

A shirt sleeve falls down the side of the washing basket so she carries it to the kitchen and begins the routine – a lilac stream of fabric softener, then in goes the programme number *punch punch punch.* The washing begins its watery spins and she sits cross-legged in front, putting her face closer and closer until it's the sea waves of a storm. She's remembering a Turner painting she saw on a school trip once, when the phone goes.

'Hello, Baker residence.'

'What the hell, Deloris.'

'Harvey?' She winds the phone cord around her forefinger.

'Mrs Morgan just rang.' There's a crackling as he breathes heavily and she pictures the tanned skin of his chest appearing and disappearing between the buttons. 'What is wrong with you? Talking like that to a frail old woman.'

'She's tougher than she looks.'

His voice becomes a low whisper. 'Jesus, Dolly, have some respect.'

Deloris is empty of words.

'I've got a meeting now but I'll talk to you tonight, OK?'

She sucks in breath.

'I said, OK?'

'Yes, Harvey, yes.'

After the low hum starts, Deloris lets the phone cord slowly unravel itself. She puts the phone in the cradle and shivers for the first time in days.

Aylesbury high street is ablaze with shoppers. High tops on the cobbled streets and bare shoulders turning brown now the sun is finally out. Nobody is whispering about any intruder or judging her choice of dress. An ice-cream van is parked by the town hall and Deloris tells the young man she wouldn't mind a lick of something.

'Oi, oi,' he says, elbows leant on the counter as he watches her go.

She's left the washing, probably now festering in its own grey water, but puts it out of her mind. Tells herself she is Deloris McKee, as she was born and made, or really anyone she wants to be. Nobody knows her here in the crowds, the noise of chattering and traffic flowing past, buses heaving into the curb and off again.

On the twenty-five minute bus ride she started to wonder if she hadn't been too brash deciding to come, but what did it matter? There is a lightness to her, and she watches her reflection as she crosses past shop fronts, lingering by a display of televisions, one on top of another. A pattern of brown outsides and glowing shapes, characters, plots. She doesn't recognise this soap with two glamorous women in power suits at a restaurant bar which then pans out to a casino with a rattling roulette board, the ball skittishly bouncing around before landing on black.

What is this show? Deloris thinks. She wanders into the shop and glances around for an assistant but the tall scrawny man is with another woman, a housewife with a child pulling on the flap of her handbag. Another woman waits behind and lifts her eyebrows at him to get his attention for a moment, a radio alarm box clutched in her hands.

Deflated, Deloris turns on her heel and goes out again. Instead she goes to Woolworths. Passes penny sweets where boys look up from the gumdrops, the laces glittering with sugar. It's the place of her teenagehood. Of buying her first Bay City Rollers record with its tartan lettering for the cover.

At the huge magazine rack, she leafs through *Smash Hits* for information on *Dallas*. A page almost tears as she goes. When is the next season? Another arm reaches out and finds the bare shelf. Deloris has the last copy, which she brings marginally closer to her chest.

'What date?' asks the woman. Her eyes bulge below a bleached fringe. She must be ten years older than Deloris but still wears an acid-wash denim skirt that exposes the loose skin around the top of her knees.

'Pardon?'

'Of *Dallas*, course.' The woman peers over the top page as if she can read upside down.

'Oh. Erm …' Deloris continues to flick and, at last, finds the double-page spread. She wants to be alone to savour the article, the quotes from the writer she always finds herself nodding at. The woman comes so close Deloris can see the lines either side of her mouth. Pores on her nose blocked with foundation.

'Not until next spring,' Deloris announces and closes the magazine, though she keeps her finger at the page.

'Typical.' The woman puts hands on her jutting hips. Most older women get fat, Deloris thinks, and become so different their younger selves are subsumed and eventually forgotten. This woman is skinny, hip bones free from dimply flesh, but really, this is sadder still.

'What are we going to do till then?' At this she laughs and holds Deloris's eye. There's something mischievous there, but in her next breath the woman is calling in a tired voice across to the next aisle of children's toys. Buckets and spades trapped in plastic nets. 'Oi, Mags, time for swimming.' A frowning girl slopes towards her mum with her hands in a bag of sweets. Deloris starts to move away but hears the crumple of paper on the floor so ducks down to pick up the bag. The girl swipes it back and Deloris is left only with a sticky trail on her palm from the little sucked fingers.

'You buying that, then?'

'Oh.' Deloris looks at the magazine in her hand. 'No, you can have it.'

'Sure? There's loads to read here, looks like.'

'It's fine,' she says and holds it out to the woman, noticing that their wedding bands match: gold and a little loose for the finger.

'When do you get off?' Deloris asks the young man in the ice-cream van. She hadn't planned to actually say anything – only to get a closer look – but the thought of going back home makes her grimace. The man's face glows one side as he leans towards her, grinning. He is younger than she first realised, with spots along his jawline, but still has a sort of boyish charm. Maybe if she squints ...?

'My uncle says not till four.'

A queue is already forming behind Deloris and she feels her cheeks flush.

'It's almost five,' she says in what she hopes is a brash voice. It's do or die. 'Come buy me a drink.'

The boy looks unsure and turns to one side, grinning to an imaginary friend behind him.

'You serious?'

'Sure I am.'

Someone in the queue tuts then tells Deloris to get out the way. Her knees weaken a little.

'Mine's a bourbon,' she says in a voice threatening to crackle. Just as she's about to turn and run, the van board snaps closed. She baulks at the sound, then – as people behind complain to each other – she realises the boy is coming.

*

They can't find a bar that's open. Deloris expected the boy –
Eddie – to know one, but he slopes along in his baggy T-shirt
which is smeared with chocolate and sprinkles stuck to the
hem. Sensing the mood will soon pass, she jerks her head to a
pub. It's an old-man type of place with dark wood and a smell
of stale beer sunk in the carpets. Eddie glances back in the
direction of the van and seems reluctant to follow her inside.

'What'll it be?' asks the balding man behind the bar.

'A branch,' she says.

'What's that?' He rubs at his nose.

Deloris has no clue. 'Fine, a Lilt then.'

'I'll have the same, cheers,' says Eddie as he scoops some
change from his back pocket and counts it out. It's a painful
process, watched over by the barman as if he's overrun with
other customers. Deloris wonders if she should pay but thinks
it might embarrass him.

'You didn't tell me your name,' he says as they sit down in
the corner. The seating has lost its springs but it's dark and
sort of sultry, Deloris thinks. Eddie spreads out his legs and
she lets her knee touch his. A group of middle-aged men trawl
into the pub and look over. Eddie smiles to himself and maybe
even blushes.

'Sue Ellen,' she tells him.

'Really? My mum's called Susan.'

'Hmm.' She angles her knee closer to his. 'Let's not talk
about your mum, all right?'

He gives a goofy grin and glances at the men again. They've
moved over to the dartboard where they're absorbed in wiping
down the chalk.

'You at college, then?' he asks.

Deloris drapes an arm across the back of the cushion, which

is a little too high. She puts it down again between them. 'I own land.'

'Yeah?'

'Oh. I'm sorry,' she says slowly with raised eyebrows. 'You don't think a woman can own a small slice of this world? A place to call her own?' She's proud of the line – a mix of Sue Ellen and Woolf. What a combination.

'I guess.' Bubbles fizz as he takes a long glug of his lemonade and she realises he's draining it. His Adam's apple slides up and down. 'You wanna go somewhere then?' he asks the empty glass.

Deloris lets a silence settle. 'You think it isn't for a woman to own but to be owned?' she says.

'My van's not far and …' he mutters, angling his shoulder away, 'we could open the vent at the back.'

'I might be married,' she says. 'But I'm leaving him. He's no good, I tell ya.'

'What?'

'He's simply no good.'

Eddie rises now, unsure of himself. Deloris stands too. 'And I'm a free woman.'

A pause and scratch of spotted chin. 'Whatever.'

He goes to move away and she takes the loose fabric of his T-shirt, then throws the soda in his face. His mouth falls open as the yellow drips down his top. 'My mum's gonna kill me.'

Deloris bites her lip. 'Oh, I …'

'You silly bitch,' he mutters.

'I am sorry,' she calls after him but the landlord suddenly has his arm clamped around her waist. The huge body presses up against hers from behind, sharp with the smell of vinegar.

'Get off me,' she shouts.

'I see girls like you all the time,' he says groping his fingers upwards. Eddie has gone and the other men are out of sight. His fingers tug at her bra. 'Think you can do what you want.'

'Please, no!'

'Don't fret, you're going.' He heaves her over to the door and with a final rough squeeze of her breast, pushes her out into the street.

Deloris doesn't cry on the bus home. She keeps her eyes fixed on the ceiling which is rounded with posters either side for Tide washing powder and some triple-action Hoover for easier above-the-floor cleaning. She sniffs and ignores the little old man who glances across and offers her a handkerchief. He asks if she'd like to talk about it, then, after a pause, goes back to twisting menthol sweets from wrappers. At the bus station Deloris had gone to the ticket office for coaches to London Victoria. She had even stepped into the queue, but it was more an act that no one was there to see.

Perhaps a part of her still loves Harvey, or maybe it was that she wasn't sure her parents would take her back home. She'd been smug about Harvey, accusing her mum of wanting the life for herself, and so even though they'd come to the wedding, they left the party early and hadn't even taken a slice of cake. Sharon, her sister, didn't approve either. Never seemed to like Harvey even at the beginning when he was all flowers and manners at the doorstep, him asking about her hairdressing one time. Why hadn't Deloris paid more attention? She really is a stupid girl. She shudders to remember the man's fingers squeezing her breast, leaving a cloying film of vinegar.

As Deloris tentatively steps through the front door, she braces herself for Harvey. It's almost seven thirty and she hadn't left a note. He'll be frantic. But the living-room curtains are pulled shut and the television on mute so there's just the sound of heaving breath, his body slumped on the sofa in his boxer shorts. A pizza crust lies on the plate by his foot, as does an empty glass; the other foot is across the sofa arm. Deloris lets out a slow sigh and feels lighter. She remembers the video of *Dallas*. Kneeling by the VCR, she rewinds the tape and sits as it makes its noisy turning, then takes the remote from Harvey's bloated side and puts the volume on three.

The opening credits start up like a familiar homecoming and she kneels right by the television, hearing her mum's voice laugh and say she'll get square eyes. The episode starts again – the argument with J.R. – but cuts out a minute in. Goes to a man who kicks a football down the pitch. *What?* Deloris shakes her head and presses fast-forward, watching the tiny men scuttle around between the stripped lines. It's a ninety-minute match that Harvey must have recorded.

Now the tears roll freely down her face and she goes upstairs, wanders around quietly sobbing. She goes from room to room, not caring if Harvey wakes up, inspecting the objects that she is bound to: the bare walls, the sockets, the dustball in a tangle of hair beneath the spare bed. Then back into the bedroom. The perfume spray is compressed again. Is it? Just a touch. A *touch*?

When Harvey later comes upstairs, Deloris is staring at the ceiling shade.

'Hi, Dolly,' he slurs. 'Silly thing.'

He heaves himself into bed, almost tripping on his boxers as he yanks them down.

'Hello, Harvey.'

He pulls her towards him into the chest that's prickly where

41

he's shaved. 'I'm sorry about earlier, you know.' Hands fumble with her hair, which catches and strains tight. 'I shouldn't have said those things. Not about my Dolly.'

'It's OK. Please can we just—'

A finger rests vertically against her lips. 'Not about the mother of my child.'

'Please, Harvey,' she says.

'I want a baby,' he whispers into her ear. She hopes she's misheard but he says it over and over as he pulls down her nightdress.

Over the next few days Deloris keeps going to the phone. It shouldn't be so hard to get hold of some. Her friend Josie used to be on it and said it worked a charm. One pill every morning, as long as you remember after breakfast. Every time Deloris dials the doctor's number, however, she puts the phone back in its cradle as it starts to ring. The practice is just in the next village and the staff are bound to know Harvey or at least his parents who've lived in the area for thirty years. It's supposed to be confidential, but nothing seems that way in these villages. Not so long ago Deloris heard Sandra talking about someone who'd had an abortion and turned up to a prayer meeting and confessed everything over a cup of orange squash; she had moved back with her parents in Winchester shortly after. And it wasn't like the men were much better. You'd hear them in the pub telling each other about how Rick makes snuff films in his caravan park, or that Ralph Scott has a deformity so awful he can't look in the mirror.

The next time Deloris and Harvey have sex she thinks of the baby growing inside her. Another life expanding with its own set of legs and arms pressing against her skin. 'A little Harvey,'

Sandra said when he told her. A limp hand wavered towards Deloris and she realised it was destined to pat her belly. 'Folic acid is essential. And eggs. Don't forget the eggs.' Deloris spends her days silently roving the house, going from room to room. She doesn't go back to Aylesbury – even if she wanted to, she is low on allowance and refuses to ask Harvey for any more. She begins to note where each object is in the house – not just the perfume bottle, but the kitchen towels on the rack, the front-door mat that meets the skirting board at a ninety-degree angle. The one time the perfume bottle disappears, put into the drawer, she spends the afternoon pleasantly agitated only to find it was Harvey. 'That gaudy thing? I'll buy you something new.'

On the following Monday afternoon she walks up the sloping hill of the high street to where the post office sits in a row with the corner shop, a small library of mostly children's books, and the church. Opposite is the village green, deserted of children, though perhaps they're still in school.

After paying the electricity bill, she wanders around listlessly even as her shoe rubs raw against her heel. They looked so nice in the shop – the velvet a deep purple – but catch slightly on the bone. It was her choice to buy them, she thinks as she skirts the edge of the churchyard, avoiding a smear of crushed snail. The stone church casts a shadow, but beyond that the sun renders the grass pale, the scene bleached of colour.

Deloris squints. Something is moving in the grass. It's Anna, who is crouched over, the floral fabric of her dress a mound among the grass. Her shoulder blades move back and forth as she picks at something.

'Hey, you over there,' Deloris says. Anna continues to scrabble.

As Deloris heads closer she senses she is intruding but is too close to pretend she hasn't seen her. 'Hi, Anna.'

'Oh.' She turns round, her face red. For a second her features are distorted with a shiny lower lip. 'Hello, Deloris,' she breathes. Her hands clutch the wings of a china angel. The gravestone is flat across the ground.

RUTH BLAKE, MOTHER AND CHILD OF GOD
1930 – 1983

'I'm sorry,' starts Deloris. 'I didn't realise.'

There is a crack along the angel's face which journeys below mournful eyes. Anna runs a finger along it without looking. For a few moments the only sound is the birds crying in the hawthorn hedges along the far edge, just before the woods.

'I shouldn't have interrupted you,' says Deloris, turning away.

'No, no.' Anna shuffles upwards. Green patches have stained her knees, cracks across the skin. 'I can't stay here all day.' She puts the angel carefully back at the top of the grave beside another to form a mirror image.

As the two of them shuffle back past the church, Jim appears from the side door. Deloris only knows him by sight even though he lives in Yardley Mews, the next road along. A white cloth covers his small chest and drapes from his arms. Some religious cloth, she thinks but it means nothing to her. RE is a mere subject she learnt at school – a question of ticking boxes and remembering which god goes with which religion.

'Got a minute?' he says.

Anna adjusts a smile on her face and neatens her fringe as she walks over. Deloris follows and observes the fifty-something man, unmarried, or married to the church, is it? No ring decorates his left hand, which scratches his neck, then stops to lace fingers inside the other. Although his white hair is clipped short, the sun highlights several stray wisps across his face as well as deeply etched frown lines.

'For the prayer meeting this evening.' He clears his throat and stops on the edge of the stone path to wait for Anna. 'I was hoping you could help to organise the drinks.'

'Of course, Jim.'

'Thank you.' Deloris waits for him to acknowledge her, but he doesn't. 'And help to put out the chairs beforehand? I haven't much time myself.'

Anna pauses to think. 'I'm not sure how early I can ...'

'Oh dear, I—'

Instantly Anna shakes her head. 'No, of course, I can.'

'Someone else could do it?' says Deloris. Both of them stare, Jim noticing her at last. 'Well, why not?' She bends down to feel the dislodged skin on her ankle.

'No, no, I can do it,' Anna insists, smiling at the two of them.

Jim's gown swishes as he turns to go into the church. 'Lovely.'

The two of them walk back together along the high street. Ahead by a few steps, Deloris bristles at the thought of Jim making Anna organise the chairs. And how Anna just agreed. Deloris should ask her if everything is OK, or say something comforting about her mother, but she can't think what. Besides, her ankle is now raw and every step brings a sharp wince. She pushes her toes forward to escape the back edge. It's still there, though, rubbing away as they pass the primary school with its empty playground and chalk lines fading in the sun.

The pavement narrows by the police station. It's more like an office building, or even a house, than somewhere investigations are held. Brian might be inside researching the Fox, though it's hard to see through the glass door between the pebble-dash walls. Deloris thinks of Anna, smiling so shyly at Brian, how she scurried off after giving him the glass of water. She must like him, and yet has done nothing about it, despite them having lived on the same street for years.

'Everything OK?' she asks as they reach Anna's cottage. The gate is fastened shut with brambles climbing higher in the front garden.

'Yes, thank you.'

Deloris crosses her arms. 'Are you sure?'

'Yes, thank you,' she mutters.

'Only ...' Deloris suddenly feels too hot, as if her blood is surging against her skull. It's far too humid. Anna's fringe sticks to her forehead but she doesn't fidget, just stands there politely on the pavement with her feet close together, like a child in ballet. 'You don't always have to be so polite,' says Deloris finally.

'Pardon?'

'Well.' She looks around the street. Sees the peeling doors of the bungalows opposite, condensation rising in patches of white against the shut windows. 'Just now with Jim. And in general. I mean, there's more to life than this village.'

For a second it seems like Anna wants to say something. Her lower lip protrudes as her face focuses on some imaginary point on the pavement where words might form. But then she stiffens and draws in her arms, the fabric of her dress wrinkling.

'Even with Brian,' Deloris starts again, frustrated at whatever is stopping Anna talking. She is probably speaking too loudly herself, but goes even louder. 'Harvey keeps making out that you like him, but is he even that much fun?' It's difficult to

46

know where this is coming from. Black spots are circling her as she swipes at a gnat.

'Brian is a nice man,' whispers Anna.

'I know, but really, why settle for the first man you meet?'

Anna's eyes flicker to her door and a stammer unsettles her voice. 'I don't know, Deloris.' She at last pulls back her fringe. 'All I wanted to do was visit my mother.'

That evening Deloris thinks of going over to apologise. Harvey is out with two work colleagues playing golf at the local range, so she is alone, trying not to scratch at her ankle, which flares pink around the ruffled skin. From the living-room window she can see the fence of Anna's front garden at the end of the road. *Anna won't be in anyway,* she thinks. *That dumb prayer meeting.* She has an urge to read Charlotte Brontë's *Jane Eyre* or perhaps Emily's *Wuthering Heights*. Some sort of long sad romance that builds to an exhilarating end of dishevelled clothing in moors of wild grass. But she has left these books at home – or rather her *old* home – where they remain under the bed with notes squeezed up the margins and hearts over the 'I's. She was supposed to be embarking on a romance of her own. Deloris stares at the spider web drifting from the ceiling.

The next morning she wakes up from a thick sleep to find it's past nine o'clock. What might once have been a thrill at missing school is replaced with the awareness that it means nothing much at all. Only a slight shadow over her bed stirred her and that was just part of a dream she can't remember – her flying above a forest with wings that calmly flap, then break and turn back to newspaper?

Deloris slopes into the bathroom for a lengthy shower and

then pulls open various drawers, vaguely looking for what to wear. The underwear all seems uncomfortable in its fussy layers of lace and bows that are now greying. She pushes the lower drawer closed and opens the top one. Taking out the perfume bottle she breathes in the scent before realising something is different – a photograph has been left in the drawer above her make-up box. It's one she forgot she'd taken from home: her in a striped one-piece by the lido in London Fields, a crease down the middle where she's bent out her dad who is an oily pink after sunbathing. With a hand on one hip, the water reflecting on her legs, she looks like a girl from a magazine. But who put it in her drawer? Her old photos are all stashed in the attic.

Something moves within her and she enjoys the pulse of life. Deloris not sure what this feeling is, knows she is supposed to feel afraid.

Hurriedly pulling on shorts and T-shirt from the clean laundry pile, she heads to the only place she can think of – Anna's. She will apologise for the afternoon before and say of course she should be with Brian. Why not? Anything can happen in this village, the most mundane of places can witness all sorts of events.

As she gets closer, Deloris sees the side gate is open a few inches. She must be in the back garden weeding.

'Anna?'

Just the usual tall grass, the birdbath in the middle claimed by moss. She reaches the back door and stops. Through the small window she can see just a dim impression of the Welsh dresser with its row of looming teapots.

The kitchen is chilly and her sandals slap across the stone tiles. 'Hello?'

It's tidier than the other day – the milk pan has been washed and is upside down in the drying rack. On the counter beside the bin, however, grapes are shrivelled with splitting skins, a fruit fly sucking on one. Deloris hesitates.

There's a shuffling from the passage that leads into the living room. A scrape of shoe. Deloris releases the breath she's been holding. 'Sorry to just let myself in ...'

But the figure that emerges isn't Anna.

'Who's that?' comes a man's voice. Jim dips his head to walk beneath a low beam and straightens up in the kitchen.

'Where's Anna?' asks Deloris, seeing the strange expression on his face. 'Is she upstairs?'

'Not that I can see.' Jim scratches the back of his neck. He's not in his white robes, but a linen shirt that seems too casual. Shorts flare over scrawny legs; bare toes protrude from leather sandals.

'Anna!' Deloris edges around him to get through to the living room. Her foot crunches on something. It's the photograph of Anna and her mum that used to be on the wall. Glass has shattered across the Oriental rug all the way to the tassels at the far end.

'She didn't come to prayer meeting last night,' Jim says to himself. 'It seems ...'

'What?' Deloris draws her feet together.

'It seems Anna isn't here.'

'Where is she?'

He peers out the small window. 'Anna is gone.'

3

Deloris kneels on the sofa, just like the evening before. This time, however, a police car is parked on the pavement opposite Anna's house. It seems over the top, Deloris thinks. Surely Brian could just walk down from the police station less than 200 metres away?

Sandra is behind her. The pearls of her necklace click one on top of the other as she pulls at the long string. Harvey and Michael have both come home from the office early supposedly to check that everything is all right. Michael is pouring his son a vodka at the drinks table.

'She'll have gone away for a couple of days,' says Deloris although her voice is uncertain. 'A summer trip.'

No one replies. A hiss fills the room as a lemonade can is opened.

'Brian has been in there twenty minutes now,' says Sandra, stepping closer to the window. 'What's he doing, do you suppose?'

'Checking for damage, compiling evidence in case it's linked to this Fox character,' says Michael.

'Seriously,' Deloris says, swivelling round to the three of them. 'We have no reason to think it was him.'

Harvey lets out a puff of air. 'Don't be naive, Dolly. Who else would it be?'

'No one. Maybe she went out and forgot to lock the back door,' Deloris says. 'She is pretty ditsy.' The others reluctantly murmur agreement. They all continue to watch though they can't actually see much of Anna's house, just the police car, and Cynthia out by her own front door in the same dressing gown.

'It's not even been a day,' says Deloris.

'She didn't turn up for prayer meeting last night,' whispers Sandra.

Michael sips his drink. 'That's almost twenty-four hours.'

'So? She is a fully-grown woman,' Deloris points out. 'She probably just needed to get away from the village.'

They all lower their eyes from the window to look at her. 'Why do you say that?' asks Sandra.

Deloris falls silent and remains on the sofa until it's time to cook dinner.

The police don't have much to go on. An article in the local *Gazette* the next morning takes up marginally more room than the first published after Elsie's intrusion, but is still relegated to near the back beside the football scores and trade union meeting times.

*

MISSING VILLAGE GIRL

On the evening of Monday, 18 June, Anna Blake went missing from her home in the village of Heathcote. Police are unsure whether her disappearance may be connected to the three domestic intrusions that have taken place over the last fortnight. A villager describes Anna as, 'a sweet girl committed to the church'. Her mother Ruth Blake passed away last year and Anna has been more dedicated than ever to the village. She had no known reason to leave and PC Brian McPherson asks local residents to report any sightings of Anna or relevant information as to her whereabouts.

Below the paragraph, a photograph shows Anna looking young and carrying a tray of sandwiches at some church gathering. She's frowning slightly, though her lips are upturned as if someone has told her to smile.

The blender pulses once, then twice, as Harvey makes his usual SlimFast shake.

'I told you,' he says, angling his head at the newspaper as if proved right all along. He tells her he's decided to go into work late that morning and she supposes she should feel touched although he's more absorbed in the news than checking the locks like he talked about.

A while later, as Deloris stands at the sink wiping down trails of Harvey's powder, the doorbell rings.

'Just some routine enquiries,' says Brian. He notices the newspaper article and anxiously tugs his shirtsleeves above his elbows. The fabric seems heavy with a collar that pinches the pink skin around his neck.

'Sure, sure.' Harvey puts a hand on Deloris's head. 'Though be careful what you note with that pencil of yours.' He laughs. 'My wife here seems to think she's riding roller coasters in Blackpool or something.'

'Oh?'

Deloris pushes off her husband's hand but stays beside him.

Brian explains he is asking everyone in the street if they have anything to report. Any idea where Anna might have gone. 'Even if it's the smallest thing. It all helps to build a picture, you see.'

'A horrible situation, eh?' starts Harvey as Brian diligently listens, pencil to pad. 'She wouldn't have stood a chance at defending herself, either. Too gentle, that girl. And now she could be anywhere.'

'You're not helping,' says Deloris. Her husband has never seemed to like Anna and now he is basking in the drama of her being gone?

Brian puts his shoulders back so the silver police badge tilts at an angle. There are slight bags beneath his eyes that don't seem to belong to his face. Deloris wonders if this is his first proper police investigation. 'We have no firm connection with the previous intrusion,' he says mechanically, 'Right now we're simply trying to build a picture of Anna's last known movements.' He raises his eyes to Deloris. 'Perhaps you might have some information as to her whereabouts?'

She tells him that she saw Anna at the church on Monday and they walked back together. 'She did seem a bit irritable, actually.'

'About what?' Harvey says, licking the last of his protein shake from the blender jug.

'Yeah, about what?' Brian's pencil lifts from the paper. 'I mean, do you know what this related to?'

'I don't know.'

'Come on, Dolly.' Harvey goes to look over Brian's shoulder at his notes. 'You girls—'

'What's that supposed to mean?'

'Mum said she saw you and Anna together by the church.' He speaks to Brian, 'Girls tell each other everything.'

Deloris shakes her head. 'For a start, we're not "girls". And—'

'It would be helpful actually,' says Brian with an apologetic smile. 'To know why Anna might've been upset.'

'I said "irritated", not upset. And ...' Deloris places her hands on her hips, her finger bare of the wedding band she'd not put on that morning, ready to tell Harvey she'd forgotten if he asked. 'Maybe she wanted some space from this village.'

Brian seems hurt. He blinks and his shoulders fall forwards. It's Harvey who goes to speak but Deloris jumps in. 'She is a fully grown woman. It's been barely a day. And maybe people didn't know Anna as well as they thought. There's always more than what meets the eye.'

'See what I mean about her own world?' Harvey says to Brian. 'All her TV shows and books.' He turns to Deloris. 'We both went to school with the girl. You only rocked up here a few months ago.'

'A year, actually.'

'A year, fine.' Harvey turns the tap and water shoots into a glass, flooding the edges. 'Did you know Anna has never left Buckinghamshire? She's hardly the type to swan off for some travelling.' He takes the glass and then mutters that he's going to sort some paperwork.

Alone with Deloris in the kitchen, Brian fidgets with his pencil, prodding it against the paper before regaining himself. 'I'm sorry, Deloris. I hate to say this but there are signs of an intrusion. A broken photograph plus a cracked window pane upstairs.' He reads a line from an earlier page. '"The profile of a violent criminal."'

'That doesn't sound right,' Deloris says without thinking. Her mind is filled with the image of the lilac perfume bottle; the almost silent steps.

'What do you mean?' Brian looks up to meet her eye and she spins round to the work surface. Busies herself with wiping the tiles again.

'Nothing.'

'Are you sure?'

'Yes.'

After he closes his notebook, she follows Brian through the hallway to the front door. He moves slowly, as if about to stop at any moment. His fingers pause on the door handle.

'If you know something, please come forward,' he says with wide eyes, white appearing all the way around the pupils. 'We're tracking the recent intruder's movements and it's vital we're told everything, however small.'

Deloris wanders out on to the patio where she goes to the back gate and peers into the road. Brian is walking up the path to the Braithwaites'. He'll soon be back at the station. Or she could leave a message with whoever is on reception? She's never been into the building or into any police station for that matter. She pictures herself in a small interview room like in a crime novel. The tape running, polystyrene cups of coffee turned cold with a film over the top. Although she tells herself

Anna hasn't been taken, she should still be honest with the police. As she thinks of what she'd say she is distracted by the sound of Harvey's voice from upstairs. He is on the phone in the study. She walks towards the back of the patio to where the silver birches have dropped leaves on to the tiles. They crunch under her flip-flops and she jumps back, skittish.

A slip of orange runs up the side of the bin, the liner of the rubbish bag showing through where the plastic is cracked. Stooping a little, Deloris runs a finger along its protruding edge. She pushes the bin back to its place against the fence. Beneath lies just a bare slab of tile. It's where she keeps the spare back door key but it's no longer there.

Footsteps send her jerking away and the bin clatters back in its spot.

'Deloris!' Harvey stands inside of the door holding the cordless phone. 'Get inside now please,' he shouts and then disappears again.

With shaking legs Deloris comes into the kitchen. The walls are moving around and she struggles to catch the edge of the work surface to hold on.

'That was my mum,' Harvey says hanging up the phone as he paces the kitchen. 'Apparently they think the Fox might be targeting young women.'

The rest of the day goes by in a strange, confused daze. Deloris skips lunch. When she later picks at a piece of bread it passes uneasily down her throat. Harvey makes her promise to lock all windows and doors before he leaves for a meeting and she walks around, double and triple checking the handles. The miniature keys rest on the brass on top of each one. But the spare back door key isn't anywhere, not even accidentally slipped down the drain cover, which she pulls up to a waft of dank moss. She tells herself to call the locksmith and finds the number in the *Yellow Pages*. But she can't arrange it without Harvey finding out – her allowance has run out for the month and, besides, he'd be sure to hear from a neighbour if an unknown van parked up outside. She pictures his face twisting as she admits to leaving the spare key outside despite him telling her not to. *See? This is exactly what I'm talking about! You might have ten O levels but you really don't have a clue.*

Instead, she sits by the back door with her forehead against the glass that turns smudgy, her breath creating clouds. Sleep pulls her under and she wakes with a crick down the side of her neck and an image of Anna's face after their last conversation in the street. Her quiet words: *All I wanted to do was visit my mother.*

The phone rings and it's her sister, Sharon.

'D? You there?'

'I am, yeah.'

'We're having a family tea. Tomorrow night.'

Deloris pictures them all crowded around the table with their aunts and cousins, everyone nudging at each other's elbows, her mum fussing over the special roast lamb she makes that always smells so good.

'Well? You coming then?'

The blank walls stare back at Deloris.

'Dad wants you to come. He's got a doctor's appointment next Thursday.'

'He does?'

'And you can bring Harvey if you want.'

Deloris's eyes flicker towards the patio doors. At any minute there could be a click of brass as the Fox slips inside the house. 'I'm sorry. I can't deal with this right now.'

Later that afternoon she finds herself turning the front door key, bending to undo the bottom bolt lock, and walking down the street. Outside Anna's house things seem too normal. Perhaps she expected to see tape across the lawn but the front garden is unchanged, with its overgrown hedgerow and windows dark behind. The only difference is the row of three milk bottles left in the rusting container by the door. The side gate has been left closed but swings forward as she pushes it. She wanders down the side of the house. Anna's garden doesn't have a proper fence at the back – wooden posts fall at different angles, the wire between them sagging and out of shape in the middle where she might have climbed as a little girl. Deloris sits down cross-legged beside the birdbath where a pool of water covers the moss.

Where can she have gone? Deloris thinks of the washed milk pan and tidied crumbs. She pictures Anna packing a small suitcase, her carefully folding and adding clothes, but on finishing, the suitcase is still empty.

When Deloris eventually wanders back to her house, she finds Sandra waiting by the front door. Her arms are crossed and she cowers in the shade of the porch, a shadow across her bony chest.

'The sun can have a disastrous effect on the skin of women my age,' she says with a nervous laugh.

'I didn't know you were coming.' Deloris tries to hurry up the drive but is too tired. The gravel slides about under her flip-flops.

'Where have you been?' Sandra asks as Deloris unlocks the

door. Before she can answer, Sandra slips past her and totters towards the kitchen. 'It's really not fair of you to wander around without a care in the world.'

'I do have a care,' says Deloris, though the words feel strange.

'Do you really?'

'Yes,' she mumbles, ending up by the kitchen counter.

'Then explain this.'

'Hmm?'

'This!'

Sandra's finger points to the ground. A trail of something. Mud in tiny clumps, a cream-coloured root curling outwards.

'You should really be looking after the floor.'

Deloris looks at her clean flip-flops.

'Especially while it's so new.'

As Deloris slowly lowers herself, her hands hit the floor first, then her knees. She puts her head on the hard surface. The soil smells savoury and blows away with the air from her nose. So the Fox *was* here?

'Oh dear, I'm sorry,' says Sandra, unsure of herself. Kitten heels edge towards Deloris and stop just short of her knees. Pearls fall outwards from her blouse as a hand pats Deloris's hair. 'I think I know what's wrong.' She pats her again with stiff fingers and moves away. 'You're worried about poor Anna, aren't you?'

Deloris takes several breaths, her eyes closed and knees still pressed to the floor, while Sandra's heels echo around the kitchen. When she finally looks up, she finds the trail of mud hasn't been cleaned away. Instead Sandra has made them a pot of tea and biscuits.

*

They sit on the same sofa in the living room, and once Deloris has chewed through three bourbon creams and regained herself, they shuffle further apart. An uneasy silence claims the room but it seems Sandra isn't ready to go home; she gropes at her pearls as she stares at the display cabinet. A picture shows Harvey at age sixteen on his first day of work at the carpet factory, the suit overly large for his frame. Beside him, his dad's hand is clamped on his shoulder while he smiles proudly at his son.

'That's it,' says Sandra after a minute.

'What?'

'If the police aren't doing enough then, well ...'

Deloris swallows the last of her biscuit. 'What are you talking about?'

Sandra stands up and smooths down her skirt as if preparing to give a speech. 'We residents need to take things into our own hands.'

'You don't think Brian is doing enough?'

'Not really, no. The villagers are as bad. The more I talk to people about it, the more infuriated I get. That awful Jim – not even a real vicar, you know – said we shouldn't jump to conclusions about the Fox.' She purses her lips and goes to the window. 'And the receptionist at the police station told me enquiries were open at this stage. As if we don't already know who's responsible.'

Over the next few minutes Deloris has trouble understanding Sandra as she lapses between fits of talking and silences. 'What are you going to do?'

Sandra turns with eyes that don't settle. 'Personally? Nothing, of course. Who knows what sort of person this Fox character is? It's one thing to watch people, but now he's abducted our neighbour?' The skin under her jaw quivers as she speaks again. 'Harvey's the man to do it. He'll lead us all, I dare say. His father always puts so much faith in him, why can't I?'

She strides into the hallway, where she stops and looks around. Deloris follows with heavy feet. 'What would it consist of?' she asks nervously.

'I'm not sure.' Sandra opens the door. 'But I'll be damned if we just sit here.'

Harvey's body is a weight above her the next morning, elbows trapping her either side. She keeps her eyes on the perfume bottle, which is standing on her bedside table. The window is shut, the hot room lacking air as her husband sweats. Afterwards Harvey frowns and pulls away to shower. 'At least you could pretend to enjoy it.' His voice is brittle as he walks to the bathroom. While the shower beats against the side of the bath, Deloris stands up and flexes on to the front of her feet – a technique for avoiding pregnancy she learnt in *Cosmopolitan*. She then pulls on the same dress as last night and doesn't bother to brush her hair. She is tired of being in the house, of obsessing about perfume bottles and milk pans. The kitchen is already stuffy with recycled air. It smells of the tuna fish they had last night, or rather Harvey had. Bones are still stuck down the bin liner.

'I want to go and see my sister,' she says as he comes into the kitchen to say goodbye.

'I'm not stopping you.' He throws a cloth into the sink. 'As long as you're careful,' he says as an afterthought.

'Well, I need some money.'

Still facing the window, he stands hunched with arms out. His shoulder blades are raised and pull at the shirt. 'I suppose that's where I come in?'

Deloris steps towards him with a hand ready to place on his arm. 'Yes please. If that's OK.'

'How about no?' He whips around. 'What've you done to deserve it? Sloping around the house like some kind of prisoner ...'

'I thought you'd want me to stay inside?'

'Do whatever you want, Deloris.' He shakes his head and leaves for the day.

The breeze is agitating the newspaper left on the coffee table. A page has fallen open and she slumps on the sofa to close it again. A series of job adverts are composed in columns – most are just a few words each, one is in a large box that says, 'Forklift drivers wanted'. Seeing these reminds her of when her mum used to look each week as soon as the paper came – though she had a job in the canteen at the shoe factory, she always browsed just in case something better came along. Deloris goes to clear it away and sees another advert in the corner: 'Kitchen porter for King's Cross hotel. Urgently needed. Come for interview today.'

She's never worked in a hotel before but a new possibility tingles inside her.

On the train she hides in the toilet cubicle. The door rattles against its plastic fitting as she tries not to step in the toilet paper strewn across the floor. She hasn't avoided the ticket fare since she was sixteen, but it was much easier at the small station with no staff. And the train showed up on time too. After rushing to the station, her heart leaping to pass every fence or overgrown hedgerow, she actually laughed to see the rusted carriages slide along the platform.

A while later there's a timid knock and a child's voice, 'Is anybody in there? I need a wee.' Deloris winces and silently apologises as the handle is pulled down a few times and then goes still. As she waits, images flit through her mind: a flat share with another couple of girls, not much money but a splurge every fortnight maybe. Going out in Croydon with her old friends, Sally and Tina. The Nag's Head on a Friday night. She hasn't spoken to either of them in months after it got too difficult to listen to their stories of drunken kisses or a new pair of wedge heels for the disco that'd started up. Even talk of factory lunch breaks together made her wince. It could all change now, though. What would her little sister say? She could come visit if she liked.

Almost an hour later she's at Euston where she joins the end of the queue behind people with large suitcases or wide buggies. The one in front has heavy-duty wheels and all sorts of things stashed into its lower compartment. A grey-faced woman pushes it forwards and Deloris follows too, trying not to fidget with her handbag. At least she is presentable in a white blouse and the knee-length skirt she dug out. It's the one her mum bought her when they thought she was going for the college interview. Depressing that she's now going for a job in a kitchen, loading a dishwasher, but she shakes away the thought. Gives a tentative smile with just a little teeth showing.

'Ticket.' The uniformed man barely looks at her from beneath his bushy eyebrows.

'I've lost my ticket.' She pats herself down. 'No idea how. I always keep it in my front breast pocket.'

The man jabs a finger at his office. 'Wait there.'

'Pardon?'

'Penalty fare.' He goes to check the next young woman's ticket and she puts it into his outstretched hand.

'I've got no money,' Deloris says, trying to keep her voice even.

'Then it's the station police.'

For a second it's all over. She imagines them calling Harvey at work to say she's been arrested. *Arrested*. A criminal and not even a clever one. What will Brian think if he hears? It isn't like they're close friends but she'd hate him to brand her some petty thief. The man still isn't looking at her and yawns as he takes the last person's ticket. He's then twisting to see the clock, leaving a gap between him and the newspaper stand.

'Oi!'

Faces slide past as she runs up the sloping entrance to the main station. A dog pulls on a lead, two young girls with ice cream of swirls of pink. Their mother cries out as she passes, hearing the man's calls behind and the comments, the shouting of another deep voice. But she is ahead and flying across the shopping area and out into the day, bright and warm air whipping at her clothing.

Whatever powered her body quickly fades as she walks along Euston Road after waiting behind a phone box and seeing the man turn back, then become lost among the crowds. She doesn't know north London all that well and roams the streets looking for the right address. People she asks barely stop to help her until she sees a friendly-looking man with round glasses in the bus shelter. 'Oh yes, Sheldon Hotel.' He raises an arm. 'It's a few roads from here past the British Library.'

The hotel is the unassuming type with just a small plaque next to the door. Deloris walks past it at first and then peers into the dim lobby, which is empty. Inside she waits for someone to appear and after several minutes a guy with an unusual accent – Russian? – tells her to take a seat. The fake leather is clammy under her thighs. She tries not to judge the cigarette burns or the shoddy display of pamphlets in the plastic containers attached to the wall.

It's a far cry from the Bermuda hotel. All high ceilings with fans spinning and potted plants she never saw anyone water. Deloris tries to think of Harvey ignoring her at dinner as he read the *New York Times* and telling the maître d' how impressed he was with all the travelling she must've done. *You're from France? Really made something of yourself, haven't you?* But perhaps he *was* just being friendly. Perhaps Deloris was the lucky one.

'Excuse me.' Deloris stands up. 'Where are the ladies' bathrooms?'

'Down zer hall.'

'Right.'

'Don't be long. Zer interview is soon and zey won't wait.'

Deloris stares at herself in the mirror. Strip lighting flickers above so her face goes from stark white to dim. Rough skin appears on her cheeks – is that sun damage? She leans in and almost slips, her arms suddenly weak. Her legs feel similarly unreliable as she opens a stall and goes inside. Maybe she should just go home again. Wait for Anna to turn up. As she sits she doesn't bother avoiding the crumpled plastic bag that gets caught in her heel. It rustles as she jitters her foot up and down. The corner of a magazine is exposed – the *TV Times*. It's a couple of weeks old with a battered cover but she opens it anyway. Harvey was never keen on ordering a subscription. *Like admitting we're TV slobs.* The page falls open on an article and Sue Ellen stares out. She has hair like a falcon – it rides high on her head in a glossy spread of brown. Her eyes stare straight at the camera. 'J.R. Gets His Comeuppance' reads the headline.

Deloris is led along a corridor and thanks the man every time he holds a door for her. Despite his shaved head and almost yellow pallor, he fills his waistcoat well and gave her a small smile at reception. At the final door, which scuffs along the carpet, he shows her to a chair in the dining room. It's a prettier place with the smell of furniture polish and just one dirty ashtray, the others clean.

'Ten O levels?' the man asks in his soft voice. It feels like there should be paper or something on the table between them, but Deloris doesn't have a copy of her CV.

'You can ring my school. Edenham.'

'Ring your school,' he repeats as if an unlikely demand.

'Yes.' She touches her hair, which is damp where she added some water. It's sinking lower but is still raised. 'They're very nice.'

He laughs to himself and shifts in his seat. 'And you're telling me you want to wash our dishes?'

'To begin with,' Deloris says. 'I can manage the hard work when I put my mind to it.' The words she prepared for her college interview come back. 'But ultimately I do want more. I've always been a dreamer. Someone who wants big things and though I know it'll take time, my dreams are what keep me going.'

He studies her with gentle grey eyes.

'Don't we all need a dream? Aren't they what count?'

The man laughs, but hopefully with her. 'I guess so.'

Fifteen minutes later Deloris finds a phone box and makes a reverse charges call to her parents' house. Her sister picks up after the first ring and sounds disappointed, hearing her voice.

'Can I meet you somewhere?' she asks. 'Please, Sharon?'

'You were rude to me the other day.'

'I know and I'm sorry.' A man in a long coat lingers outside the box. 'But please – just tell me where to come.'

Deloris waits in a café by Covent Garden near where Sharon is due to start work in half an hour. It's for tourists, mostly, with plastic menus and overblown prices. Deloris sits back in the chair, letting her shoes fall off her feet and listening to the kettle boil, the pleasant hum of conversations around her.

'You never said why you're here,' Sharon says as she arrives in her hairdressing uniform. A comb sticks out of the pocket above her breast.

'I just went for a job.'

'You never!' Sharon seems affronted by this. She wrinkles her nose as she plonks herself down and leans chubby arms on the table. 'What for?'

'Just as a kitchen porter, but still, it's something, isn't it?'

The owner bustles over and asks what they fancy. Sharon orders a jacket potato with coronation chicken while Deloris, who hasn't yet admitted she has no money, asks for a black coffee. Her stomach horribly empty, she almost calls out to add her own food but doesn't want her sister to think she's spoilt.

'You get it then?'

Steam curls up from the potato as Sharon slices it open and Deloris leans forwards. She has forgotten all about the job interview. It's nice sitting with her sister, sort of like old times when they'd be bored at home and eat their tea in the kitchen when their dad had tennis on the TV.

'D?'

'They didn't say.' She tries to sound cheerful. 'But the guy was impressed with my school results. He said to phone him tomorrow once he's seen a couple more people.'

Sharon ends up lending Deloris four pounds on the promise she'll pay it back within the next month. Though she's been promoted to junior stylist it's not like she has much to spare. Deloris agrees and says it won't happen again. She's not used to being like this with her younger sister who's supposed to be asking *her* for things, not the other way around. But she treats herself to a scone with butter and each bite comes with a little relief.

'I'm leaving Harvey,' she says as Sharon pays at the till. Hearing the words out loud makes her dizzy. She's thought them once before the week after their honeymoon but just as an experiment like trying on shoes you know won't fit.

'Eh?' Sharon scowls into her purse, pushing coins between the plastic slats.

'I am. For a better life,' she says uncertainly, then trails after her sister who is winding her way past a line of people that's formed from nowhere. 'Did you hear me?' she asks outside on the side street.

'You could come home, you know.' Sharon glances towards the salon where she works. 'I've put posters up your side of the room but suppose I could move them.'

'Well …'

'And you can come to the family tea. Dad's properly ill, you know. The doctors say he's got something on his lungs they can't get off.'

'I didn't realise.'

'Why would you? You're not around any more.'

Deloris feels her chest tighten to picture their dad in a hospital bed, its railings shaking with every cough. The two of them used to share a cigarette after dinner until she realised her nails were yellowing to resemble his own stubby fingers. She told him it was a gross habit and so he sat in the back yard on his own, humming a Johnny Cash or Leonard Cohen song, until it was time to start his night shift at the car parts warehouse.

Now Deloris takes a slow breath and Sharon, seeming to properly look at her for the first time that afternoon, puffs out her own cheeks. 'What's brought all this on, D? You was never s—'

'Spoilt?!' Her arms whoosh in the air as she says it. As they come down again she feels jittery and grabs hold of the handlebars of a bike leant against the wall. They shudder and fall away, leaving Deloris staring at the pavement, which is dusty with cigarette ash stubbed out. Silvery ash lost its glow.

'No.' Sharon scrapes her canvas shoe on the pavement. 'I was gonna say "sad".'

Deloris sidesteps the bike and lets herself drop backwards to the café's wall.

'Stuff is happening in the village, it's on my mind,' she says but doesn't want to talk about it.

A minute or so passes and they both stand there watching tourists go past.

'I think you should,' Sharon says. 'Leave him, I mean. I never thought Harvey was all that, even if you and mum did.' She nods at Deloris as if deciding herself. 'You got carried away, that's all. Not a crime.' After another crowd ambles past, she pulls back her shirtsleeve to see her watch.

'I'll walk you,' Deloris says as she pushes off the wall. 'See you get there safe.'

'Safe?'

'You never know who's watching you.'

Sharon rolls her eyes but lets her sister put an arm through hers.

It's past five o'clock when Deloris gets off the train and makes the walk back to Heathcote along the main road, past the village green. The smell of barbecued ribs and pork sausages comes in whiffs and she smiles to herself. Maybe she'll have a barbecue when she first gets to London. The idea of setting up a new life buoys her. It won't be easy, but then what is? She strolls past a group of teenagers by the corner shop who kick at the faded ice-cream sign, cans of Boddingtons in hand. Deloris holds her head high and flashes a grin. She can be anyone she wants, she thinks, waiting for the hoots. As one of the boys in his tracksuit begins to approach, she carries on down the pavement. She reaches her road and pauses in front of Anna's empty house. Perhaps they can both be free.

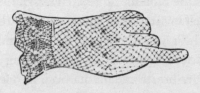

4

Harvey is waiting in the living room with the television on mute. He turns to her as she steps into the hallway and she's gripped by a feeling that makes it difficult to keep moving forwards. Hearing the zap of the television turning off, she tilts her chin slightly and goes through to the kitchen for a gulp of lemonade.

'You're bloody selfish, you know that?' Harvey says, appearing at the door. He's still in his work clothes though his tie hangs loose either side of his vein-striped neck. 'Coming home whenever it suits you.'

'What? Because I wasn't here to cook your dinner?'

'No.' He's genuinely shocked. 'Because I was frantic when I got home and you weren't here.'

'Oh.'

He fills the doorway. 'Swanning around while our friend is missing.'

Deloris feels herself deflate so pushes past him to go upstairs. *Me making plans doesn't hurt Anna.* Expecting Harvey to follow, she yanks the suitcase down from the cupboard above the wardrobe, then realises it belongs to him. Where is her old duffel bag? Thrown away most likely, with everything else. The thought makes her shake. She takes things off hangers and throws them on to the bed. Hears Harvey's footsteps and forces herself to carry on, as she waits for him to see. Whatever he shouts she'll ignore. She's made up her mind.

His footsteps come across the landing and stop in the doorway. Her breath catches halfway in. He says nothing, so Deloris takes a red halter-neck dress and folds it over one arm, not wanting to look up and see the contorted expression on his face. He's never been violent with her before, not properly, but then she's never left him before.

He carries on standing until she can't bear it any more. She turns to see his face calm and smooth. His arms hang limp by his sides with a remote control in one hand. As if she's a channel he might be able to change.

'Harvey?'

'I got an interesting phone call earlier.'

Her voice comes out in barely a whisper. 'You did?'

Flesh is sucked in one side of his mouth, then the other as his jaw moves. There's a grinding noise she's not heard before. Teeth against teeth. He whitens them, looks after them with various implements and a bottle of purple mouthwash.

'What was it?'

'You betrayed me, Dolly. We were planning to start a family and you ran off.'

She lets the skirt in her hand fall to the floor and grips herself around the middle. 'It was shitty of me but I've got to get away. I hate this house.'

'You hate this house?' he says and throws the remote control against the wall. A crack of plastic before it slides down. Batteries roll across the carpet. 'You think it's been easy for me? Paying for this huge place? The goddamn microwave oven?'

He paces across the bedroom where dresses lie discarded on the floor, over the bed and its Egyptian cotton sheets she picked out. 'I stress all day to buy this stuff you said you wanted, but I come home and . . .' He takes a breath. 'You look so *disappointed* in it all.'

'I'm sorry.'

His chest begins to heave, sweat shining among the prickles of hair. 'You used to look at me like some sort of hero. Like you couldn't wait for our lives to start together. And now you'd prefer to work in some poxy two-star hotel? I suppose they might give you a room too. You'd never need see me again.'

'Please, Harvey.' She's scrabbling with her clothes, trying to pick them all up though she's got no bag ready so stands there with them expanding in her arms.

He stops in the doorway. His eyes drop to the loose batteries. 'Are you really leaving me, Dolly?'

'I don't know.' She sits on the bed and the clothes fall around her. Creases in all her summer dresses.

'Well?'

'I don't know,' she repeats without looking at him.

'No?' There's an edge to his voice, 'I do.'

Deloris looks up. His jaw is stiff again and there's a glazed look to him like something has come between the two of them.

'I told this gentleman at the hotel no thanks.'

'*What?*'

'Say "Pardon", Dolly. See? This is what I have to deal with.' He chuckles to himself as he paces into the hallway, shaking his head dramatically.

73

'They were impressed with me!' Deloris shouts. 'I'm not just some housewife.'

'Yes, they were.' He stops and turns to nod at her. 'Pity you're not fit for work.'

'What?'

'I told them about you having a baby soon.' He starts to pace again and disappears from sight. A surge brings Deloris to her feet.

'What the hell?'

'You'll be busy at home. Looking after our child.'

'I'm not even pregnant yet, thank God.'

An odd laugh. 'Is the idea *so* awful?'

Shocked by the pained look on his face, Deloris goes to catch Harvey's arm but he throws his weight down the stairs and thuds into the kitchen.

'I guess this isn't enough for you.' The Magimix rattles as he grabs its handle then throws it to the floor. A pile of their dinner plates wait by the cupboard, each forming a white blur as they skim through the air from his outstretched hands. Deloris watches in a daze, stunned by the explosions of china.

Harvey starts to list the price of each gadget and she's suddenly aware of the space between her hips. 'But now you think I'm some sort of creep,' says Harvey, his words half-swallowed.

'Of course I don't.'

She goes to him, but he won't meet her eye. She takes his arm and nudges him round until they face one another. Their bodies are less than an inch apart but not touching, just like when they first danced together in a bar in the West End, a spread of silver reflections over the dance floor. They'd been the only two people there; it was too early for the rest of the crowds.

As she steps towards him, her foot crunches on a plate. The crockery from their wedding day is in broken pieces around them.

'Can you sit with me?' she asks quietly, a heat flushing through her middle.

Harvey slumps against the counter and helps her down. His hand is quickly removed from her damp palm as he picks up the handle of the Magimix and tosses it towards the bin.

She wants to lean her head on the cabinet but something wet is expanding between her legs.

'I don't feel right,' she breathes.

Harvey fingers another piece of china, then reluctantly stands to get her some water. The tap goes, ice cubes tinkle. And then he is saying something to her. He says it again but she can't make sense of it. All she can do is clutch her skirt as a trickle of blood slides down her inner thigh.

Deloris later sits in the bath. The light is dimming so she can only imagine the pink clouds of water forming. She closes her eyes and listens to the silent house. Harvey has already gone to bed for an early business meeting the next day. *An important talk with a guy visiting from one of our Chinese suppliers,* he explained after asking again if she was all right. She hadn't said what happened exactly, only that she had stomach ache. How could she explain when she could barely say the word? Surely it belonged to women who'd already picked out a name for their boy or girl, a layer of paint for the spare bedroom wall and a mobile spinning above a cot. *I can't miss something I never had,* she tells herself and realises the water has gone cold.

It's almost ten o'clock by the time she is wrapped in her bathrobe. The landing is dark and she peers out to see Anna's house where no lights are on. To the outer edge of a pool of streetlight stands a figure: Mary Braithwaite. The Irish woman lives next door to Anna and, together with her balding husband Donald, runs the post office with a resolute cheerfulness even when people complain of her being too slow with the franking machine.

Deloris slips on some shoes and goes out.

'I thought I heard a noise,' Mary says as she approaches. The woman is pressed against the front gate, her eyes wavering across Anna's house with its dark windows and the crack in the paintwork by the guttering.

'What sort of noise?'

'Like a scratching.'

Deloris listens: just the drops of rain spilling on the bushes and milk bottles. She gestures to go through the gate but Mary doesn't move.

'I used to hear her, you see. And I suppose it plays on me.'

'What? The sound of scratching?'

'Oh aye. Who knows what Anna was doing, though. It was quite a surprise – after twenty-odd years living next door, I'd barely heard a peep from the two of them. Then it started up most nights during the weeks after Ruth's death. I held off going around to see her, wanting to respect her grief, like. But it went on and I ended up knocking on the door one evening. The poor thing was terribly embarrassed to see me. I remember she tried to hide something behind her back, and when she went to close the door, I saw it was a small crucifix snapped in two.'

'And you heard the scratching again tonight?' Deloris nudges an arm to the gate and walks towards the front door. She listens again but there's nothing.

'Such a private family,' Mary continues, still hovering

behind. 'Though they did so much around the church, they never spoke much of themselves, even when Ruth became ill and Anna nursed her. You couldn't get either of them to complain about it. That's what makes it worse.'

'What does?'

'This Fox character being inside Anna's home; her bedroom, maybe. And how long was he watching her beforehand? It's so easy to get into her garden with that toppled fence. And it's an old house without double glazing. Donald once offered to fix the windows but Anna refused.'

A door creaks open next door and Donald, in a string vest, motions at his wife to come back. 'She's not there, love.'

Mary doesn't turn. 'And to think she might now be with him? That animal?'

The two women gaze up at the top window of Anna's bedroom. Not much can be seen since the curtains are drawn, although as Deloris tilts her head she can make out the shape of a crucifix leant against the glass. Slightly bent where it's been stuck back together over and over again.

At home Deloris is too restless to sleep so sweeps the rubble of the kitchen. Bristles against floor the only sound, she comforts herself with thoughts of nights at home; the noise of her dad clicking on the kettle after returning from the night shift, her and Sharon giggling in their bedroom following a night out dancing, one of them tripping on the hair dryer or a high heel left on the carpet.

The phone rings seven times before her mum picks up.

'Hello?'

'Sorry to call so late,' Deloris says, smiling to think of her mum's hair in foam rollers.

'Who is this?' she asks with a croak in her voice.

'It's me, D.'

A silence. 'You'll wake up your father.' There's a creak in the background and she speaks in a hushed tone to him. 'Go back to bed.'

'Is he OK?'

'He's on a ventilator,' she says matter-of-factly and Deloris thinks of his night shift uniform forgotten on the chair. Then, 'You took your sister's money.'

Deloris hugs her middle with one arm. 'I'll pay her back.'

'That was for her next hairdressing qualification.'

'I said I'll pay her back.'

'Course you will. The money don't mean anything to you, does it? Now that you have everything you want.'

Deloris tries to find some words. 'Please can I come see you?' she starts. But her mum is distracted again. 'Sorry, Deloris. I have to go.'

In the darkness of the bedroom she slides open the drawer of her table and feels for the photograph of her in the one-piece. Her dad had insisted on them spending the day together by the lido and paid for the deckchairs so they wouldn't get grass stains, then fallen asleep with his face right in the sun. When he'd later printed out the photograph at the chemist, it hadn't occurred to Deloris that he might have meant it as a family portrait, not just a picture of her looking pretty. Now, even as she flattens it against the windowsill, it remains rough where she's bent it to hide him from the scene.

Deloris wakes the next morning with a start. Chilled sweat is a film across her skin. All night she lay rigid in bed with a throb across her empty womb. In the mirror she now sees a gaunt face stare at her, its eyes rimmed with pink. She scrapes her hair back with an elastic band from Harvey's study and ignores the sour curdling in her stomach. Voices are speaking outside so she goes downstairs to the living room to see better into the street. A police car is there again on the pavement.

Deloris almost trips up as she runs outside in her flip-flops, through shrunken puddles to Anna's house.

The milk bottles have gone from the front door and Deloris thinks she'll do anything to have that mean Anna is back, sitting indoors, making tea in the floral dress. What would she give? Deloris runs a list in her head – her home, her marriage, a fistful of hair – but it's an idiotic child's game she won't win.

The back gate is left open and a large uniformed figure is winding something – orange tape – around an area beyond the fence. Brian is hunched over, writing, while a few steps towards the trees, Rick from the caravan park watches with his greyhound rubbing its back into the wet earth.

'What's happening, Brian?' Deloris says.

He takes a minute to finish what he's writing.

'New evidence.'

The man has finished with his tape and picks up a clear plastic bag. Inside something is crumpled and leaves a brown residue down the side. As the man walks closer, Deloris can see it's matted with soil.

'What is it?'

Brian wipes his forehead and sighs. 'A purple glove.'

'That belongs to Anna,' she says, and thinks of her touching the lace so carefully, removing it before washing the glasses. 'It was in the mud?'

'Buried,' says Brian. He takes a long breath and stops just

short of her. 'We all hoped she'd gone away for a few days, but it's time to face facts.'

'I know,' Deloris says, her temperature rising. All these days wasted with her indoors, or in London, lost in her own world. 'She's been taken by the Fox.' Everything is crowding in on her, shouting her awake.

'We're recruiting more officers.'

'It's not enough,' Deloris says to herself, walking through the garden and over the fence to the scrubland where the police tape wavers flimsily in the breeze.

To think that not so long ago she'd defended this person? Had known he'd snuck into her house and said nothing to the police? Her and Anna might not have been close but she owed her more than this. She'd make up for it, she promised Anna, furious at the thought of the sullied glove. A few feet beyond, the mass of branches of the silver birches block out the light. A wind blows and carries dead leaves on to her bare feet but Deloris doesn't move. From now on she won't be afraid. She will do everything she can to bring Anna home.

PART TWO

5

The pulpit towers over the stage, a chunk of dark oak carved with thistles that wrap around the base. It must be from the Victorian era, when religion was supposed to inspire breathless children to kneel in its long shadow. Jim is reluctant to climb its steps, never has done even when he's been alone in church, but maybe now's the time. The few who've turned up for the impromptu Friday service – Sandra, Elsie and two other elderly women – all sit together, three aisles back. Their elbows jostle each other as they flick through their hymn books, Elsie's copy shaking in her arthritic hands.

'We must take much courage,' he says. 'Dark times like these can make an animal or a saint of us.'

Nobody looks up so Jim speaks louder, 'We must keep love in our hearts because that's what makes us strong.'

Elsie takes a noisy sniff and he pauses. The others fold their arms, even Sandra who is ashen-faced without her usual paint-work. A silk scarf is the only concession to her usual styled self and is tightly knotted against her throat.

Jim lifts his choir gown and climbs the pulpit's stairs, which creak and tremble under him. At the top he can see Elsie's patch of thinning hair and casts his eyes away, ashamed. Instead he looks just beyond as if to a full congregation. As if he's a revered speaker who can inspire real faith in the villagers.

Although Jim pulls himself up tall, his position only seems to incense the women. They mutter and turn down wrinkled mouths as he speaks his rehearsed lines, encased in the vast wood.

'Please now,' he says, suddenly intent to be heard. Sandra meets his eye for the first time that morning. 'What good is our fear and anger doing Anna?' He forgets the sermon. 'Surely, after all God has done for us, we trust Him to show us the way?' His voice quietens as he stoops again and earnestly asks the women, 'What else can we do?'

After the service has ended, Jim walks to the vestry. Its darkness is soft with patches of blue cast on the floorboards. The only place he feels truly at ease in the building. He stands still for a minute before he takes off his scarf and lays the weighty material on the back of the chair.

Beyond the curtains that separate his room from the nave, he sees Sandra talking to the women.

'What happened about that man outside the school?' one asks, interrupting her.

'He was a dad waiting to fetch his daughter.'

'You sure?'

'A soldier, apparently. He'd been away in the Falklands and no one recognised him.'

They're not sure what to make of this so let Sandra speak.

'We're meeting tonight at my Harvey's house to share the plan,' she says. 'Seven o'clock sharp.' The other women step away like startled hens and give small nods at no one in particular. Sandra is left alone. 'Seven o'clock,' she trills after them.

The vicarage door is stiff to open and Jim has to nudge it with his shoulder. Envelopes fold back and catch as he enters. Mostly it's junk mail and free newspapers, a coupon for the local hairdressers. There's a letter from the Diocesan Director too – postmarked Oxford five days ago – which he slides into his satchel for later. In the kitchen, he sees he forgot to water the spider plants last time. *Why keep them?* he thinks as he holds each plastic pot beneath the tap. But of course he knows why: he's wary of someone from the local parish visiting and the place looking uncared for. Almost three years without the vicar position being filled – him giving every service – and still they indulge the idea that he's just keeping the post warm, the house ready for a real vicar. Whether he'll ever begin his official training he's given up wondering. Let God show him the way. *Any* way, he thinks.

He goes into the living room where dead fruit flies lie shrivelled on the ledge. A brief prayer, then swept into the bin. The house is arguably nicer than his own – it's three doors down from the church, with a working fireplace and a garden he could sit in for breakfast, the Bible perched on his knee. Although the director once said he could stay here if need be, the offer seemed begrudging so he ended up renting his own house on Yardley Mews.

Jim has almost let his mind wander to a more serene place when he sees the embroidered cushion on the armchair. He winces and the week's waiting and hoping fill him with the now familiar sense that the world is souring, colours spoilt with a cold yellow filter.

The cushion was made by Ruth Blake, one of the first people he'd met in the village when he arrived three years ago. He'd been startled at the sound of the doorbell, having spent so much time alone, gazing at his few boxes of remaining possessions.

'Good evening – I hope I don't disturb?'

Ruth was a plain-faced woman wearing a shawl he'd later see draped over her robust shoulders in church twice a week without fail. Another person was behind and appeared as just an elbow and a rustling plastic bag.

'Go on, Anna,' Ruth instructed as they crowded into the porch. Anna shuffled forwards and he could see she was in her mid-twenties and dressed in an old-fashioned blouse and skirt. She brought out a cushion between delicate fingers and presented it. For a second it didn't occur to him who the present might be for.

'It's to say welcome to the village,' Anna said. The cushion showed three lambs in silver and white thread with a starry sky above. Its stitching was so small it must've taken, well, he didn't know how long. 'My daughter here made it,' said Ruth.

Jim, still unsure how he ended up in this village, was overcome. 'How utterly kind. I can't tell you—'

Ruth cut him off. 'It's nothing to get excited about.'

'No really—'

'God teaches us to be kind,' she said matter-of-factly and ushered Anna around, who followed without another word.

Over the next couple of weeks Anna struck Jim as a lamb herself. She was often at her mother's side in church, helping to hand out the prayer books or prepare tea after service. Soon enough, however, Jim noticed how her pale green eyes took in everyone around her: a dropped scarf would quickly be returned to its owner, and she asked fellow churchgoers all about their children, husbands and even newly planted dahlias without her ever forgetting a name or detail. Likewise she remembered when Jim himself mixed up words from a passage of the Bible and would later tentatively ask if he had a different interpretation.

'I think love of God can be subjective,' she said one time while her mother was busy snuffing candles. 'And it's up to us to shape our understanding, isn't it?'

They began to have discussions during the minutes Ruth was out of earshot, Anna silencing if her mother did come along and Jim following suit. The next month she volunteered to be church treasurer and spent Sunday afternoons with him at the vicarage where, after counting the coins from the collection plate, the two of them would sit drinking coffee and discussing passages from Luke and Peter or her favourite Corinthians. She seemed to look to him for answers, or for new angles at least, but it soon became clear that her understanding was far more advanced, that she had studied the Bible from a young age and knew all the routes a debate might take, nodding patiently while he spoke but, at the end, flummoxing him with another question. Jim found himself going for days without turning on the television or radio, instead poring over pages of the Bible he thought he already understood well, then waking hours before his alarm each morning to imagine their next discussion and what objections she could possibly raise to his revised arguments.

The question of female roles in church was a reccurring topic between them. Anna believed humility was a crucial aspect of religion but then this applied to both men and women, didn't it? And after all, she went on, some of the prophets of Israel were female. For the most part Jim remained unsure and, instead, was simply taken with the fire with which she spoke, her fingers grasping the air as she paced about his kitchen.

It now makes him smile to think of Anna that first summer. How he'd naively hoped he might be some sort of father figure to her when really she was the one teaching him to be a better man.

But he must shake himself from these indulgent memories. Five days gone and no word. Where can she be?

Jim makes his way down the high street where a hard shadow spills in front of him. Its arm forms a triangle as he scratches – a prickly heat working across his neck. At least the choir dress prevents him from tearing at himself with its high collar. Now, in his ordinary shirt he has nothing to stop his fingernails finding skin.

As he turns left down Yardley Mews, a voice shouts to him.

'Reverend Thomas!'

Brian is standing outside the police station, a few metres away. Jim crosses the road towards him.

'Please, call me Jim.'

'Not very professional to shout, I suppose.' Brian pushes the door open. 'Only Trish on reception took a report from you the other day and I wanted to follow up, what with this further evidence.'

'The glove?'

'That's right.'

The station doesn't have a proper interview room. Just a corner of a larger room with two desks – one with an Ordnance Survey map laid across it and a banana hidden under a plastic file. A radio is there too, like a prop of police work left out for effect. Brian indicates the second desk that's empty and, seeing there's only one chair, Jim pulls another over.

'Oh. I should've set up properly.'

'It hardly matters,' says Jim and immediately regrets his impatient tone. He doesn't know Brian well but the young man has always seemed enthusiastic enough with a wide, honest sort of face. His house is a few doors down from Anna's, with a garden consisting of nothing but a patch of close-mown lawn and a wheelchair ramp. His brother Beattie is said to have been in a rugby accident, though Jim's never spoken to Brian directly about it. He occasionally sees the two out on the village green and thinks such trips must be hard work.

'Sorry we're going over this again,' Brian says.

'Please don't apologise.' Jim sits down and crosses his legs. 'I'm willing to do whatever I can to help bring Anna home safe and sound.'

Brian smiles gratefully and retrieves a tape recorder from a single drawer under the desk.

'Righty then, let's run through the events of the night of this Monday, 18th June.'

Jim suddenly feels on edge, irritated by how the table feels like the kind from school, as if chewing gum might be stuck to the bottom. He sits on both his hands.

'I'd seen Anna earlier in the day,' he says. 'And she assured me of her plans to attend prayer group but didn't show up. So, after I had cleared away for the evening, I thought I'd pop round to see if everything was OK.'

'Did you have reason to believe it might not be?'

'No, I don't think so.'

Brian stares at him with his plain face. He blinks but nothing can be read in those wide-set eyes. Jim wonders if that's some psychological technique the police are taught or just how Brian is. It's not helpful, Jim thinks, and tries to refocus.

'And anyway, I had planned to knock on her door, of course, but I noticed someone through the window.'

'Which window?'

'Her living room one. A Virginia Creeper partly obscures it, but yes, it's certainly her living room.'

Brian flicks through some notes. 'An unidentified woman.'

'That's correct. I hadn't seen her before.'

'Can you describe the woman?'

'Tallish, dark hair possibly. And something on her arm like a bag. Yes, a handbag on a chain strap.'

Brian continues to look at him expectantly.

'That's it, I'm afraid. I only saw her from a distance.' Jim's fingers escape from under his thighs and scratch at his neck. 'I thought I'd leave them to it, so turned for home.'

'You didn't knock on the door? Go inside?'

'No.'

'You're certain?'

'Of course I am. It was only a few days ago.'

Brian grimaces. 'Sorry, it's just this woman might be the last person to have seen Anna before she disappeared, Mr Thomas.'

'I know,' he says testily but only now realises what that means. 'I wish I could remember more. I suppose I assumed it was a family friend who'd just popped over, or ...' As his words trail off he hears how stupid they sound – the Blakes didn't have visitors from outside the village who just popped over. In all the time he'd known Anna, she had barely mentioned any more family apart from her father who hadn't written in years. 'I wish I had gone to the door and said hello and that none of this ghastly business had ever happened, Heaven help us all ...'

They discuss more details of the case. Although Brian says more staff are being sent from the Eddlesborough station, he seems grateful to have someone to discuss his ideas with. 'I'm trying to build up a picture of the intruder's movements. Deloris has come forward with information on a stolen key, but I don't think it's just young women he's targeting. Mr Whitley lives alone and last night went to bed and found blankets across his study floor.'

'You think it was the Fox?'

'Possibly. He might have been making himself somewhere to sit and wait. Like a sort of den.'

'A den?' Jim pulls at the skin of his neck until it hurts.

'There's still so much I don't understand.' The notebook in front of him remains blank. 'And why take Anna?'

'Because she's loved,' Jim says, suddenly angry again at the man who is too young for this case, too naive. 'Surely he wants to upset us as much as possible. This kind-hearted girl everyone knows.'

'Maybe.' Taking a long breath, Brian meets Jim's eyes. 'But the truth is we don't know for sure what he wants.'

After Brian thanks him for his time and escorts him out, Jim is still shaking. A heat surges through him to think of how he walked away from Anna's house on Monday night.

Now, children stand in groups in the school playground next to the station. Around them teachers are twitchy and cast glances over the beech hedgerow on to the footpath beyond. Desperate to escape the high street, Jim hurries the fifty metres to his semi-detached house at the top of Yardley Mews.

He goes upstairs to his cubby, which is lined with shelves of books and a few shoeboxes. A futon sofa is covered in a wool blanket he found in a charity shop. Above is a window that he gazes through. In the street opposite, with scrubland between, waits Anna's house. Beyond the branches he can see glimpses of the white paint turned grey in the shadow of late morning sun. Something awful is welling inside him, coming from the base of his stomach in coils. He looks away from the window and slides down the sofa, taking muffled breaths.

Theological college has broken up for the summer and Jim isn't sure what to do for the afternoon. It wasn't like when he worked in insurance, a manager with his own company car and parking spot right by reception. Days would be so busy with shareholder meetings and lunches in glass-walled restaurants, then home to Belinda and Lucy, whose hair would be damp with the smell of chlorine or her tiny body wrapped in an apron for cooking iced biscuits. Always some activity, mess strewn across the polished hallway floor and up the stairs. He'd watch his Italian leather shoes climb each step, designer dolls or building blocks beside them, and regard himself as a stranger. Hope that Belinda didn't follow him up with heavy musk perfume and arms snaking around his waist.

Although they were married for twenty-two years, he always goes back to the part of their marriage when things began to change. It had started out with family holidays at her parents' cottage, Wimpy dinners eaten straight from the box and swimming in the river whenever it was warm enough. Then Belinda was made chairwoman of the Society for the Protection of Historic Buildings and everything became overblown. All photoshoots at galas, Belinda heaving her ever-expanding bulk around hundreds of guests, reminding waiters to ice the shrimps while he and Lucy would sit somewhere near the back, hoping not to be called for more meet-and-greets. Sometimes Jim reluctantly circled the room – *be witty*, Belinda would insist – and grit his teeth while people thanked him for his donations. *I hardly do much*, he'd tell them, thinking about the backpacking trips he and Belinda made as students, their month around India with little more than their passports and candied apricots for the street kids. *It's not supposed to be about the money, is it?* They'd agree, and eyes would drift to Belinda in her sequinned pantsuits, picked out by some assistant who promised the shape was flattering.

She was a good mother to Lucy, at least. All the personal tutors and foreign exchange holidays a girl could ask for. And even though he and Belinda have barely spoken since he left Guildford, they'd always have their daughter.

Jim wonders what Lucy is doing now – in France with her husband and her baby, who must be learning to speak French though he doesn't know for sure. And what faith, he asks himself, feeling the familiar tingle of wanting to write another letter. Times like these, family is so painfully important – but then, none of them know about Anna.

Jim unpacks his satchel and takes out the envelope. It doesn't seem right to open it – to worry about his own vicarhood at a time like this – so he puts it in one of the shoeboxes on the shelves by the little portable television set. Instead he takes out his writing pad and, sitting on the sofa, tries to compose the sermon for Sunday. Guidance, that's what the village needs. A strong voice to connect them to God. His pen hesitates on the page. The ink bleeds larger and larger as he considers, like so many times before, how he can help others if he can't help himself.

*

Stan is crouched in Elsie's front garden. She watches over him in her crooked form, the fuzz of her hair alight from the evening sun behind. It's hard to tell what he's helping her with – usually it's leaf-cluttered drains or crisp packets and cans that shine silver amongst her geraniums. Jim can't help speculate about why he isn't asked – after all, he lives next door to the old woman, unlike Stan who is four doors down – and offers assistance whenever the sound of her stick rattles along the driveway. She *has* known Stan longer, Jim assures himself.

He lets the door click behind him and pauses in the warm breeze. He has decided to go to Harvey's house for the meeting – a last-minute decision after stepping out the shower and realising the village would be discussing a plan without him. Heaven knew what the villagers were capable of. By and large they were an inward-looking group who used so-called pride in their woods for an excuse to distort any sort of rational thinking. (His suggestion of a car park at church had prompted several letters to be shot through his front door.) But perhaps he is being unfair.

'A tripwire,' Elsie says to him. 'I thought of it myself.'

Stan pulls a thread around a section of cane that juts from the grass. He's dressed in a cream shirt with his tortoiseshell reading glasses slipped into the pocket.

'That should do it,' he says, carefully securing the end.

Elsie is peering at Jim like she's expecting a response. He says nothing. Filling the silence, Stan tells him 'good evening,' and unfolds to his full height, a good two inches taller than Jim, plus he never slouches. 'Do you know what this meeting is about?' Stan asks.

'I told you,' says Elsie. 'The lad who broke into my kitchen.'

She points a shaking knuckle towards the high street and Stan offers his arm so they can walk together. He's his usual quiet self as the three of them make slow progress, Elsie wittering on about needing more security in the neighbourhood. Too many youths unemployed with this government. She misquotes the Bible and neither man corrects her, though perhaps Stan doesn't know himself. The two men sometimes chat over a glass of wine but Jim senses his friend doesn't like to talk religion. Instead, it's mostly Stan's trips to London where he likes to see the symphony orchestra or else just gardening tips.

Stan waits for Elsie to get her breath at the top of Glebe Crescent. Almost a minute goes by and Jim grows aware of the long evening shadows that fall across the road, the overgrown hedgerows that obscure views into front gardens where anyone might be hiding. At number eight the Jewish couple hover inside their front door before darting out into the street, past a Neighbourhood Watch signpost propped above a bin.

The three of them eventually arrive at Harvey's house: a large gaudy affair with his car left across the middle of the gravel driveway so they're forced to traipse round it. Several parking tickets lie across the dashboard, like souvenirs of where he's been. Of course Jim knows he was the same at that age, although with Harvey's looks and salary the man needn't try so hard.

The front door is opened by Deloris, who stands in a simple dress without any of her usual make-up.

'Don't worry about taking off your shoes,' she says before anyone has a chance to ask. She acknowledges each of them and throws Elsie's cardigan over the bannister. As always, Jim is struck by how attractive she is.

'Elsie, Stan, Jim,' sings Sandra, striding towards them. The same silk scarf is around her neck but the rest of her is painted, including a streak of orange across her mouth.

'Apologies if we're late, only—'

Sandra taps Jim's wrist before he can finish. 'Say no more. We're all friends here.'

She's more comfortable on her own family territory, Jim thinks as she leads them down the hall into the living room. A silver tray of tumblers sits on the coffee table and she offers them one with a well-practised smile while Deloris carries on to the next room.

'Soda water with mint from my garden?'

Elsie sniffs at her glass before lowering herself into one of the two white leather sofas while Jim and Stan stand next to the other neighbours who take small sips of their drinks. Elizabeth from number sixteen jiggles her red-cheeked baby on her knee, the fabric of her tie-dye skirt riding up to show unshaven legs. Behind, her husband Pete flaps his flannel shirt. It's strange to be among everyone like this, seeing as so few gather for church. They're usually just fragments of each other's lives – faces seen here and there on lawns or queuing at the post office – not many real friends, not in his case anyway. Jim might otherwise be depressed by this realisation, but is pulled by his earlier sensation of being detached. Voices talk around him, polite mumblings about the wet weather, and he stands letting his eyes un-focus so the carpet becomes an expanse of beige.

A minute later someone rudely slurps the last of their drink and he moves away, avoiding the hallway in favour of the back of the house where it's cooler.

'You don't mind, do you?' Deloris's voice floats through

from a few metres away. She is standing in the connecting garage beside Harvey, who's illuminated by an open freezer. 'Only your mum liked the idea and before I knew it—'

'Of course I don't,' he says and takes a tray of ice. 'I'm glad you're on our side at last.'

She seems stumped, then finds some words and leans towards him. 'I always want to be on your side.'

'Hasn't seemed that way …' He lets out an uneasy sigh. 'Anyway. I'll make some more drinks.'

'Harvey.' She takes his arms and their bodies turn to one in the dim. 'I hated fighting with you yesterday. I don't want to leave. I hope you know that.'

The two begin to kiss and Jim slopes off, embarrassed to have watched.

Back in the living room, Jim sees that Rick, the caravan park owner, has turned up and is slumped on the other armchair, thighs spread in some grease-stained overalls. A space has been left around him, which makes Jim wonder what the fuss is about. The two have only had a couple of conversations in the time he's lived in the village – both short and mostly involving grunts – but the man diligently looks after his dog which is an elderly greyhound he rescued from being shot. Whenever Jim sees him walking it around the village, he's carrying a bag of meat that he doles out in delicate slithers.

'Evening, folks.' Harvey saunters in with his oddly tanned face and unbuttoned shirt. People move out of his way as he heads for the cabinet and helps himself to clear liquor from a tall glass bottle. 'Good of you to make it.' Another man puts out his glass, ready to thank the host for a tipple, but the lid is already refastened.

Everyone turns to the corner where he stands, twisting themselves around on the sofa and adjusting positions to see him in the crowd. There might be fifty people or more, so even in the spacious living room there's little free elbow room. Sandra waits in the doorway to lookout for latecomers.

They're all waiting for Harvey to do the talking when a high-pitched ring comes from beside him. Deloris is standing with a teaspoon and wine glass, which clatter as she puts them on the cabinet. Harvey frowns as she adjusts her neat dress then smooths her hair. A murmur goes around the crowd and she waits for quiet.

'I know the police are doing their best …' Her voice is not quite steady and she takes a breath. 'But they're only a small team.'

Jim realises Brian isn't in the room. Perhaps the only villager who isn't, apart from Ralph – an elusive man that Jim hasn't met properly – just a wave here and there from a figure at the front window. Cynthia now loiters at the back with a sceptical look on her face. Her dressing gown is gone and replaced with an old-fashioned striped dress from the seventies. Thick-skinned, Jim thinks, knowing how the others talk about her husband despite the couple never causing any harm, as far as he knows.

'Us residents can't just sit back and do nothing when, with every minute that passes, the Fox has Anna.'

Elsie nods vigorously and others follow suit. Murmurs of assent encourage Deloris who lifts her chin to speak again, 'She's our friend and our neighbour and we have to protect her.'

'That's my girl,' booms Michael. They all turn to him, including a startled Sandra, and he winks at Deloris.

'What my wife's trying to say,' starts Harvey, stepping forward, 'is that we need to arm ourselves. Set traps. Do anything we can.'

This time Elsie is the only person nodding. Rick raises his eyebrows. 'Weapons?' he says.

'Yes – cricket bats, knives, rifles. Even a brick by your bed is better than nothing.'

Jim hopes he speaks for the group. 'And how will that help Anna?'

'By taking out this guy in the next house he comes into,' retorts Harvey with a frowning smirk. Beside him Deloris looks hard-faced.

'No one is trained to use firearms,' says Jim, putting down his glass, which he now sees as a trick to make him feel indebted to the hosts. 'We'd be a danger to each other.'

'What rubbish,' says Michael, and Rick nods. 'Only people like—'

'So what do you propose, Jim?' Deloris interrupts, angling her head towards him.

The room goes quiet and Jim speaks evenly. 'Let the police do their work. We can all pray that she's safely found, which she surely will be in time.'

Michael scoffs. 'Spiritual guidance eh? You're not even a real vicar, are you?'

'Well . . .' Jim is overcome with a heat that shudders through him. He edges back but someone is there, another face waiting for an answer as if the whole village has always wondered. 'Faith can be anyone's,' he hears himself say. 'Everyone's.' He grips his neck, pressing fingers into prickly flesh.

He looks to Stan but he is standing with his eyes lowered to the carpet.

Around him, the crowd starts to speak in layers of whispers – *could we find a gun? It sounds pretty extreme. We've got that Samurai Sword in the attic. Really? It's a collector's item but sharp as anything.*

'God can save us,' Jim says desperately. He's never felt so alone, so exposed, and with just words that don't add up to enough. He could lie down right here on the floor and hope the Lord might be kind enough to take him. Foolish, he thinks.

He sees Deloris moving ahead and realises she's trying to catch his eye across the preoccupied group. She tells him, '*We're* not the ones who need saving.'

'What've we decided, eh?' Elsie asks a minute later. 'While we're sat here drinking pop this lad could be back in my kitchen.'

'Or doing something awful to Anna,' says Sandra, clutching at her neck scarf.

The crowd falls to a deeper silence. Deloris takes a breath and speaks. 'There's another possibility we have to consider.' In a pause she stares at the carpet, then dares to lift her eyes again. 'Most abductions are by someone the victim already knows.'

'Come on, honey.' Harvey goes to grab her hand but she pulls away from him.

'We have to consider all possibilities.'

'She's got carried away with her theories,' says Harvey before taking a sip of drink that goes down uneasily. 'Dolly isn't from round this area.'

'What *is* she talking about?' asks Mary Braithwaite with a polite raised hand.

Deloris's voice comes out low and travels across the room. 'How do we know it's not someone here?'

'Beg your pardon?' cries Elsie. Others uncross their legs and cast her wide-eyed looks.

'I'm not trying to be facetious,' Deloris says defensively as the crowd pulls away from her. 'I'm going off reports, statistics I've found in the library. There are dozens of cases on microfilm and ...'

She turns to Harvey who grinds his teeth as he stares into his empty drink.

'And who knows what anyone is really capable of?'

Sandra's voice is shrill. 'This is not what we discussed you'd say.'

'Isn't there the devil in all of us?' Deloris looks to Jim. Her face suddenly looks older than its years. Large eyes are fixed on his, imploring him for help.

He mutters, 'Yes, arguably so.'

The room bristles at the thought but stays quiet.

'See?' says Deloris. 'We have to accept the Fox might not be far away.'

6

Jim wakes in a crumple of damp sheets. The swift that's built a nest just inside his roof is calling, but this isn't what woke him. Through the window that's open a crack – the way he leaves it otherwise the bedroom gets humid – voices are talking. Jim keeps his head on the pillow and hopes sleep will take him again. It's Saturday, and he doesn't want another day to be here so quickly; another day having passed without word from Anna. He lets himself imagine the voices saying she's back. Shaken, yes, and hungry. In need of prayer. But home in her cottage with the milk pan on the hob, releasing that warming smell as they discuss the next church meeting.

The voices continue and he recognises Stan's. Jim props himself up on one elbow. Could it be?

His heart shudders to action and lifts him from the single bed to the window. A few doors down, Stan is standing on the pavement by his house with a newspaper. He's speaking to Elizabeth who lives next door and clutches her baby with a bangle-clad arm. 'Don't patronise me,' she says, flicking her long auburn hair. 'Not when our neighbour's missing.'

Jim's heart rate gradually slows and, as he descends the stairs, is replaced with the numb sensation of not being quite there again. Anna isn't back and might never be. He opens his front door and steps out, not caring who sees him in his checked pyjamas.

'Everything all right?' he calls to them.

Stan turns around and lifts his hand in a wave. 'Morning, Jim.'

'What's happened?'

'My hallway smells of wet earth,' Elizabeth cries, gesturing to the house where the door is open. 'Only Stan here thinks I'm losing my mind.'

'I didn't mean to imply that,' Stan says gently. 'I just remember what it's like when you have a young child. You never get enough sleep.'

'He could still be in there.' Elizabeth skitters up her driveway, her baby now whimpering. 'Pete!' she shouts through the door. Her husband emerges and, seeing the two other men, gives them a sheepish smile. 'I've checked all the rooms, love.'

'And?' she breathes.

'Everything's fine,' he says, scratching his beard. 'None of the locks have been tampered with.'

'Under the beds?'

'No one's there.'

Elizabeth can't believe this. She furiously pats the baby, which remains flopped over her shoulder and then hesitates by the door. 'Surely you can smell that?'

After retreating to his own home Jim goes upstairs and turns on the television. It's part of his usual routine – watching

Breakfast Time with Frank Bough and Selina Scott – but he can barely understand what they're saying: advice on your summer wardrobe, gardening equipment – all so inconsequential. Had the Fox really been inside the Robinsons' house? It seemed likely to be Elizabeth's imagination. She could be highly strung at times, complaining to the council about the infrequent bin collection, although maybe Jim just expected her bangles and henna to mean she'd fully subscribe to the laid-back hippy mentality, not that such a thing ever really existed apart from for the sake of selling records.

He flicks to BBC1 and watches the local news about a cinema closing down. Just before the weather, a photograph of Anna appears on screen, her eyes staring straight back at Jim so he kneels in front of the image. Green eyes turned to grey, the black-and-white image poor quality but still, it's her, back with him. And then, a second later, she's gone and a balding man in a suit is reading autocue lines, 'Police are searching the village of Heathcote where the close-knit community is on high alert for any suspicious activity.'

Ten minutes later Jim is still in the snug when the doorbell goes. He really should have got showered already but has just been staring at the television where his reflection slides round its curved edges.

'Hello, Deloris.'

'Sorry to interrupt.' She hands him a yellow laminated poster reading 'Neighbourhood Watch'. A sketched group of figures huddle together.

'Not to worry, I'll put this in my window.'

Deloris lingers on his doorstep, hair falling around her shiny forehead.

'Would you like some water?' Jim asks, assuming she'll decline. But the next thing he knows she's glancing to the street behind her, then following him inside.

Jim chooses the best of his glasses, all mismatching, from a car boot sale.

Deloris thanks him before choosing her next words carefully. 'I heard you were married. Where's your wife?' she asks.

'Oh.' Jim sits down at the table and opens his hands so the palms face up. 'She's in Guildford, where I used to live.'

'Why didn't she move with you?' she says. Then adds, 'If you don't mind me asking.'

Jim has never been asked so plainly but reasons she's not trying to be rude. His hands find his neck. 'We aren't friends these days.'

A silence lengthens as Deloris frowns and Jim waits until she speaks again. Still in his pyjamas, which are growing damp under his thighs, he wonders what she's waiting for. A minute or so goes by. 'I don't really talk to my family either,' she says at last. She is distracted by the thought and gazes at the plughole. 'Why's it so hard?'

He considers going over to her but decides against it. 'People can be complicated,' he says. 'They can want all sorts of different things at the same time. But eventually a path does reveal itself if we're patient enough.'

Deloris's chin dips so the angle of her jaw is lost. Now Jim rises and quietly moves over. She doesn't flinch as he places a hand on her shoulder.

'I should be going,' she says, and moves away.

'Of course.' Jim edges back, unsure what's happened between them.

As she steps round him her eyes dart about the room. At

105

the empty worktop, the black spots of mould between the tiles. And him there in his pyjamas, unshaved and flushing to see her so unnerved.

'Deloris? Are you OK?'

He leaves a distance between them as she walks to the hallway but notices a slight turn of her head – her glancing up the stairs – before she opens the door and hurries away.

Deserting some uneaten toast and herbal tea, Jim makes more than a dozen phone calls to parishes. *A blonde woman with a heavy fringe, sort of girlish, though aged twenty-seven. Yes, missing for almost a week now. Have you seen anyone like that? No? Well, thank you anyway.* One woman is particularly interested and he tells her all about Anna's kindness, how *she helped her mother do everything in the end, even brush her hair,* but the woman has nothing useful to say.

His throat is dry by the end of the final, unsuccessful call. He at last removes his pyjamas to shower and, having left some messages on answerphones, listens out for the telephone ring. The only noise is the clumsy patter of water on the bath's floor, though, as it cascades from his body which is wrinkling with age. He used to go on runs in his work lunchtime, around the park or even along the river to St Paul's, a way to keep himself lean. He stares at himself in the square, unframed mirror above the sink and applies skin cream in overly thick blotches. He's covering over himself, disappearing.

Jim later picks his way over the cobbles of one of Aylesbury's back lanes. After driving the twenty minutes, he's left his Ford Estate in the market car park and tries to think what he needs from the butcher. It's horrid to think he'll be eating and Anna might not be. Jim shudders and hurries down the set of steps to the lower passage. A whiff of urine sharpens the air as he walks through the graffiti-lined tunnel under the road. If only paint sprayed on a public wall was the worst society did, a clumsy line dripping with colour as the vandal scarpers at the red flash of siren. But the devil always demands more.

A queue of people clutters up the butcher's, the podgy white arm of Mr Harris pushing ham against the slicer, the whir of the metal blade.

Jim carries on past the row of shops – the newsagents with its sticky floor, a shop where toys and boxes are piled against the window so no light must get in.

At the end of the lane stands a sandwich board made from woodchip.

DIY TOOLS
PAINTS
VARNISHES

and then, written on a sticker attached at the bottom,

WEAPONS

Jim steps into the room. His eyes take a second to adjust and he can make out only a few shelves in front of him that stand empty. He blinks. The smell of wood shavings scents the air like in their old shed in the house where they first lived in Surrey. Not that he used it much – just to store Lucy's bike – but it was oddly reassuring to keep the rows of tins left by the previous owner. The solid walls, a heavy padlock you could grip in your palm that left a trail of oil.

But the tools of men are frightening in the wrong hands.

A Samurai sword. That's what Jim heard last night, wasn't it? He has little idea what one looks like. The words make him think of the books Lucy used to read as a girl. Set in Japanese towns, exotic places with ink drawings of rooftops and midnight-blue skies. Not any place he knew. Not Heathcote, anyway.

Now Jim's eyes have adjusted he sees revolving stands of nails in plastic boxes. Many shelves are almost bare, with plastic labels rendered useless below dusty expanses of wood-chip. Jim reaches the end of one row and carries on around.

'You looking for a weapon?' A large man emerges from behind the counter.

'No,' says Jim, startled. 'No thank you.' Then, feeling the man's eyes on him, 'Just an extra lock. Nothing fancy.'

The man heaves himself down the aisle, the straps of his overalls straining at his shoulders. Jim decides to buy whatever he recommends, reflexively edging away from the man's bulk.

'We're sold out,' the man says.

'Pardon?'

'Completely cleared of any sliders. Padlocks. Sashlocks. Deadlocks.' He seems almost impatient with the news like Jim should really have expected it. 'Now, how about summat else?'

'No, that's fine.'

'Don't want to protect yourself?'

'No thank you.'

A flash of chipped tooth. 'Then why you still stood here?'

Jim hurries out, though his shirt catches on something. A nail protruding from a shelf. The fabric is frayed but not quite torn.

*

The phone is ringing as he unlocks his front door. Jim hurries to its place in the hallway, not wanting to miss any of the parishes returning his phone call. He doesn't have an answering machine and wonders if he has enough savings to buy one.

'Hello? Jim speaking.'

'It's you.' He knows her voice instantly.

'Sarah.'

She says something about having been trying him all week. The gentle notes of her voice – the anxious lift at the end – are so familiar he aches to hear them again. He wishes he could keep them in a box to take out whenever he wants.

'I've been worried, would you believe it?' She gives a breathy laugh that crackles down the line. 'An article in the *Mail* said there's been break-ins in your village. And now a girl is missing.'

'A woman, yes.' It's bizarre to speak to Sarah about this, though he's played a similar conversation in his mind more than once. Still, it's like a part of his old life has slipped to form a layer of the new one.

'I'm sorry, Sarah,' he hears himself say. 'We shouldn't be talking.'

'It's only a phone call.' She presses the consonants like she did when angry, her nostrils most likely flaring as they did whenever he told her not to write him notes or stand so close in the lift.

'It's not though, is it?'

'Please, Jim.'

His hand shakes as he goes to put the phone down. Before it reaches the cradle he thinks she says, *I still love you*. It's too late for all that, he tells himself, though he presses his forehead against the stair wall until his skin is sore.

Jim had planned to make more phone calls that afternoon but instead takes down one of the shoeboxes from the shelf above the television. Dust falls as he does so, particles glistening in the light, and he ponders whether God is watching. Of course He is. Still, Jim unpacks the cassettes so he can see the videotape at the bottom. The cover has 'Bambie' written in biro on the side in Belinda's handwriting. Sarah had found that disturbing and they almost hadn't gone, even once the car was packed with the towels, the picnic basket and the bikini she slung over the backseat with its frilled edge decorating the leather.

Later he watches the back of Anna's house. His shoulders are stiffening as time passes, his knees pressed into the futon sofa, arms folded on its back. But he doesn't deserve to go make himself a cup of tea. The video is left stranded on the carpet and he hasn't pulled out the tape as he should have done. So he waits and he waits, even as his thighs begin to move under him as the muscles tire.

He's barely looking at anything, in a trance, but at some point a movement catches his eye. A figure has appeared in Anna's back garden. The angle isn't right for him to see much – a man's face appears through the tree branches in parts: a mouth set in a hard straight line, grey hair ... He's moving about slowly with something in his hands. Making notes, perhaps. A reporter from the local newspaper? Or a national one, for that matter, since the news has reached the *Mail* and who knows what other tabloids. Some flagrant newspaper headline is not what Anna needs.

The last newspaper article mentioned Ruth too – her charity work with the church. Not an incidental detail, but added to make it all that much sadder, more tragic. It seemed wrong. More so because Anna never spoke about her mother after she died. Jim tried several times but she would instantly clam up and sometimes even shake, the collar on her dress quivering as she looked around for a cup to wash or prayer book to tidy. Neither did she visit her mother's grave for the first few months after her death, so Jim himself took care of the potted flowers villagers left. It's ridiculous to think of the lengths he went to replant the roses, but of course he felt he had to do something. Anna wouldn't open up and he just accepted her silence like a coward. In part, he did have some sort of excuse: he'd never particularly liked Ruth. Although she'd always been cordial with him, they'd never got past pleasantries and she hardened if he dared suggest Anna and she might eat dinner with him one evening. It therefore seemed disingenuous to insist Anna share a memory or two. Surely there were other villagers who'd have comforting things to say? In truth, though, he wasn't sure this was the case.

And now somebody is on her land without her say-so. Inspecting her and Ruth's grass, pausing at the birdbath to see … what, exactly? Jim pushes himself up from the sofa.

The air is cluttered with gnats that stick to his face as Jim hurries up his mews then turns left on to the high street. Above, a plane is roaring but is hard to see in the colourless sky. He wonders if Anna is looking up at the same plane. Some P.D. James novel might tell him she's in some dingy cellar with ropes around her wrists, that she's in pain and sleep-deprived, with dirt clouding her cheeks. Jim's breath wheezes as he turns down her street. At least he can do this for her.

But the car parked on the pavement outside Anna's house

is a police car. Brian's, he supposes, though the male figure wasn't him.

Cynthia is watching from her driveway opposite. She's in her dressing gown over leggings and a T-shirt, an arm lent on her kitchen window ledge like she's been standing there a while.

'What's happened?' Jim asks.

Cynthia shrugs.

The side gate is wide open but Jim hesitates on the street, not sure he should even unlatch the gate to Anna's front garden. Perhaps he should simply go home now he knows it isn't the press. Yet he lingers. Maybe it's all the waiting in the cubby that makes him reluctant to leave. Or maybe it's a sense he's needed here. Jim waits and fills his lungs with the subtle scent of roses. Ruth used to prune them regularly – the short, clipped buds always struck Jim as over-loved. Now they're almost overwhelmed by the brambles and have greyish leaves curling at the ends.

'Mr Thomas.' Brian walks through the side gate towards him.

'Any news?' asks Jim tentatively, afraid of the answer.

Brian wipes the sweat from his forehead beneath the police cap. 'Nothing that's easy to write up: smells, shadows, a broken tree branch. I'm showing Mullins around. He's been assigned to the case.'

Despite wanting to ask more, Jim watches as Brian bites into a cling-filmed sandwich from his car seat and then heads back towards Anna's house. It must be his dinner, the evening already upon them.

Mullins, the grey-haired officer that Jim saw, stands in the hallway. A man in his late thirties, perhaps, he has a long crooked nose and fleshy cheeks. He waves Brian in, who leaves the door open as if Jim might follow.

'We need the natural light,' Brian explains.

'Oh, I see.' Jim flushes but can't help peering inside. Two clear plastic bags lie on the hallway tiles, which Brian slides over his shoes. The older officer, who must have been drafted in from the Eddlesborough station, has gone upstairs and a rattling echoes.

'This door's locked,' he shouts.

'Hang on.' Brian says, heading towards him. 'I've got the key.'

Brian's feet are light compared to the angry rattling. There're some muffled sounds as the men talk and Jim hovers on the doorstep. It must be Ruth's bedroom door that's locked. Perhaps Anna was preserving it, Jim thinks, and winces to imagine the room. From a glimpse one time he used the upstairs bathroom, he remembers many small framed pictures hung in lines on the green walls, the end of the bed covered in a quilt made of endless tiny hexagons.

Her wool shawl will most likely still hang in the wardrobe for Anna to press to her face, flowers from the garden dried and piled in a china bowl.

Another rattle echoes from upstairs.

'Careful up there,' calls Jim angrily. 'Must you even go in Ruth's bedroom?'

But the two men don't hear him or at least don't answer.

After another uneasy creak of wood, Jim steps into the hall and touches the bannister. The air feels chilly, untouched by summer outside. He climbs the stairs and jerks at movement to his right: his reflection in the glass across a piece of embroidery. The cross-stitch spells out 'My Angel' in neat gold with a picture of a wing below.

At the top of the stairs is the bathroom, then at the end of the corridor is Ruth's room. The two men stand outside it with Mullins cursing at the key that won't quite turn the ancient lock. 'Why didn't you just keep it open?' the man asks.

Brian says nothing, just fiddles the lock again, then pushes the door with the toe of his boot. It creaks open and he stands back, letting Mullins gawp before going in.

'What is it?' asks Jim, pausing on the top stair.

Brian turns and blinks several times before answering him. 'You're not supposed to be here, Mr Thomas.'

'What's in the room?' Jim asks again, venturing forward.

'Nothing.' Mullins moves away to another room.

It's just Brian left, who fidgets with the corner of his shirt. 'Please go home.'

Jim expects Brian to reach out an arm to stop him but he lets him pass. Inside the room Jim doesn't know what to feel. The carpet has been peeled away so the elderly wooden planks are exposed and scuff marks bruise the skirting boards. Jim sees the walls are empty of all the pictures too – just holes remain, plus a crooked nail near the door. In the middle, four dents are the only sign a bed was there. No shawl or single item waits in the wardrobe where even the metal bar has been removed. It's impossible to comprehend: the whole room has been stripped.

7

'I don't understand it,' says Jim later that evening.

Stan fills the kettle and carefully spoons tea leaves into the cream ceramic teapot.

'Did Anna strip the room?'

The tinkle of a teaspoon against the saucer is the only reply. Stan arranges a tray with various items, his hands too large for the small jug of milk yet not letting anything spill. Jim had knocked on his door after returning from Anna's and found him with his reading glasses perched on his head. His wife and son are away visiting family for the summer and the house is orderly, with music books piled on top of the upright piano in the hallway.

'What do you think?' Jim is starting to wish he'd called on Elsie's door. She at least would have an opinion, however outrageous it might be. The two could've picked over the details and offered some sort of theory, even if Jim would later have the sting of knowing he'd gossiped about Anna.

Stan pours water into the pot and, amid the curls of steam,

recites a familiar quote, 'There is no grief like the grief that does not speak.' He then picks up the tray and carries it through to the living room.

Jim scratches at his neck. 'But that's an odd thing to do, isn't it?' He doesn't want to sit in one of the low armchairs, as Stan places the tray on a table of light ash, smoothed to round edges.

'I suppose she couldn't bear looking at Ruth's possessions after she passed on,' continues Jim.

'That sounds right,' says Stan.

And with that he settles in an armchair as if the conversation has reached a natural close. Jim watches him pour the tea through a strainer. He's closely shaved as usual but his skin is especially pale and smooth around the dip under his cheekbones. His wife being away must give him more time for such things. Jim considers asking how she is over in the States with Elliot – holidaying with her family somewhere mid-west is it? – but it doesn't seem the right time for casual conversation. How much he misses them is hard to say, though Jim gets the feeling he enjoys the quiet house.

They drink their tea in silence. It's a serene, well-balanced room with the two armchairs facing a two-person sofa. An abstract painting of a vivid blue box streaked in red hangs over the fireplace. Jim doesn't recognise it from previous visits, though he remembers they've never had a television set.

About to leave for home, Jim thanks Stan for the tea.

'Would you like to see some photographs from school?' Stan asks as Jim is rising.

'Oh?' It seems a peculiar offer until Jim remembers Stan's family is originally from the area.

'My younger brother was in her year,' he says as he hands

the photograph album to Jim. It's a heavy bulk of a thing with a red leather cover. The weight of memories, Jim thinks, and remembers Ruth's stripped room, the four dents in the wood where her bed once stood.

'Our dad let us use his Polaroid camera occasionally,' Stan says, leaning forwards to look at the pages too. 'To the envy of all our friends.'

'Oh yes, I can imagine.' Jim perches the album on his knee. The first page shows sporadic images – a Christmas tree with flared white patches where lights must've been; a dog in a garden ...

'We were almost afraid to press the shutter.'

'It did feel like magic, didn't it?'

Jim turns another couple of pages and stops at Anna who must be five or six. She's staring across in a corduroy tunic dress with podgy arms at her sides. A crayon is snapped in two in her hand.

'Easter 1962,' says Stan easily. 'The photo comes with a story my brother told me.'

'Oh yes?'

'They had an Easter art competition at school, with crêpe paper and pipe cleaners and the likes. Most children did rabbits and chicks with yellow fuzz.' A smile glides over Stan's mouth.

'Anna insisted on a representation of Jesus on the cross with blood in red paint flooding the grass. Another girl cried and cried until the teacher took the painting away and called Ruth. Needless to say it didn't win the competition and Anna seemed to accept that, but when they all got back from the Easter holiday it was pinned to the middle of the blackboard.'

'Anna did that?'

'Or Ruth.'

'Really?' Jim can't help but laugh.

The two men have supper together. Stan steams some fish and serves this with green beans and new potatoes he got from a pick-your-own farm near the caravan park by the Aylesbury road. They sit at the dining-room table without any cloth and the radio on, though when the news comes on Stan goes to turn it off. Jim thinks how nice it is to be casual like this. The only dinners he has these days feel overly formal with visiting church people. He isn't himself but a role he plays. It's always in the vicarage where a wife will busy around doing the washing-up. No matter how much he protests, he can only watch as she puts plates back in the wrong cupboards.

Stan tops up his tumbler of wine from the carafe.

'It's just so strange,' Jim says after a long silence. 'To be sitting like this with her out there.'

Stan slowly chews the rest of his mouthful and swallows, then reaches out. His warm, large fingers form a protective cave around Jim's hand. How long it's been since he was touched, Jim thinks and rests his fork on the plate, not wanting the evening to end.

'She is stronger than people think,' Stan later says at the door.

'Of course. You've known her a long time.'

'I have.'

'I'll try to take comfort in that.'

Jim ambles the twenty or so metres home. A warm breeze plays with the hedgerow as the sun is slow to sink below the school buildings the other side of the high street. It's Saturday night but you wouldn't know it from this village. He passes Elsie's which has the lampshade on in the red living room, the lace curtains open – she says it's so she can keep an eye on the street but Jim suspects she also likes seeing people go by, feeling part of something.

Jim unlocks the front door. It's not yet ten o'clock, too early to sleep, so he goes to make some herbal tea to take into the snug. He's fingering the chip in his mug when a voice upstairs catches his ear. Through the ceiling it's a murmur – faint but definitely there. Jim freezes for a long moment as the kettle obliviously chugs out steam, then forces himself to turn and walk into the hallway. He hopes he's imagined something but the voice comes again, rounded at the edges so he can't understand what it's saying. Is it speaking to him? Jim reaches the phone and directs a finger towards the turning dial, then pulls on the round plastic hole. A shrill tinkle makes him stop.

Looking around in the dim hall, he finds no obvious weapon. It doesn't seem real as he goes back into the kitchen and slides open the knife drawer, then decides against that and goes for the utensils, settling on the rolling pin.

The Lord tests the righteous, but his soul hates the wicked and the one who loves violence.

Self-defence, Jim tells himself as he edges forward and stops at the bottom of the stairs. The first step lets out a cry under his foot; a warning. He slides his shoe to the edge where the boards are firmer. Up he rises, again and again, holding the rolling pin over his shoulder. The dim hall turns to darkness that's lit only by the slit of glowing light along the bottom of the cubby door.

A familiar laugh. Sarah's.

Then his own voice.

'Hello?' Jim calls in a shaking warble.

No answer. *What did I expect?*

Christ, please help me, he silently pleads and takes the last step, then walks forward in the inky dark, left hand out in front like a blind man.

Jim finds the door handle and summons something from deep within himself. Not the place that loves Anna. Or God. The place where he takes what he needs, a place of sharp-fanged savages. The door bursts as he throws himself through, his arm throbbing as he waves the blunt wood. A low guttural noise is swirling around him across the walls, through his core. He stops.

No one is there.

There's only the open window and a haphazard scuffing. Jim struggles to the window. Below lies just shadowy scrubland, a drainpipe looking up at him where it's come loose from the wall.

Sarah speaks behind him, 'Like this?'

The video is perhaps three or four minutes in. They're at the beach, him holding the camera in his clumsy way where the picture jerks about so different parts of her appear. She's on the wet sand and facing him running backwards in her frilled bikini, a towel wrapped around her waist.

Jim lets the rolling pin drop from his hands.

The wind whips at her hair that straggles across her laughing face, catches on her tongue.

'Take off the towel,' comes Jim's voice. It's like another him, one that makes him shudder.

'It's freezing!'

'So?'

She turns and gazes at the waves that churn and crash behind.

'You look like Grace Kelly,' says Jim.

'Who?'

He laughs and the picture shakes and fills up with greyish sand. Only the sound is left. Him chasing her and Sarah shrieking – she can't run fast enough.

Jim lunges at the screen, punches the stop button and sucks breath as he waits for the machine to spit out the video. His fingers draw it out, then work the tape, feverishly turning the plastic rolls and pulling it free. Images torn from their device, a history destroyed but still a stain on his memory ...

Despicable, he says into the carpet as he hunches into a ball and pounds his fists, though it's a feeble motion, him an aged man with so little left apart from faith in a god who can feel so distant.

After an indefinite time Jim unfolds himself, stands up and cradles his neck side to side. What now? He checks all the windows are locked, then goes to phone the police. His body is working without his mind.

'PC McPherson is out on another call. Should I request a second uniform?'

'No, that's quite all right.'

'I'll ask him to visit as soon as he can.'

The itch of what just happened skirts around his mind, trying to penetrate. In the kitchen Jim starts to reboil the kettle but stops. He finds the pages of his sermon from his satchel but the words jump across the page, refusing to make any sense. On returning to the cubby he is drained and lies face down on the futon with his warm breath dampening his lips. When the distant ringing sound works through the layers of sleep he can't pull himself awake – away from the dreams, away from Sarah.

*

A line of people form outside the church. More than usual for the Sunday congregation. Some are fidgeting in suits, most likely the husbands cajoled to attend for once. They peer round the heavy oak door and aren't sure what to talk about, carefully avoiding the grass verge as if regressed to school-children afraid to be scolded. Jim watches from the back door of the porch. Usually he'd stand by the entrance shaking hands and welcoming families but something isn't right inside him. When he rang the police again that morning, his voice felt tight and strained.

The church bells clang in uneven succession. Jim pictures the ropes yanked downwards and jerking up the stone bell tower. The bell-ringers come every Sunday, have done for years since before he even arrived, and always sit on the back pew in a series of sombre faces, protecting the bells themselves.

After the last bell releases its low looping ring over the village, it's time for service.

'How nice to have so many families with us today,' Jim says as he walks down the aisle.

Sandra and Elsie are perched on their usual row and inspect the newcomers.

'What're all these folk doing here?' Elsie asks with a scowl.

Sandra stays tight-lipped but raises her head to see across the church. People are unsure where to sit, how many to fit in a pew. Usually relaxed men clasp their thighs together to allow elderly neighbours to join them.

Jim reaches the front where the pulpit towers over him. He suddenly wants the shadow to hide him and for someone else to lead the village in prayer. Everyone is sitting and gazing at him now, wanting answers. He isn't here to provide definitive truths, he tells himself. He doesn't *know* all the answers. What is it all these blank faces expect him to say? Their eyes search his face, hands neatly folded in laps over pleated skirts or trousers with folds down the middle.

'The redeeming power of faith can heal us all.' He committed his sermon to memory early that morning and he's glad to know each line word for word. As he describes the community offered by church, so vital in these difficult times, people begin to settle and his voice fills the room.

He's chosen the passage from Matthew that warns against revenge. Though it's debated and often misunderstood, Jim is enlivened by the scent of burning candles behind.

'You have heard that it was said, "Eye for eye, and tooth for tooth."'

He sees people nod. It's not a call for revenge – the opposite – but what might be so wrong with revenge?

Jim lifts his arms as he takes in the vibrant reds and blues illuminated in the stained glass window above the chapel, a heart ablaze in a circle of sharp petals.

In the next moment he is uncertain again. This wasn't a call for the shedding of blood but the crowd are restless once more. He wonders if he should clarify, but is losing his nerve. He goes to arrange the bread on the table and when he turns back, the room is somehow changed.

Something has been said out there.

Chins point in different directions and mutterings are hushed, rise up again, are hushed more loudly.

After the service Jim puts out the candles, cupping the flames with the brass snuffer. Each wisp of smoke is quickly lost to the air. Above, the carved disciples loom across the ceiling.

Matthew, Nathanael, James the Elder – they all wait and watch with their unblinking eyes.

'He's been arrested,' someone says behind him. Jim turns and sees a mass of men in black suits like a crow.

'What for?'

'Caught in the Robinsons' house on Yardley.'

Jim is drawn over. 'Who?'

A pair of tall shoulders rotate outwards, a face appraises him. 'One of our neighbours, in fact.'

'Who is it?'

'Ralph Scott.'

Jim's gown brushes the pavement as he walks to the police station. He could sense people talking as he left the church, almost tripping up the path before he passed the idling groups outside.

Inside reception, Cynthia is slumped in one of the three plastic chairs that line the back wall.

A grey woollen blanket is over her shoulders, which she clutches to her, though her head has fallen back against the wall, mouth cracked open. Is this woman the wife of the Fox? Would she know if she was?

Jim asks Trish on reception to let Brian know he is here. The fifty-something woman agrees and makes a scrawled note. She has the confused look of someone who's found herself in a situation no one warned her about, all wide eyes and smudges of ink up her freckled arms.

All Jim can do for the minute is wait. As he hovers by the chairs, Cynthia wakes with a start and gropes the blanket tighter beneath sharp knuckles.

'May I?'

Jim indicates to the seat next to her.

'Suppose.'

A red vein across Cynthia's eyeball makes Jim blink. Her usually neat curls have flattened in a patch where pressed against the wall.

'You here to accuse us 'n' all?'

'Not one bit.' Jim realises how little he's ever spoken to Cynthia. She is usually just a figure on her driveway in that dressing gown which he can see poking under the blanket now. The lace trim is folded within the standard police wool. 'Would you like a cup of tea?'

Cynthia gives just a slight nod as if not wanting to fall for a trick. The task of making hot drinks, however, has Trish readily deserting some paperwork to bustle around offering sachets of sugar and milk. She hums tunelessly before handing over the polystyrene cup.

'It's not him,' Cynthia says once she and Jim are alone again. 'He thought he saw something in the back garden so climbed the fence, that's all.' She says the lines blankly, as if they're worn with use. Her pinkish eyes fix on the door. Outside villagers are walking home from church and slowing feet to peer inwards, their faces distorted in the thick glass panel.

'Most people, they'd crown a hero for going after the Fox like that,' she mutters, having found herself a willing audience. 'Not us though; never gave us the smallest chance, them lot, even though we've lived here all these years.' Her eyes slide down the length of Jim's gown. 'Dunno about you.'

'I try not to judge.'

'Try?'

'We're all prone to our bias. We each have a single perspective with which to view the world. Can only really know ourselves and even then there are surprises.'

He says the last line more to himself but Cynthia is alert.

'I know my husband.'

'Well ...'

'I bleeding do. Spent the last twelve years in that bungalow with him. Side by side, every day. I know every scent of his body, every milk bottle named and numbered.'

Jim hears a faint mew from Trish.

'Don't tell me I don't know him.'

'It's settled then, I won't.'

Jim has difficulty picturing Ralph in his cubby, climbing from the window, but his mind is blank. All he can process is the room around him: the savoury smell of tea, the soft cracking of polystyrene as Cynthia squeezes the cup's rim; she angles it from a circle to oval, the brown liquid inside reshaping.

'No one listens to me round here.' She eyes the interview room door.

Jim adjusts himself in the seat, wondering when Brian will be ready. 'I suppose the police must be curious as to why he was outside the Robinsons' house.'

The cup bulges back into shape.

'Since he doesn't usually leave home,' Jim quickly adds.

'Sometimes I tell him to leave me to my things. You can't spend your whole life indoors. So he goes walking.'

'At night?'

'Helps him work things out.'

'What things?'

She shrugs. 'Things in his head that are wrong.'

Deloris turns up, out of breath, with her hair a mass of un-directed strands.

'Where is she? Where's Anna?' she calls towards the corridor.

'Excuse me,' Trish says uncertainly, glancing at the door to the interview room.

Deloris clocks Cynthia opposite and goes quiet.

Cynthia's face tenses. Her lips are pulled to one side with lower teeth showing.

'Say it's not true,' she says under her breath. 'You were meant to be nice.'

Cynthia baulks and begins to say something but Deloris is now raising her chin, stepping forward.

'People are saying you might be in on it too,' she says to her in a hard voice, a South London accent coming through. She hesitates by reception. 'That's not true, is it?'

Jim rises to stand in Deloris's way, although, as he does, he suddenly wants to believe that Ralph has Anna. That she's somewhere in the village, somewhere close to them, waiting for Brian to ask the right question in the interview room. It might all be over so soon.

Just as Deloris is taking breath to shout down the corridor again, Brian appears. He rubs his face, surprised to see all of them in reception.

'Has he told you yet?' Deloris asks.

'Sorry?'

'Where he's hidden Anna?' Her eyes shine, the rest of her paralysed.

Brian frowns wearily. 'Please, all go home.'

'We should be scouring the woods.' She wipes her eyes, twists round to face the door.

'We have been.' Brian is grey-faced. 'But there's miles to search.'

'So?' Deloris says but without conviction.

Jim steps to one side. Behind him, Cynthia sits with her

lower lip still downturned. The blanket has fallen around her and is partly on the floor, revealing her dressing gown and shoulders set forwards like an animal braced for attack.

It takes Jim a second to hear Brian, then realise he's saying his name.

'Do you want to come this way?'

'Ah yes. Sorry.'

Deloris narrows her eyes as they go into the other room. The place has been cleared up since he was here last and he wonders if it is the other officer's influence. Brian must be used to having it to himself. Several cups sit upturned on the drying rack by the sink. The Ordnance Survey map is pinned to the corkboard on the wall with two lonely pins protruding.

'All right if I make some coffee first?' Brian says.

'By all means.'

Without asking if Jim wants one, Brian shakes coffee granules from the pot straight into two mugs, then slops in some milk and water from the kettle.

'Bad form I didn't come sooner last night,' he says putting the top back on the coffee. It goes on at the wrong angle; he twists it in reverse, then gives up. 'Staff shortages, you see. Apparently they'd usually pull other officers but too many are up north with the miners.' He grimaces. 'And I was busy at the Robinsons. Elizabeth was beside herself.'

Jim tries to clear his head. 'That must have been when I rang, yes.'

'The call came in at ...' Brian trails off as he picks up the coffees and plonks them on the table. Jim lowers himself into one of the chairs.

Brian takes a noisy sip. 'The call was at eleven-oh-one.'

Just past eleven? The awareness shivers through Jim. *Around the time the Fox was in my cubby.*

He's only vaguely aware as Brian removes a tape from the recorder and writes something on its label. His tongue slides into view. *Ralph probably isn't the Fox.*

'Perhaps Ralph is telling the truth,' Jim says, a cold penetrating him. His mind is turning too slowly to think it through.

An attempted smile. 'That's what I plan to find out. If you don't mind, I'm going to record your statement on the matter. Did you see Ralph Scott last night?'

'No.'

'Oh?' He rubs his forehead then across both cheeks. Flesh is pulled in all directions. 'So what are you reporting?'

Outside a door slams open, then someone shouts down the corridor, 'You sick pervert! We all know what you did.'

There's a scrape of chair leg and the receptionist says something.

'I'm too tired for this,' Brian mutters, slowly rising. 'Excuse me for a minute.'

Voices shoot back and forth beyond the wall. Alone in the room, Jim realises he's sitting in the same chair Ralph must have been interviewed in, in the same position facing Brian, a tape running. Only he's the one with the criminal record, the video at home, pulled apart but surely repairable. He imagines the police reassembling the tape, sliding it into the VCR …

'You won't get away with this!' screams the woman again. It's Elizabeth. 'You freak!'

A door closes and Brian comes back in. 'Where were we?'

They'll think it was me.

'Mr Thomas?'

'Nowhere,' Jim whispers. 'I mean, I only wanted an update.'

Brian rubs his face again, leaving white fingermarks on his cheeks. 'You don't have any more information, Mr Thomas?'

'I'm sorry.' Jim shakes his head like a twitch. 'I don't know anything about last night.'

8

The whole village surrounds Cynthia and Ralph's house. Many are still in their Sunday best – not long home from church – and one woman even wears a plastic apron like she's about to start preparing the family roast. Jim hovers behind the main crowd who stand in the road, unsure of themselves, feeling too close and fidgeting with fingers sliding inside tight collars and reddening faces, yet unable to walk away. Jim left the police station less than five minutes ago and now finds himself here, talking to no one, simply standing watching. His white robe falls around him like a protective layer but is surely smudging with dust as his body involuntarily sways, picking up dirt the longer he does nothing.

The midday sun beats down, causing them all to squint and shuffle, but they continue to watch as the house is searched even when the front door is closed and there's no movem apart from the odd haze of navy uniform by the kitchen dow. The last of the rainwater is dried from the cracks driveway bricks. After a while a few people in the cro away, including Harvey who announces it's a waste of his time. He stalks off in his golfing outfit with the collar turned up, followed by Michael who has been standing with Sandra some distance away. Deloris stays where she is, however, transfixed on the pavement with arms awkwardly at her sides.

Mullins has parked on the pavement and must be inside. Jim pictures him rifling through drawers in that careless way of his – a lifetime of clothes and jewellery and trinkets up-turned as he looks for evidence that most likely doesn't exist. Family photographs pulled from their frames? The bedroom door flung open? Jim knows he is the only one who can stop all this. The act of stopping it, however, seems so far removed from his position amongst the crowd, quietly watching with all the other neighbours. He's supposed to walk to the house and say what? That he lied to Brian earlier. That he was afraid of being accused himself because … He wipes the sweat that trickles from his forehead. Because in some ways he and the Fox aren't so different.

After a while another police car turns into the road and they scatter to one side as it steadily continues before stopping a few metres ahead of Cynthia's house. The driver takes his time getting out. It's a woman who appears, putting a cap with an inspector's insignia over her dark wiry hair that's secured in a net. She trudges over without casting an eye at the villagers and says something to Mullins who holds the door open for her before disappearing again.

A plane chugs across the blue sky above them and the crowd ·mporarily distracted. How lucky to be off away, somewhere ·nt where turquoise water ripples in a swimming pool ·er umbrellas loll in cocktail glasses. Jim's not sure he'll ·ure anywhere again. How would he deserve it? His thoughts are interrupted by murmurs breaking through the crowd. Following the angle of shoulders, Jim sees Cynthia's face at the kitchen window, a haze of white with shadows for eyes like a theatre mask. An elbow nudges in front of him, a man then points a finger although Cynthia has already re-hidden.

'She shouldn't be in there,' someone says.

'Hiding evidence of what he did,' says Elsie, leaning on her stick by Anna's front gate.

'We don't know he did anything.'

'It's the only explanation.' The last voice is Pete Robinson's. He has his arm around Elizabeth, lips pressed to their baby's head. She babbles an incoherent lullaby whose words have got scrambled. 'He said he saw someone in our garden but he looked guilty as hell when we found him.'

The door opens and the inspector comes out with a black bin bag, which she carries to her car amid the sound of clinking glass. Everyone surges forward to see.

'Is that the milk bottles?'

'He has hundreds, doesn't he?'

No answer comes from the crowd – it seems no one has visited them lately, if ever.

Someone else begins to speak but is cut off as Cynthia flies from the house. Her dressing gown flaps open as she strides across the drive. 'They're bloody Ralph's!' Mullins follows and catches her arms from behind. Her breasts flop forwards, unhindered by any bra. Jim winces to watch as Cynthia sticks out her lower lip but says nothing more.

A reporter is suddenly in the crowd. Jim recognises him from his visit after the initial break-ins, as do the rest of them who aren't sure what to say as the young, suited man strid‑

through them all and they part as if for a prophet. He quickly reaches Cynthia who hesitates on the drive.

'Howard Mills from the *Gazette*,' he says, wonky teeth flashing. 'What's going on, Mrs Scott? How do you feel about your husband's arrest?'

Mullins tells him to get off the property but just rolls his eyes when the young man pushes a recorder near Cynthia's mouth. The policewoman gestures to Mullins and he follows her inside.

'They're taking his bottles,' Cynthia says.

Howard is lost for a second, then switches to a sympathetic stance. 'Is it true your husband is disfigured? From an accident with glass when he was a boy?'

Jim grips at his neck, his wrist, at any loose skin.

'And that's why he doesn't go out much?'

Cynthia sneers. 'Would you want them lot judging you?'

The crowd shrinks back, suddenly aware of themselves. Jim can't see for a second as Elizabeth jiggles her whimpering baby and its robust legs drop from the folds of cashmere.

'Is that why he abducted Anna? For revenge?'

'*What*?' Cynthia backs away towards the house.

Howard stays where he is. 'Did you do it together?'

Cynthia's shoulders hit the front door, which is closed to her. 'Pack of lies. Get away, the lot of you. Please.'

But Howard isn't letting up. 'All these people seem to think so and they're your neighbours, aren't they? The people who've known you and your husband for years.' He indicates casually to the crowd. Jim finds his mouth falling open. The moment slows as Cynthia veers back against the closed door again, like he might push through the wood. But the dressing gown, which she grips beneath her knuckles, is her only protection.

Jim shuffles forward through the crowd at last. He reaches the pavement and speaks, or at least he imagines he does. In his mind, he is crossing the drive and taking Cynthia in his arms, protecting her from the crowd who begin to strike his own body with slaps and fists. They scream at him as their rage lashes down in a torrent, the two of them in the middle. Only Cynthia squirms free from him. She knows he is guilty. She joins the crowd as they cuss and spit in globules that land like sticky rain as he curls on the ground. Deloris's hand reaches to pluck an eye from his socket and the street around him runs red with a river of his blood.

Something touches Jim's shoulder and he awakens. It's Stan, asking if he's OK. Jim realises he's down on the pavement. He mutters an apology and Stan quickly steps back to avoid an elbow. The crowd want to see Cynthia. Legs edge forwards, shoes scuffing and accidentally kicking gravel that skitters about. They step round him to mount the pavement. Jim's gown is still draped over his legs but is dirtying badly, becoming black. As he stands, all he can see through the shoulders is a glimpse of Cynthia collapsed in front of her house, knees pulled to her chest like a scared child, the door not opening even as she begins to wail.

He is slow to walk away but finds he isn't hurt, nothing apart from spots of red that expand on his inner wrists. Dead skin is wedged under his fingernails, which he notes with a strange detachment as if the body part isn't his own. Jim takes two steps towards the high street. A freckled boy turns to look and Jim tugs down his sleeve to hide the blood. On the far side of the pavement, up from Anna's house, he observes the crowd a few metres away. Their anger now defused, they hover in huddles. Cynthia is taken back inside by the police. Howard talks to Elsie and the Robinsons who speak into his recorder, giving shakes of their heads that seem exaggerated now. Deloris glances over but stays near the house. Stan is standing next to Mary Braithwaite and her husband. So many people who aren't fully known to him or to each other, neighbours going about their lives side by side for years, decades, certain strands woven but with holes through which light or dark can seep.

Jim takes a few steady breaths and lets his thoughts begin to order. The Fox is still unknown, someone lurking in the village who came into his house and played his tape. Granted, it had been left out on the floor but there were plenty of other things to look at. Now this person knows not only what Jim did but that he kept the tape as – as what? A warning to himself of what he's capable of? Worse, a memento? He recoils at the thought as he walks along the street, away from the crowd, although for all he knows the Fox could be watching him this very second.

Passing by the other homes, Jim is struck by another question: why him? Out of the entire village, why was *he* visited last night? And this visit marked by the television's volume turned up, the tape left running, the secret he's hidden for years displayed on screen.

At home Jim closes the kitchen curtains left by the previous tenant. He then finds the videotape snaked across the snug's carpet and carries it downstairs to the kitchen table. The sun casts a sickly orange over the walls as he works scissors through the tape, slicing it piece by piece. He lays the narrow strips across the kitchen table and moves the order around – the front to the end, the middle shuffled. How different his life might be if things had happened in another way. Now he just has fragments that curl upwards, a smooth plastic under his fingertips. Jim sits and stares for a while, slumped in the chair with his lower arms across the table. The blood on his left wrist is drying, darkening to a crust. In a few days it'll fall off, fresh pink underneath that'll soon be healed.

He pushes himself up and pulls off the gown. His vest beneath is grubby with a hole by the seam. He runs upstairs to pull on jeans, a shirt, and the thick-soled boots he hasn't worn in months. The police will soon release Ralph, but in the meantime he can't just sit here.

Leaves crackle under his feet near the edge of the woods where a police sign reads: *Under surveillance.* It looks overly small and flimsy, stuck to a tree with tape. Jim heads to where Anna's lace glove was found buried a few metres behind her house. He stares at the ground and a shiver runs through him – did Anna flee or was she dragged? But the ground is giving away no secrets. Nothing more than mounds of earth that lie bloated with water.

Away from the scrubland the narrow path slides under his feet as the trees grow more dense – first silver birches in pale beams, then ashes and oaks and another sort with purplish bark and spindly branches that feel their way outwards like fingers. They throw shade that roves the floor, the gaps creating slits of light like shards across Jim's body. He finds a stick and begins to swipe thick brambles ahead, then stops. How does he know what's beneath?

Jim's hand goes limp. He continues along a slight ridge but still can't see much. The trees are in all directions now, standing in their solemn rows, faint scratching sounds falling as squirrels and rats scavenge for food. Some people make a home of woods like these – they spend their lives tramping along the footpaths, understanding the cycle of the buds, the strength of branches to climb and see across to the village.

Not Jim, though. His boots are becoming weighed with mulch as he tramps onwards. He is losing his sense of direction as the sun is blocked overhead in the dense canopy. While others see nature as being close to God, he now realises he's never quite reached this point. The odd photograph might strike him, or the passing of trees in his car window. But to be immersed in nature like this doesn't make him feel God. Where *do* I feel God? Jim asks himself abruptly.

Time passes and it might've been an hour or two. The sun is lower in the sky and turns shapes to silhouettes; light briefly splinters out from behind them, then fades to a dim glow. A clearing opens up ahead – a huge log lies on its side with a flattened part on top. No doubt ants and creatures have burrowed into its festering pores but Jim is tired and leans against it. This might be the area where the local primary school had its barbecue in May, before Elsie's first break-in set everyone on edge. Schools will be stopping for the summer holidays next month. What if they don't find him? He is sure it's a him. Will kids be kept inside? A hot sensation pulses in Jim's head to think of children frightened to venture past their front lawns, bikes rusting in sheds. What do they understand of Anna being gone?

A scrunching sound starts behind, then turns to footsteps. They're fast and uneven and Jim glances through the darkened trees to see a person get nearer. It's Deloris.

She seems to have clocked Jim a while off and comes within several metres of him in the clearing.

'What are you doing?' she asks, dressed in jeans and a purple anorak.

'Looking for Anna.' Jim attempts to push himself from the log, feeling guilty for stopping, but feels too tired. To his

surprise Deloris sits down next to him. Maybe her earlier sus-
picions have evaporated now everyone thinks Ralph is the Fox.
Or maybe she's simply decided he's not so bad after all.

'Should you be out here?' Jim asks.

'Not you as well,' she says with an exasperated laugh. 'I can't
just sit at home. And Harvey's out helping the Robinsons with
a new alarm.'

Jim didn't think he was the neighbourly type.

'He's changed the last few days,' she says as if reading his
thoughts. 'Paid for all the Neighbourhood Watch signs too.'

They tramp together for the next half an hour or so, staying
several paces apart, but with Deloris stopping to wait when she
gets too far ahead. She seems to have a system and narrows her
eyes to take in the horizon. At one point she marks a tree with
two sticks she crosses over one another at its base. Gone is the
young woman he once saw check her lipstick in a car mirror
and rolling her eyes when the post office didn't have her magazine. This Deloris picks her way along the river, unconcerned
about the mud rising around her ankles, and even offers him a
hand over a wide section. But then, maybe she was always that
way and people just didn't see it.

She shows him a hideout she's built for watching the Fox
and he's too stunned to ask what she means, only gawps at the
mass of branches.

Once they're back near the fence to her patio she turns to
him. 'I know you and Anna were close,' she says gently. 'You
should keep the faith.'

Jim is startled. 'Well, I—'

'I don't believe myself.' Deloris frowns, as if solving a
puzzle. Then says, 'But it's what Anna needs. If she believes in
this God, it makes sense to pray, doesn't it? To do everything

in your very fibre? You can't give up on God now. You'd be giving up on her too.'

Back at home Jim stands at the kitchen sink as he drinks a few sips of water. He doesn't let himself turn to the strips of film on the table. Instead he puts down the glass and clasps his hands together. How right it feels to cross them over, palm to palm. He tells God he is sorry for everything. Please can he keep Anna safe? He thinks of the 'My Angel' embroidery on Ruth's staircase and holds the image in his mind.

Later, as he is climbing the stairs for bed, the phone rings.

'Mr Thomas? This is the DDO.'

At first Jim can't understand why the reverend would be calling.

'I've been trying you for the last hour or so. We sent a letter but didn't hear.'

'Oh, I'm sorry. Is anything the matter?' Jim hears another voice in the background – his wife perhaps. It's late.

'I'd like you to come see me first thing tomorrow.'

Jim agrees and feels for the phone cradle in the pitch-black hall.

9

Jim drives to the village of Little Finchley, a few miles to the south of Oxford. After parking beside the duck pond in the centre he walks down a sloping lane and breathes in the warm, fresh air that's flavoured with rosemary. He slept fitfully the night before but now here it's like everything is laid out more simply. Inside his pocket is a list of parishes to contact about Anna after this meeting. Whatever the DDO wants to discuss pales in significance to her and it's this later task he fixes his mind on.

He finds the DDO's cottage near the end of the road where a lawnmower waits unattended in the front garden.

'Evelyn,' the man says as he stretches out a hand. He's tall, and although in his sixties, perfectly upright. Until now Jim has only had phone conversations with him – polite but brisk talks about the running of St Katherine's church. The heating all right? Enough funds? This is the first time he's been invited to his home and he self-consciously wipes his feet several times on the doormat.

'I thought we'd go for a ramble, actually,' Evelyn says, reaching for some wellington boots left against the wall.

'Of course.'

Jim isn't dressed for a countryside walk but nevertheless picks his way behind Evelyn. It's a thin path beside a field of high, brittle corn that releases flecks into the air. For a time the two men walk in quiet and Jim resolves to let Evelyn decide when to speak. He does so a minute later as they turn a bend and the field path widens.

'It's not until the winter I retire but I need to start getting affairs in order.' Evelyn sets his eye on the view ahead: a church spire rises from a crop of trees, the sky patterned with a drift of smoke. 'I hear you've been telephoning a few of the parishes.'

'Ah … yes.'

'It's quite all right to do that, only there are some gaps in your files.'

Evelyn continues to walk with his eyes ahead so Jim searches for some words. It's a conversation he's been delaying for over two years. 'I had some chats with the Bishop,' Jim starts, pretending to admire the bramble bush to his left though it has no fruit this early in summer. 'He said we should wait to discuss them further.'

'Well, I'd like to get it all cleared up today. The process has been rather sluggish but there's no reason not to rattle through some of this paperwork.'

'It's not just a matter of paperwork, I'm afraid.'

'Well.' Evelyn waves a hand in the air dismissively. 'A disagreement, then.'

Jim waits for Evelyn to climb a stile, which he does in a series of careful movements and a swift swing of leg. He pauses, momentarily overcome by the swell at his throat, but forms the sentence word by word. 'I had an affair with a fifteen-year-old girl.'

Evelyn is temporarily still, his hand paused on the wooden plank which is splintered at various points. A bird flies overhead in the colourless sky.

'She cried rape?'

'No, I did, on her behalf,' Jim says. 'I had no idea she was so young. Her name is Sarah. She lied about her age, but of course I should have known. There's a caution on my record, which is why there's been a delay with my vicarhood. The Bishop said redemption might be possible but he needed time to consult the relevant orders. And, well, that was two years ago.'

The words lighten him though he knows they shouldn't. He's never said them before in such quick succession. It took him a long time to realise he should have known. Arguments with Belinda lasted hours. Though he was guilty over it all, him not knowing was like the last thread he clung to, as if its snapping might be the end of his last claim to not being some monster. The weeks with Sarah had been a throng of impulses, vivid colours, and him consumed by something that gripped and didn't let go.

'I suggest we have this conversation back at the cottage,' Evelyn says turning round.

Jim agrees and they walk back the way they came. Neither speak, apart from when a woman with a Labrador crosses them and smiles brightly at Evelyn. He scratches the dog behind its ears and says hello. They're quickly off again though, Jim recognising a brisk manner in him as his boots swish against his trousers.

They go up a steep staircase to his study and his wife calls to ask if they want a pot of tea.

'Not now,' he calls back, pausing on the landing where wooden beams support the ceiling. Then, 'OK, fine. Bring one up.'

They wait until the saucers and cups are assembled, the pot left on a brown envelope on Evelyn's large maple desk that fills most of the room. It's too large an item, really, and Jim's back is against a sloping ceiling wall.

'I have wanted to do it before,' Jim says once they're alone. The lawnmower starts a soft chug outside. 'Of course, nobody ever admits to being attracted to girls – you're not supposed to. We have a culture of women looking so young, so few clothes, but a man should never admit it.'

Evelyn seems to be nodding, though he doesn't meet Jim's eye. One leg is crossed loosely over the other, his back reclined in the leather armchair with studs along the seams.

'But I joined the vicarhood,' Jim continues. 'Not that I wasn't religious before, but I resolved to devote myself to it, to become a better man in every way. The church seemed the only place.'

'A refuge,' Evelyn says decidedly. He uncrosses his leg and sits more upright at the desk.

'Not exactly. I wanted to help people. I still do.' Jim shifts unsteadily. 'It hasn't been all that easy. People wonder why I'm not a vicar myself but I am trying.'

His tiredness is dragging at him. He's been away from Heathcote well over two hours and wants to get back home to make those phone calls. 'And, quite frankly, I understand if you don't want to recommend me for discernment. I wanted it for a long time but really my work is just the same and ...' Jim trails off as he notices Evelyn's face.

Evelyn speaks slowly, carefully placing each word. 'I might have to call a halt.'

'To my vicar training?'

'No. To your position at St Katherine's.' His eyes are pale but steady. 'Your role as lay reader might no longer be possible.'

The words are like pebbles sinking in dark waters.

'Although, as I understand it, you don't reside in the vicarage?'

Each pebble is lost so quickly under the sliding layers, the froth.

Evelyn moves his armchair back. 'No? Well, that makes matters simpler.'

'I gave everything up for this,' Jim says into his own lap. A thread has come loose on his trousers. 'I gave the house to my wife. Lucy doesn't speak to me. I live in a hovel. I give myself to God.' He grips the underneath of the chair as if to stand would be to accept what this man is telling him. 'I'm happy to do that but it needs to be for something.' He thinks of Anna. 'And it is.'

'It's simply not responsible,' Evelyn says curtly. 'And while we're here, please stop phoning parishes.'

'Why?'

'It's not your job any more. Am I clear?' A tinkling comes from downstairs and Evelyn glances towards the door. He stands and signals with his arm. Neither has touched their tea, which sit cooling on their saucers. 'We shall speak more in the next week or so. I need to make some phone calls.'

Jim shakes off the hand that Evelyn rests on his shoulder. 'My only purpose is to help Anna. It's all I have left.' As he says the words he realises how true they are. A rare, perfect truth around which the rest of his life drifts.

'There are others who can help,' Evelyn says and shows him to the door.

Cars overtake as Jim drives along the motorway. His hands rest loosely on either side of the steering wheel on the endless straight road. The sides seem monotonous – an unknowable stream of greenery, the trees planted for the sake of meeting a quota of green land, preventing floods, but where no one really goes to walk with families. He lets his foot press on the pedal though there's no longer anywhere he can think to go.

In his mind he's back driving Belinda to the hospital. She was in the passenger seat with a flannel across her forehead that kept sliding off, a giddy look on her face. She told him to slow down as he overtook a motorbike but said it with a laugh and Jim was pleased. After all the nausea Belinda had been through, the difficulty sleeping on her side, it was his chance to make sure their baby was OK.

The rain was streaming and the torrents of water on the windshield glowed red. Cars were stopping ahead as traffic piled up. After several gut-wrenching screams, Belinda had Lucy on the back seat, an unusually quick birth especially for a first child, the paramedic said when the ambulance eventually turned up. By this time Jim had cut through the grisly chord with scissors a woman in another car had produced. From the pick-your-own farm, she said. Belinda was flat out and laughing again, great ripples through her thighs and belly, Jim wrapping Lucy in a towel. A squirmy, soft child he couldn't possibly be responsible for. As the traffic began again, wheels spitting out water, Jim prayed to God for the first time. Not just knelt among his family for service, self-conscious of the draft, the creak of his dad's knees. The first time he'd felt how utterly lost he'd be without Him.

Now, the 'SLOW' paint of the road disappearing under his

car, Jim wonders at what point God left him. Or he left God. It was hard to keep track – life wasn't so many big moments like births, but a succession of tiny ones that pieced together. Any day was a battle between good and bad, though there must have been a moment he started to lose? Sarah brushing her hair and the smell of patchouli across the corridor? Him agreeing to take her to lunch at 'the good place' where she ordered a white wine, told him about the Kant she'd been reading. *Thoughts without content are empty.*

No, at that point it was just simmering under the surface. He knows the rupture. He was supposed to see Lucy in a ballet recital that weekend – a stiff sort of thing with competitive parents whispering in the audience. Sarah was quick with an alternative and he saw the lands part, let himself walk right up to the edge. *A holiday house by Sheringham beach? It'll be chilly, but what the hell?*

Jim now feels the car begin to shake as he speeds along the A road that has met another straight patch. He eats up the distance, the white stripes sucked under the wheels. It's freeing to rest his hands on the steering wheel and lose himself to the engine's roaring cogs, the smell of gas like a veil of death.

The road begins to curve away from him. Jim's foot reflexively lightens on the peddle to slow and he wonders at what his body does, what it wants and demands through a series of impulses, twitches, though it's ageing and weakening, his hands wrinkled with tendons, age spots mottling the skin towards his elbow.

'A sick fool,' he says and thinks to make a prayer but his mind is shuddering with too many images as he should really be turning the wheel, but is going straight. Straight up on to the grass verge. A better man might think something profound but too soon he's shaken by a rattle of bank and green and sky till the final chosen tree greets him through the windshield.

The room gradually arranges itself among the white. Jim blinks and he sees a long rectangle of strip lighting. It gnaws at his eyes so he tries to turn his head but there's a pain holding him still.

Jim is later apologetic to the young doctor who is feeling his chest with a cold instrument. Whether any words have formed he's not sure. The doctor doesn't respond and another person in a light-blue uniform walks up with a clipboard. Jim's body is seemingly pressed against many cushions, which hold him in place. Antiseptic mixed with stale urine hangs in the air.

'You'll need a neck brace,' the nurse tells him. 'And a prescription of Co-codamol.' He helps Jim from the bed, and though the bulky item rubs against his shoulders, Jim's shocked to find he's balancing with no assistance. For a minute he stands just as he is, waiting to tell someone he doesn't see the point, has nowhere to go, but the nurse has gone. The hospital busies around him with appointments to make, jars softly clinking as a trolley is wheeled past.

'You're alive,' a guy in the reception area says. His turquoise shell suit is too short in the legs; a goofy sort of lumbering walk. 'Tony,' he tells him. He explains he was the driver who stopped on the road. 'A crumpled bonnet. Hope you've got some ace insurance.'

Tony keeps glancing over as he walks Jim to the taxi rank. An ache is rankling at his left shoulder. 'I can't believe you're all right, man.'

Jim tells him he's fine now. 'Thank you for your concern.'

'I just can't believe it.'

When Jim gives a stiff wave and joins the queue of people waiting, Tony gives him a grin of yellow teeth. 'Come on, I can't just leave you now.' He insists on giving Jim a lift and though he declines several times, the aching shoulder is becoming more insistent.

He doesn't want to think about his own car as he sits in the passenger seat, just looks through the window as the hospital car park changes to road, a roundabout, then the familiar stretches of farms, the metal sign for Heathcote, the high street towards the church ...

Anna had turned white as chalk when he told her. It was September, two months into his move, and following a Sunday service she'd inspired him to write. On forgiving others, forgiving yourself. They'd talked about it the evening before – mostly in abstract terms about the strength required to let something go – and her words had itched inside him.

'I've barely slept a full night since,' he said when she hurried away into the hall. 'Or eaten a meal. Nothing tastes right.' He knew he was babbling but couldn't stop, afraid to touch her arm or even say her name as she pulled on her coat.

He didn't hear from her for three days and considered moving parishes to somewhere people wouldn't be afraid of him. But the following morning she turned up on his door with a paper bag of fresh mint, parsley and tomatoes. 'Everyone should eat,' she said. Whether she ever fully understood, he couldn't be sure, but nevertheless Anna never told another soul.

He now asks to be dropped at the police station. Tony gives another grin then, realising he's serious, shrugs and parks clumsily on the pavement outside.

After thanking Tony again, Jim takes the three steps in turn. He'd barely noticed the steps before but a headache has joined forces with the shoulder ache, meaning each movement sends a wave of hot pain vibrating through him.

The female inspector is standing outside the door of the interview room. She must have been drafted in especially for the case and grips a thermos of coffee, her wiry hair almost escaping its net. Beside her, Howard, the reporter from the day before, holds a tape recorder near her mouth.

'Does someone like Mr Scott fit the profile?' He dares to angle the tape recorder even closer to her. She looks out from her heavy eyelids at Jim, ignoring the younger man.

'A sexually frustrated type?' Howard pushes on. 'A voyeur who likes to watch people?'

'That's what "voyeur" means, correct,' she mutters.

Jim hovers at reception.

'Is it urgent?' The woman is suddenly alert.

'No, no, I can wait,' he says, shaking his head. He's grateful to have time to sit. Back in the middle of the line of three plastic chairs he realises that only a day has passed since he was last here.

The inspector strides back into the interview room and Howard is left alone. He glances about, putting the tape recorder in his pocket.

'Howard Mills,' he tells Jim. He's older than Jim first thought – around thirty, perhaps, with thinning hair gelled over his scalp. The suit he wears is polyester and paired with black trainers that look like shoes.

Jim gives a vague nod.

'He's been released, you know. What do you think about that?' He brings out a recorder but is preoccupied twisting the reels where the tape's loosened.

'Ralph isn't being held?'

'There's been another break-in while he was inside. A rope taken from Mary Braithwaite's shed. Got a comment?'

Jim's feet slip free of the floor as he leans back, a lightness in his head for a moment.

Howard sticks around a while longer, pacing about in his trainers, and then openly curses and leaves. It's just Jim in the reception area for a time. He listens to the clock's hand work round the face until it reaches one o'clock. Trish comes in with a plastic bag and a can of pink lemonade, says hello, and plonks herself at reception.

It's not until almost two that Brian walks up the steps, followed by Deloris who's dressed in the same anorak as before, the buttons mismatching so spare fabric hangs at the bottom.

'You have to come now,' she tells him.

'OK, Deloris. Just give me a minute.' Brian is pulling down his shirtsleeves, neatening himself for work. The inspector comes to the interview door.

'McPherson,' she says.

'Afternoon, Inspector Jackson.'

Deloris is in a flurry. She hangs by the door, which she doesn't let close, a foot wedging it open, and shoots Jim a wild look. He rises from the seat and, ignoring the ache, goes to her.

'Everything OK, Deloris?'

'Not at all. You have to come. *All* of you. Now.'

Brian and Jim follow Deloris outside on to the high street. She walks straight on to the road, stopping skittishly for a car, then heads for Glebe Crescent. The two of them traipse after her. Clouds have closed over the sky, which makes the village feel hemmed in, as if a weight is pressing down, trapping the hot air.

As they reach the end of Deloris's road, fat spots of rain are staining the pavement, giving rise to a concrete smell. Several yards ahead she waits impatiently for them before passing alongside the gate of her house. Brian takes out his notebook as they walk and holds it at his side against his navy sweater. Jim notices he now has a radio clipped to his trouser pocket, and shorter hair so you can see his scalp.

'Please hurry,' she says in an odd, high-pitched voice that makes Jim want to do the opposite.

She takes them several minutes behind her house, along one of the paths she and Jim followed the evening before. Jim stops to let the stitch in his lungs subside and Brian carries on.

It's hard to see through the branches but Jim hears their voices. Brian is speaking into his radio. 'Assistance needed, approximately half a mile south of Glebe Crescent.'

Jim almost trips on an upturned root as he nears them, his eyes trying to understand the scene segmented by the branches, brambles and shadow cast across Deloris. Her expression is unreadable but her body is tense, arms wrapped around her waist.

As he passes the gushing stream, Jim recognises the place where Deloris told him she was building a hideout. To watch the Fox.

'This is the exact spot,' she says, pointing to the mass of branches piled at an angle against a fallen log.

Above it, a piece of rope hangs from the branch of an oak. It's tied at the end to a noose.

It isn't long before Inspector Jackson comes with a steady traipse of feet, the same tired eyes that only widen when she sees the rope. It sways slightly, almost imperceptibly, bulges along its length that must only be two metres up.

'What does it mean?' asks Deloris who is almost at the rope.

Jackson raises a hand and signals to Brian to speak with her.

'Tape off this area,' she tells him. 'I'll put in a request for more officers.'

'More officers?' Brian gazes again at the rope.

They begin to walk back along the path and the two others follow.

'We're not dealing with some sexual deviant,' Jackson says quietly, an edge to her voice. 'Someone much more intelligent is intent on sending us a message.'

'What message?' Brian asks.

The others are not far behind but Jackson is preoccupied in her thoughts. She pauses and gropes the hairnet, stuffing strands back in.

'What message?' Deloris repeats.

Jackson's eyes are heavy again. She walks on with arms rigid at her sides. 'It's only so long until there's a murder in the village.'

PART THREE

10

Brian gingerly walks over to the huge, bulging screen and plastic board filled with rows of letters. *For faster information retrieval*, Jackson had said the evening before. She hadn't explained the mechanics, though, had just walked off without another word, the engine of her Panda starting up a minute later. Brian now stares at the machine that takes up most of the desk. If the kids play on them at school, surely they can't be that complicated. Can they? He presses the A key, which clicks back in place but does nothing to the black screen.

It's not quite 6.00 a.m. and Brian has arrived early to get a jump-start but now at the station is letting the minutes trickle past.

Just as he reaches a finger towards the S key, a figure appears the other side of the small square window that looks on to the street. The person doesn't return Brian's wave, so he's not sure who it might be as he hurries into reception.

'Gupta,' the man says with a quick dip of head.

Brian hasn't properly met anyone from India before, let alone worked with them.

'Constable?' the man says patiently.

'Sorry, yes.' Brian shakes his dazed head and holds open the door. 'I'm Constable McPherson. Come into my humble abode.' His laugh isn't echoed by Gupta, who gives a polite smile and waits at the reception desk without removing his helmet.

'Coffee?' Brian asks.

'Not for me.' The Indian man observes the room – the plastic chairs, log book and papers spilling across the reception desk – and then folds one slender hand across the other. He looks a little older than Brian with flecks of grey in his eyebrows.

Stuck for something else to say, Brian drifts back into the main room. Presumably it's Jackson who will give the patrol officer his instructions but he isn't sure. Everything has changed in the last day. After finding the noose around the tree, Jackson came back to fill out a report, then made a series of phone calls including one for the Intel computer. Meanwhile Brian fidgeted with the files of index cards kept in the cabinet beside the sink. When he'd joined the local police four years ago it was just him and Sergeant Stephenson, a soft-speaking Scot who was so unlike any of the men Brian met during his training. They spent their days tending house calls about a neighbour's phone conversation too loud past ten o'clock or, one of their more unusual complaints, a ferret drowned in a pond after becoming trapped in the weeds. They'd sit till the teapot was empty, listening to every word, but didn't write many reports afterwards. *Bureaucracy*, Stephenson would tut, *sent to keep the polis off the streets. Pay no attention, lad.*

Now Brian is embarrassed by how the files fall about when

the drawers are opened. He tries to open them gently around Jackson but this too causes the heat to rise under his starched collar. With Stephenson retiring the year before, it's just him who has to answer to this woman with her heavy eyelids that barely flicker as she walks about in her skirt and stockings with bobbles around the ankles.

'My office?' she had asked the first morning she'd come, three days ago. Brian cleared the storage room that he and Stephenson had almost bought a table tennis set for (to play during lunchtime breaks, as the handbook allowed). It was a long, awkwardly shaped room with scuff marks where the door didn't open properly, but Jackson had just nodded and hung her female's cap on the hook, along with the navy coat she'd brought and a plastic bag holding a thermos and a photo of a bulldog she placed on the desk. Since then Brian has been waiting for a proper conversation. He assumed she wanted to settle in before they discussed how he was coping with the case, maybe even how he'd ended up in the police force, but it seemed not. She only shuttled from room to room making phone calls and using that thermos to brew her own coffee.

After double-checking that Gupta – he resists his instinct to ask his first name – doesn't want a drink, Brian settles down to write up his last few pages of notes to index cards. People have spoken too quickly and, as Brian is reluctant to ask them to slow down, his handwriting has turned to a series of unruly loops. The interview with Elsie is particularly hard to fathom – her waving her arthritic hands towards the street as she gabbled away about a broken tripwire – and Brian now feels the first tickle of sweat on his upper lip where hair should grow but doesn't. *Maybe I'll be taken off the case*, he thinks as he flicks through the warbled notes. He wouldn't blame Jackson, although the thought comes with another hot sting to know he'd have let everyone down. Let Anna down.

This past week, in the moments between work, he's wondered what happened between them. Growing up on the same street, they'd exchanged Valentine's cards as kids. Had got pretend-married in her back garden when they were just five or six, Anna wrapping a clover around her finger before they celebrated by throwing raspberries at each other, pink streaks down their clothing. People thought it natural they might end up dating later on. Two nice-looking youngsters, Elsie liked to say, nudging him in his school uniform. And he did once think they might be right.

But it never quite happened between them. Probably he just didn't make enough effort and she the same. The one time he did ask her over for dinner – a spontaneous idea after he'd finished sitting his final school exams – 'Wouldn't it be nice to see her?' his mum said, 'She's not been around much these days' – Ruth answered the door and told him Anna was busy with her sewing. A few days later he got a card through the letterbox. It was an old Valentine he'd sent her with a Post-it note attached: *Sorry I missed your dinner. Please let's never divorce! Anna x.* Smiling at the carefully preserved felt design on the front, he tucked it away in one of his favourite *Beanos* where it must still be, covered in dust beneath his bed.

It's warming up outside by the time Jackson arrives. A flask of coffee releases a strong smell as she walks into the room. Mullins follows, having got a lift from their home station of Eddlesborough, and grunts at Brian. They're the same rank but Mullins has experience in missing person cases and talks like he's been on the job for decades. The sort of man who never says please or thank you but – as Brian has noticed these past days – listens carefully and has a special cloth to clean his police badge.

'A word please, McPherson,' Jackson says.

Brian follows into her office. He realises he should have made it nicer. Put a spider plant on the window ledge or something. Do policewomen like that sort of thing? He's not met any before now, though they can't differ *that* much from the regular sort.

'I've been reviewing the case here.' Jackson doesn't meet his eye as she sits down, her solid fingers already working through piles of paperwork.

'I can do better,' Brian says and suddenly feels sick. The early mornings have got to him. Too much instant coffee, the neighbours constantly asking if he's any closer to catching the Fox.

Jackson's eyes flicker upwards, then return to the paper. 'No,' she says matter-of-factly. 'What I mean is: I want you to lead this investigation.'

'Sorry?'

'You've lived in this village all of your life. You know these people, the woods.'

'Oh, yes I—'

She raises a stiff hand. 'And although you've much to improve on – and frankly, this is rather unusual to admit …'

Brian feels a smile stretch across his lips.

'You may well be our best chance in this case.'

Barely two minutes later Brian is surprised to find himself briefing Gupta who joins him in the main interview room, along with Mullins hunched in a chair and Jackson listening by the door, arms folded over the robust material of her jacket.

'Anna went missing on the night of the eighteenth between the hours of 8.00 p.m. and 9.00 a.m. the next day,' he starts, then pauses for Gupta to write notes. 'There were signs of a struggle, including the broken glass of a photograph although no damage to the back door which was left unlocked.'

'So Anna could have let the intruder in voluntarily?' Jackson prompts.

'Yes.' He smiles again, despite himself. 'We have reason to believe it might be someone she knew.'

Talking like this makes Brian feel funny. He thinks of Stephenson, long gone to his retirement village, then Anna too, urging him to hurry with those pale green eyes.

Brian walks to the Ordnance Survey map pinned to the corkboard and the others follow. Mullins, grumpy at first, listens and asks questions, which reassures Brian how much he knows about the case.

'The lace glove was found in the scrubland behind Anna's house, uncovered by Rick Cranner's dog which was rooting in the wet earth.' They all crowd round. 'Woods surround the village to the south and east for just short of two miles. There's no through road, meaning the area is cut off and doesn't attract many visitors, even though it's a National Trust protected site. The only potential tourist place is the caravan park the most southerly side which is connected to an A road leading east.'

'What a shithole that was,' Mullins grunts, shifting his weight.

'We've searched the caravan park already,' Brian tells Gupta. 'Right now there are only two families staying and an elderly couple from Hull booked in next week. The notes are in the index cards. Apart from that, the other important features are the river and the hill that allows a view of the church and top of the high street. This might provide a vantage point from which the Fox … Sorry, from which the *intruder* watches for lights to be turned on or off, people going to bed, spending time in their sheds, etcetera.'

Mullins dips out the room and comes back a minute later and says he's arranged some CCTV cameras for later that day. 'Dunno how many. Depends on the budget.' Brian nods along and makes a mental note to find out how they work. He then goes on to outline a plan that includes him patrolling the woods that evening and Gupta around the high street. 'The intruder could be hiding in all manner of places, so we need to be careful.'

'I understand,' Gupta tells him but glances towards the window where shapes are moving behind the glass.

'Another aspect to consider,' Jackson begins, 'is the suspect's motives for taking Anna and not someone else. It's not as if her home has been the only one broken into.'

Brian nods. 'So far I've interviewed everyone who has reported a break-in, although I'll be speaking to the Robinsons again.' He thinks of Elizabeth in a dizzy whirl of red dressing gown and tears after he arrested Ralph on Saturday night.

'And who are the suspects so far?' Gupta asks.

It's the question Brian has been dreading. They've found no more evidence against Ralph. Someone pointed to Rick but for no solid reason, just that he was rude and didn't let them birdwatch on his caravan site. Which of his other neighbours was he supposed to point a finger at?

'Jim Thompson is an unusual character,' Jackson says. 'And now it looks like he's made some suicide attempt in his car?'

'I don't think he's involved,' Brian says, thinking of how frail Jim had seemed after they saw the rope.

'And you know that for sure?'

'Well ...'

'Don't let your relationships with these villagers blind you,' Jackson says as she pulls her jacket straight. 'Everyone is a suspect at this stage.'

After they're finished, Brian rewards himself with a coffee, pleased to offer the others one too. Gupta at last accepts and he shows them where he keeps the mugs and digestives too for a sugar boost, even though it's obvious in the kitchenette.

'We've got plenty of work to get through,' says Jackson as she sips from the cup of her own thermos. It's hard to know whether she was pleased with the brief or not. Brian wants to ask but then has another thought.

'We could hold a television appeal?' he says eagerly. 'I know someone down at—'

'No.' The hand comes up again. Jackson sighs and it's as if his work has already been forgotten. 'This isn't about fancy press conferences or the things you see on TV. Nine times out of ten, cases like this are about community policing – the answers lie in what villagers already know, even if they themselves don't yet realise it.'

Brian later crosses the high street and walks towards home. He instinctively steps from the pavement into the road as he passes Ralph and Cynthia's bungalow.

Ralph hadn't resisted arrest. In fact, his shirtsleeves were already unbuttoned and in neat rolls by the time Brian parked. Having waited outside – Elizabeth at the doorstep holding a kitchen knife across her nightgown – Ralph seemed almost relieved when Brian slipped the handcuffs over his wrists.

It was only when they were both sitting in the main inter-view room that Brian properly saw the scar for the first time, a white line running down one side of his face like a crater on the moon. No incident was ever reported to the Hampshire police, Mullins had discovered after some phone calls. Ralph had grown up in an affluent village near Romsey where his father worked as the local headmaster. The man was once accused of bullying by a parent but he went on to work at the grammar school for another eight years. 'Milk every day,' Ralph said pointedly when Brian asked about his childhood. 'Or a boy never grows strong enough to defend himself.'

This was one of the few things Ralph volunteered. For the most part he sat silently with his legs crossed at the knee and ankle, so his corduroy trousers formed a knot of brown. The silence wasn't sullen, exactly – more the type studied over time. Every now and then he adjusted his elbow on the table and a sour odour drifted outwards, but perhaps the smell was in Brian's mind. For years this man had been nothing more than a shadow at the kitchen window, the guy whose door his friend Roger once pelted with eggs at Halloween when they were fourteen, lights flickering off inside with the final drip-ping yolk.

'Anna was a special girl,' he said abruptly after over an hour of ignoring Brian's questions. His voice was unnervingly clear. 'She waved at me from her bedroom window every night till her mother put a stop to it. When Ruth later became ill and almost bedridden, I thought she might start waving again but she never did.'

Brian had felt uneasy about escorting him back to the cell afterwards. Before Ralph it had barely been used apart from the odd drunken night by Rick Cranner from the caravan park.

Even though he'd given Ralph blankets and plenty of bread and chicken soup, it wasn't the bed or the food that worried him. It was the thick, hot air that made the walls drip and the sour smell take hold.

After Jackson said they didn't have enough evidence to hold him any longer, Ralph had trouble stabilising his legs from lack of walking. Brian ended up reluctantly accompanying him home. They crossed the road together and it was then Ralph began to speak again in that pointed way of his.

'That Ruth was a difficult sort, was she not?' He said it as a statement so Brian gave no reply, stopping to let a car pass. Ralph went ahead and continued to speak, still audible over the passing engine. 'But then family relations can be so terribly strained, no matter how much love is involved.'

At the bungalow, Brian felt relieved when Ralph slipped straight upstairs. He went to turn back for the station before noticing the imprints in the dark blue carpet of the hallway.

'I'm sorry we can't return the milk bottles,' he mumbled as Cynthia gave him a stony glare. At least her hair had returned to normal, curls in place. 'Jackson didn't let me.' It was a weak statement he knew and he began to walk down the driveway.

'Women can be as cruel as men sometimes,' Cynthia said. She jerked her head down the road. Brian asked if she was referring to anyone in particular but she just closed the door.

His parents are waiting in the living room when Brian gets home.

'Your brother's upstairs with his cassettes,' his mum says as she taps her cheek for him to kiss. 'You don't look too hot.'

'I've been really busy ...'

'You've got to look after yourself, sweetie.' The sofa squeaks as she jumps up past him. Her high-tops look like something a teenager might wear except her laces are tied in a floppy bow.

'I know, enough veg and—'

'You need energy for your brother.' She goes through into the kitchen and can be seen in square patches of white jeans and floral apron through the serving hatch. 'You know he'd love to see a few rugby matches this summer.'

'Right.'

After shaking hands with his dad who instantly reabsorbs himself in the newspaper crossword, Brian heads upstairs past the chair lift and collection of family photographs that line the wall in matching frames. The house is still owned by his parents who last year moved into a retirement complex but let him and his brother carry on living there on the condition they *look after each other.* Of course it's Brian who does the looking after, what with the cooking and the hoists and piling wet bed sheets into the washing machine.

He never realised how much his mum did before they moved out; whenever people asked after Beattie she'd say it was nothing really, *he's such a strong boy. Captain of the rugby team three seasons in a row.* By then his final match had been over more than a decade ago but friends would just nod and change the subject before the photograph album was whisked out from under the coffee table. It was only when his mum strained her arm on the hoist one time that she suddenly came home with brochures for Goldenacre Village. *A twelve-hole golf course and this lovely flat with a balcony.* Brian had been stunned – wasn't he supposed to be the one moving out of home? But his mum reassured him it wasn't a big deal, they could visit whenever they liked. *Every weekend if need be.*

On helping his parents move, however, it became clear that

Beattie's wheelchair would barely fit in the spare room, already filled with a set of golf clubs. Several months later they still hadn't fitted a railing beside the bath. And so it was just the two of them in their childhood home, routines continuing but without their mum to tell them not to tie up the phone line, or their dad cooped up in his study.

Some good came from it, he supposes. His mum hired Jeanette who every day plods into the house in her white smock, once her nurse's uniform, now relegated to that of a carer since she turned sixty and could no longer handle the nightshifts. Plus Brian has moved into his parents' room with its double bed and a huge wardrobe with mirrors he keeps meaning to remove (too much staring at his hairless upper lip). There were arguments at the time – his mum pointed out that she still kept a few clothes in the cupboard at the top. What if they wanted to move back? But Brian maintained he needed the main bedroom for himself, even though a part of him knew this was untrue. At twenty-seven he has no wife or children of his own. The only other person ever in the bed is his brother who he lets stay on each of their birthdays, Beattie letting out a low, silly giggle as he grasps too much of the duvet.

He pokes his head into Beattie's room. Two years older, his brother has become bulky, his once handsome jawline lost and his hair turned soft and shaggy. Sitting wedged in his wheel-chair, he smiles faintly with eyes closed. The cassette playing is Stephen King's *Carrie* which has reached the section where the lightbulb smashes – the first step in the unleashing of the girl's telekinetic powers and thirst for violence. The tape crackles where it has worn out over the years.

'All right, Beatts?'

His brother gives a jerk of head.

'One of your fairy tales again?'

On the shelf behind is the row of trophies and ribbons stuck with Blu-Tack to the pinewood. Three bronze figurines in the shape of a man with a rugby ball are in the middle: the dates show 1970, 1971, 1972. That's where they stop. Beattie never looks at them and when their mum wipes a cloth around each dust-covered figure, he starts to rewind his tape over and over.

Downstairs his mother has laid out a lunch of tuna fish sandwiches and a large bowl of Smiths square crisps.

Brian carries Beattie, who lets out rupturing giggles, over his shoulder. Although the familiar ache in his back surges up again, it's easier than using the hoist and stair lift. His dad pretends not to hear as his mum huffs. 'You need to take him shopping too,' she says, continuing the thoughts in her head. 'His pyjamas have seen better days. Haven't they, Ted?'

The final letter inserted into its box, Ted's work is done. He puts the fountain pen back in his shirt pocket and waits for his plate of sandwiches. Beside him Beattie lets a tongue slither over his lips, eyes glistening at the crisps.

'I'm not sure he should eat so many of those,' Brian says, rubbing his lower back as his mum throws a few on Beattie's plate.

'They're his favourite,' she says and proceeds to cut his sandwiches into triangles.

They all chew their food and talk inevitably turns to the case. Their parents visit every Tuesday so were here just after Brian received the initial call about Anna being missing. Brian tells them now about being made case lead and they congratulate him before remembering themselves.

'I always thought that family an unlucky one,' his mum says sadly. 'Ever since Ruth's second daughter died of cot death.'

'Oh yes, I'd forgotten that.' Brian tries to picture the funeral, the flowers too big for the coffin.

'It was a long time ago now. You must have been seven or eight, I suppose. Some families suffer such tragedies,' she says, ignoring Beattie who's crumbling a sandwich between his fingers. 'We're lucky to have never had anything like that.'

Anxious to get back to work, Brian leaves his parents with Beattie and heads for the Robinsons. It takes several minutes for Elizabeth to answer and even then it's through a latched door. 'We don't want strangers in the house,' she says.

Brian feels bruised to realise she means him. 'I only need a few minutes of your time.'

After a moment's pause she works several bolts and allows him into the hallway, which is pungent with the smell of nappies and talcum powder. Toys clutter an Oriental rug that gives way to wooden floors of the kitchen, equally busy with dropped tissues and a guitar leant against the cooker.

It's a fairly new house – only built in the late seventies – but it's already ageing and Brian suspects Pete isn't one for DIY. He's what people might call a 'new-age man' with an unkempt beard and ankle bracelets that rattle as he comes down the stairs with the baby sleeping in his arms.

'Have you seen this woman around the village?' asks Brian after unfolding some paper on an uncluttered patch of the kitchen table.

Elizabeth pulls back her auburn hair to inspect the drawing. It's one that Brian had an artist put together, based on Jim's description. It was Jackson's idea to depict the woman and Brian still wonders what use it'll be. Held the evening before, the session was time-consuming with Jim bad-tempered in his neck brace, which he scratched at with a borrowed pencil.

No matter how the artist's hand hovered on the page, meticulously forming strokes of pencil, he scowled. So in the end the drawing was simple with a chain-strapped bag at one side and a gap where the nose should be.

'It's difficult to tell. Pete?'

He lays the baby in its pram that is parked against the overflowing bookcase. 'This woman was seen in Anna's house the evening she went missing.' She repeats Brian's words verbatim so he just stands by the door into the patio. Cracked terracotta pots sit on the slabs, some with green stuff crawling out. Brian lets himself think about Deloris who he's just seen in the street, a halter-neck dress tight around her neck, eyes so bright he stepped back. 'I'll find you later,' she'd said, swinging a plastic bag over one shoulder. Although he wasn't sure what she meant by the offer, he wouldn't complain to have some company, especially if that company was Deloris.

'Shouldn't you still be holding Ralph?' Pete now asks.

Brian pretends to update his notebook, not wanting to explain it all over again.

'I know I said we understood, but really, who else could this Fox be?'

The baby lets out a squawk and Brian is grateful to the tiny foot kicking above the velvet trim of the pram. Seeing her husband occupied, Elizabeth reluctantly goes over. 'Where's her rattle? She had it last night.'

Brian taps the piece of paper. 'This woman could be the missing link to Anna's disappearance,' he says, trying to sound authoritative. 'I'd like you to take a look.'

Pete scratches his unwashed beard. 'I can't be one 100 per cent but –' he squints – 'I have seen a woman with a bag like that go into number fourteen.'

'Really? Fourteen of this street?'

'That's it. Stan's house. A couple of times, in fact, though only late at night.'

Stan's house is the next one along on Yardley Mews. As Brian walks up the pathway, he notes the bench that sits beside the front door. Carved from ash, perhaps? Stan never likes to talk about his woodwork, just smiles vaguely if you try to compliment any of his furniture or the birdhouse he made for the school wildlife area with its roof made of shingles imported from America.

Before ringing the bell, he takes out his notebook. He doesn't want to jump to conclusions about Stan, but still, why hasn't he come forward with this information? He and Anna had spent time together, with her befriending his son at church, so surely he's upset about her disappearance?

He presses the bell. Behind the dappled glass, the hallway remains empty.

The path along the side of the house is newly laid and paving slabs tilt as Brian walks to see into the garden. No one is there. Across the neat lawn stand several more birdhouses at different heights, plus a set of saws and hammers left deserted on the grass.

The warmth of the day gradually collects and, once evening time comes, breathes through the birches, unsettling the moss that skims the edges of roots and fallen trunks, a blanket of dark green that stretches out indefinitely.

'Are you sure about this?' he calls to Deloris who's walking ahead in her purple anorak.

'We can't all cower at home,' she says gesturing towards the village. 'Even if we're shit scared.'

Brian knows that it's really his job to do the searching. That he's meant to be protecting the villagers, not letting them come out with him. Still, he knows that Deloris won't go home even if he asks. As she traipses onwards her plimsolls glow amongst the shadows of the trees. Only occasionally does she skitter at a snap of bracken somewhere in the distance or the shadow of a bird's wings cast across the path. He steadies his own heart with a series of long breaths and tells himself the woods are the same they've always been, the place of camping trips with the Scouts, where his brother once climbed the huge oak all the way to the top. But he knows this isn't the case.

'Here?' Deloris asks a few minutes later.

They're almost at the brow of the hill. It's no longer just a hill, he remembers. It's a lookout. The rain-soaked hedges have overgrown but you can still see the church with its marble graves reduced to patches of grey, roofs just beyond – the vicarage, then Sandra and Michael's thatched cottage before the high street curves from sight. Further west, plumes of bonfire smoke coil into the humid air.

Deloris's idea of a hideout seems bizarre. But then the whole situation isn't making sense in his head. Jackson did approve of his plan to spend the evening in the woods, didn't she? Or had he got that wrong? A potentially violent criminal on the loose and here they were gathering sticks.

It takes a while for them to assemble the hideout, needing to go further down the slope to find enough material to make a thick wall. Too many branches are waterlogged, the fingers of leaves sagging inward, and it's difficult to tell how conspicuous the hideout is to someone else. He never learnt this in his police training which seems to have equipped him so badly for the evening ahead.

They eventually settle in the narrow space between the wood floor and the branches. Their bodies are side by side with a toggle of Deloris's anorak touching Brian's thigh. Every time she raises her head, her hair catches in the dried leaves and strands are pulled in all directions. The scent of hair spray comes in faint wafts, sweet, like coconuts. If he could relax just a little he might enjoy having her so close but his mind feels stuck in place, thoughts not ticking over like they should.

An hour later his radio blares to life with a furious crackle. It's Mullins, asking where he is. Self-conscious, Brian edges away from Deloris though there are just a few inches between him and the log, his truncheon in the way. After giving his update, he tries to refocus on the path in front, and on the brambles he can see beyond with the inside of a crisp packet shining silver. 'Do you think Anna still might be OK?' she asks.

Brian doesn't let himself linger on the thought. 'We're working on that assumption. I mean, the rope is almost a positive sign.'

'Really?' She pulls a face.

Brian nods. 'Whoever this is might be trying to get our attention.'

'So it is some sort of sick game, then?'

Patches of light play on her face so that, just as one part is known, another is lost. Brian makes himself focus on the path again.

'I'm compiling a list of likely attributes: nimble, strong. Not necessarily sexually motivated.'

Deloris gives an angry sigh. 'I keep trying to hate him,' she says, scrabbling along her belly out of the hideout. 'But there's so little to latch on to. If only we knew one definite thing.'

Another half hour goes past without anyone walking by. Brian looks down at his calculator watch more and more. 'My old boyfriend had one of those,' Deloris says, touching his arm. He shouldn't have let her come, Brian thinks again. It isn't right to be next to her and feeling what he knows he shouldn't.

She hasn't mentioned Harvey all evening. Brian reminds himself of what everyone always says: that the two of them make a handsome couple. It's true. Whenever they go to a village event, mostly dragged along by Sandra, they walk in with their arms elegantly linked and smile at people as they stand by the drinks table, clinking glasses of fizz with the Morgans and other local business people. It's only later that Harvey laughs with the other men, their loosened ties draped over shoulders, as she stands alone. At the May Ball, Brian had ended up dancing with Mr Whitley's granddaughter – a large, giggling girl who bounced up and down to a Cliff Richard song – but couldn't help notice the glazed look on Deloris's face as she swayed in the crowd. After the song finished he excused himself and crossed the dance floor to her. Asked if she wanted to request a song for the DJ. Only she mustn't have heard as she continued to sway beside the vibrating speaker, the end of her skirt sticking to its static so her ankles were outlined.

A few weeks later Brian had spoken to her in the pub. He was choosing Barbara Streisand on the jukebox and she threw her head back in laughter, red lips open wide. Rosy with drink, she'd poked him and his whole body rippled. Later that night he'd replayed that moment, wondering what it meant.

'Why did you become a policeman?' she asks him now. She drags her fingertips through the mud and inspects the half-moons of brown.

'To impress my dad,' he says, wanting to be honest, for this to mean something between the two of them. 'It was always my brother Beattie who was going to be the star. Now it's just good old Brian.'

She smiles mischievously, releasing a throaty laugh. Brian puts a finger to his lips but chuckles softly himself.

'Seriously. I almost didn't make it through the training,' he says. 'Apparently I need to do more press-ups or something. Boost my testosterone.'

Deloris lets her hand collapse in the dirt. 'Brute strength is overrated.'

As the light dims, Brian insists he's not scared even though he's realised he should've brought the night-vision goggles Gupta mentioned. It won't be fully dark for another couple of hours but already it's hard to pick out anything more than the path ahead. Shadows spread out beyond, seemingly impenetrable, until something moves, a flick of moss or wet snout catching the eye. As Deloris fidgets more and more, Brian tries to keep still though his belly and tops of thighs are growing cold. Perhaps Deloris will go soon, he thinks.

At some point Brian shudders from a daze as he hears a snap of bracken somewhere behind. He hopes it might belong to a muntjac, but it comes again: *crunch crunch.* The steps are too slow and clumsy. Deloris hooks her elbows to the ground and scrabbles forwards a few inches. Brian isn't sure what to do. He's meant to alert the others by radio but suddenly his throat is stiff.

'Hang on,' he squeaks and catches her shoulder.

They both wait, paralysed. It goes quiet again and the only sound is their breathing.

'Where are you?' a man's voice says from close by. It might be familiar but Brian can't place it. The whole woods seem to be shaking as the footsteps crunch and thrash, getting louder to his right.

Deloris's lower lip drops, her face still.

'Please come home,' the man says in a slurred voice.

It's Harvey, Brian realises, feeling himself soften. He's about to crawl out when Deloris turns to him. Her breath is hot on his face. 'He can't see us together.'

So Brian stays where he is and his racing heart gradually steadies. He enjoys the warm flood through his legs as he bends his toes to the ground, his thighs touching Deloris's as they wait for Harvey to pass. His footsteps are louder still but clumsy too like he's not bothering to stay on the path. Brian pictures the lumbering figure – catchweed sticking to his suit trousers, his suede loafers slipping on the uneven banks.

Eventually Harvey's legs come into view ahead, just beyond the path. As he pauses, it seems like he might have seen them. What is the man doing? Brian's fingers reach for the pepper spray hooked to his belt but instead find Deloris's hand, which curls around his palm.

Harvey kicks at a tuft of moss several times, cursing himself. 'Anna!' he calls half-heartedly. 'Where are you?'

Deloris pulls back her hand.

He continues to stumble around in no obvious direction. A tree cracks from the force of a kick and Brian freezes.

'I know you're out there,' he moans. 'Christ, I only want to talk to you.'

Eventually Harvey stumbles off again. The two of them lie still for a while longer until the calls of birds fill the sky.

'Him and Anna?' Deloris asks, her shoulders slumping.

Brian isn't sure what to say except to suggest he walks her home.

11

They pick their way back along the path. As Brian shines his torch for them both to see, he tries to avoid damaging their earlier footprints, as if the first part of the evening might be left intact. But it's no use. Having forgotten their hideout, Deloris rushes to get home.

'He was with Anna?' she says to herself breathlessly. 'When?'

Brian finds it hard to picture the two of them together. Before Deloris, Harvey had dated heavily made-up women who carried no money in their purses and dropped cigarette ends on the street. He barely seemed to notice Anna around the village, changing the subject if her name came up in conversation. Brian recalls Harvey's eighteenth birthday party and someone asking if she was invited. A screwed-up face, lager can squeezed until froth overflowed. Maybe they had more between them than people knew.

'I can't believe anything happened recently,' Deloris goes on. 'Anna and me were getting to be friends. She wasn't the type to lie, was she?'

That might've been the problem, Brian thinks. What if she wanted to tell Deloris about their past and he blew up in a temper? Scared her off into the woods?

In front of them the torchlight is stark on the bumps, the potholes. Everything else is utterly dark across the miles of thickets and undergrowth where anything might have happened.

At Deloris's house a single light is on upstairs. She hesitates by the front door.

'Harvey has other sides to him,' she says without looking Brian in the eye. Her voice is muffled so he edges closer. Feels her breath again. 'Last night he was in such a foul mood with me.' Her next words come out so quiet he's not sure he hears them right. 'I'm allowed to do what I want, though.'

'Deloris …' Brian reaches for her but she's turning away, shoving her hands inside her anorak pockets. He wants to ask her to stay with him – just on the sofa or wherever she likes – but she brings out a key and disappears into the house.

The street is deserted as Brian wanders home, feeling oddly bereft. His brother will no doubt be asleep and he'll have to watch television alone. That is, if any programmes are still on. He often thinks the BBC's image of the girl playing noughts and crosses with the clown is the loneliest ever; he doesn't even have proper arms to join her in the game. Passing by the new developments, Brian groans when the streetlight next to number eight flickers and turns off. Gloom. He should be used to it by now. Arms out, waiting for the pavement, he feels like a child in a stupid game. Pretending to be blind – isn't that what he used to do? He stumbles forward, no longer caring what happens to him, but finds his way clear for several yards.

It's only when he's at his driveway that his boot makes contact. There's a racket of breaking plastic before something skitters and lands beside the drain. He bends down to pick it up: part of a CCTV camera – the one that was installed near the woods. With a sobering shiver, he realises what must have happened. It's been taken down and deliberately smashed to pieces.

'Stay inside, Beatts.'

It's the next morning and Brian has hardly slept. Having made some toast for his brother, he hurries for the door. All night he's been turning things over in his mind and now braces himself to confront Harvey. Maybe he'll take him down the station, past the neighbours who'll come to windows to see what's happening. Brian has never been an aggressive police-man but someone in the village is growing violent.

Harvey is about to get into his car when Brian runs on to the driveway.

'I'm late for work,' he says, a tie carelessly knotted around his collar. 'We'll talk later, OK, Brian?'

'What were you doing in the woods last night?'

The words come out in a rush and it takes Harvey a second to understand. He then glares at the houses around him, rub-bing the stubble on his cheeks. 'Dolly isn't the only one who can look for Anna,' he says, alcohol fumes souring his breath.

'So you were—'

'I'm late, all right, mate?' Hands pat down his pockets. 'Another time.'

Brian's about to ask him to the station when the door behind opens. Dressed in a long T-shirt, Deloris stands with bare legs and blushes to see Brian. He nods, waits for her to come out before realising she isn't going to. Instead, Harvey walks over.

'Why were you back so late last night?' she asks him. He pulls her in for a kiss and she pushes him away. Brian feels for his truncheon.

'Seriously, Harvey. I got home well after dark and you weren't there.'

'I was doing some thinking, that's all,' he says testily, rubbing his shoulder. Then: 'What's up with the two of you this morning?'

They exchange a glance but Harvey is already getting in his car.

Ten seconds later gravel spits upwards and he speeds away, Brian cursing himself for getting distracted.

Mullins has trouble recovering the CCTV tape. Grey crackles across the screen while they crowd around the small monitor.

'Whoever damaged it must've seen us install the camera. It was hidden in a hedgerow.'

After several minutes more crackling, an image collects: the street with the long shadows of early evening. Mr Watkins parks his Volvo and hurries inside. A bird pecks at something then becomes a blur of movement. Everything is still again until a woman walks along, handbag gripped under her arm, and looks up at the lens. Mullins leans forward to see if it's the mystery woman, but it's just Sandra who nervously purses her lips.

With Gupta on a break, Brian paces the streets for a while. He can't stand to think of them empty of a uniform, even if he's only one man, unable to be everywhere at once. The late-morning sun casts a glare across the street, bleaching brickwork so everything looks white. But as Brian walks, his eyes slowly pick up details. Patches of condensation dampen glass where owners have resisted opening windows, despite their wooden frames softening with rot. Down Yardley Mews, no bent figures stretch gloved hands to prune flower beds. Instead, moss has claimed the grass in its spongy clumps that creep on to pavements. The only person out is Howard Mills who holds his interview recorder up and waves it as Brian passes. Related to some newspaper tycoon, Howard was pegged to be 'a rising star' after scoring an article with Sid Vicious at just nineteen but hasn't had the same success since and these days seems increasingly desperate for a story. 'McPherson,' he calls after him. 'I hear the Fox is biding his time for the next victim. Any new leads?'

At midday Brian goes to speak to Stan, who he finds applying varnish to an upturned chair in his garden. While Brian recounts details of the mystery woman, Stan scrapes yellow smears from his hands at the kitchen sink.

'I have no idea what woman you're referring to,' he says. 'I think the Robinsons must be mistaken.'

Brian pushes the drawing along the kitchen top, though Stan gives it only a brief glance before turning to put the kettle on.

The chug of the steam feels like it's inside Brian's skull. He rubs at his broad forehead, trying to caress away the ache.

'The night she went missing, I took the train to London for the London Symphony Orchestra's charity concert.' Stan's voice is stiff. Despite the painting, he is still in his supermarket uniform with his name badge clipped above where his heart is. 'As I said in my original statement.'

'Of course, but I'm talking about this woman more generally.' Brian taps the vague sketch of her face. There are fold lines where she's been in his pocket, the paper already greasy around the edges.

The kettle clicks and steam shoots out. Stan doesn't take mugs from the cupboard though. He says he must remove washing from the line and slips out the back door into the garden.

Brian keeps rubbing his head as he glances around. The kitchen has a carved spice rack. A single plate by the sink with crumbs and the rind of a cheese. A pile of post sits on the counter – the letter on top is from the local primary school. Brian skims past the formalities to the second sentence:

> *We are concerned that Elliot is missing out on vital schoolwork. His abrupt departure means Mrs Barnett had little time to prepare work in advance.*

Stan comes back in. A drop of water is caught in his eyebrow though the rest of his face is smooth, cleanly shaved. He goes to hang a pair of cargo shorts on the stool in the utility room. As he's gone, Brian calls from the kitchen counter.

'When are Judy and Elliot coming back?'

There's a pause while he waits to get closer to Brian, in case the words are lost in the space between them. 'Frankly, I'm not sure.'

'She is coming home soon, though?'

Stan looks taken aback and reaches a hand to his pale throat. 'Yes. Of course she is.'

After regaining himself, he walks through into the sitting room and Brian follows. 'Apologies for not being a good host.' He lets himself fall into one of the armchairs, then stares at the table as if a tray of tea might materialise. 'It's just a matter of time. Some space can do wonders for a family.'

Not sure what to say, Brian glances around. A large blue painting hangs over the fireplace at an odd angle, unlike everything else in the room, which seems so precise. The throw over the sofa is folded neatly in two. No mug-rings pattern the coffee table.

'I'm not sure what's happening between Judy and you,' Brian says. 'But it's important I find out who this woman is. I'll be discreet with everything else. Any affairs—'

'I beg your pardon?'

'Any affairs,' repeats Brian, feeling himself colour, 'or other private matters will be kept confidential by the police.'

'I wish I could tell you more,' says Stan, abruptly rising to a stand. 'I really do.'

Brian sits at the computer for the rest of the afternoon. The curser blinks impatiently. His thighs stick to the plastic seat as he thinks of what to type. With each rattle of key – his fore-finger then hovering about to find the next – it's as if the lives of the villagers are indelibly assigned to this vast machine.

Out in reception he can hear Trish talk on the phone. Since the first break-in the station has received more and more phone calls: people reporting information and Brian logging each one – an unknown car parked on the high street, a smear of soil on someone's hallway rug. Just yesterday a woman reported a neighbour strolling up his driveway past midnight. 'Who knows where he'd been. In fourteen years living next door, I've never known him to be out so late. And when I asked him the next day? He said none of my business. But it's *everyone's* business now, isn't it?'

The room becomes uncomfortably warm. Slumped at the other desk with more files, Mullins releases a hacking cough, which sends his clammy back beating against the chair. Brian looks through their copy of the local electoral register to compile information on villagers' backgrounds. It seems pointless. Just names, addresses, dates of birth ...

Ruth Blake has been taken from this year's edition, just Anna left as the sole occupant of 1, Glebe Crescent. He thinks of Anna still clipping the rose bushes after Ruth died, wearing her mother's gloves that she patiently adjusted, a rip down one finger.

Jackson asks if he can work overtime later.

'By all means,' says Brian.

He tries to smile but his cheeks twitch instead. Since walking round the streets, he can't shake off the feeling that he's missing something important. A sharp noise now drills through the room.

'Brian? It's Deloris.'

Something leaps in him to hear her voice. They've not spoken on the phone before.

'Hello?' she says.

'Oh hi, Deloris.' He wants to take the phone under the desk, to go to the dark space away from Mullins who stands in the kitchenette.

'I can't help you tonight.' Her voice croaky like his mum's is when she's been crying.

'Oh?'

'I've got to talk to Harvey again. He says he never liked Anna. And apparently he went out drinking with Rick last night because I wasn't home. I don't know whether to believe him.'

Brian stays quiet. A part of him wants Harvey to be guilty of

186

it all, to be this awful guy they can both hate, but how could he wish that on Deloris?

'Anyway, I have to go.' She clears her throat. 'Talk soon.'

For a second longer Brian holds the phone, looking at the tiny holes of the receiver. Mullins makes a remark so he puts it down in its cradle. He then turns back to his computer, which lets out an angry beep as he presses the space bar. He rubs his head again. The bones seem sharper; it's as if he can feel his skull.

'Actually, I think I need some sleep first,' he tells Jackson in her office.

She looks up from her paperwork and nods. 'Of course.' As he's almost out the door she tells him, 'Good work today' or at least that's what he hears.

At home the landing is filled with the bangs and splashes of Jeanette giving Beattie a bath. His brother lets out a yelp as she asks him to lower his head. Her voice is soothing, like a wash of warm water, and Brian almost wishes he were the one in the bath with the sponge on his back, between his legs ...

'Hope it's no bother but I can only stay till four thirty today,' she tells Brian through the open door as he walks past. Inside Beattie is clawing a hand down the tiles above the bath like something from a horror film. He giggles and does it over again. Then rubs the fluff of his belly that protrudes from the water.

'All righty, then,' Brian hears himself say.

'I haven't got time to shave him, either.'

'I'll do that later.'

'And a new story?' squeaks Beattie. Amazing how high his voice can become. Makes you realise how artificial a voice can be. Everything an act, Brian thinks pointlessly as he holds on to the bannister.

'Not today, bro,' he says. 'I've got no time for shopping and Woolworths won't be open anyway.'

'It might, actually,' says Jeanette as she cloaks Beattie in a towel. 'That big shop in Aylesbury stays open till 5.30 p.m. Scandalous, if you ask me. Those poor workers.'

'No no no,' is all Brian says as he drifts away. Downstairs the sofa is feather soft under him, though insubstantial too. His leg keeps sliding off. Next door the hum of life vibrates through the walls. Brian can hear the wife's sing-song voice as she cooks tea, the two kids rattling around with their toys. How nice to have them just beyond that wall, their lives playing out next to one another's. It's only as he's slipping off to sleep that he remembers: there isn't a family next door. Mrs Watkins never had children. It's just her and a radio show.

After waking at just past five o'clock, Brian finds his brother already in his dressing gown. Their routines are often confused like this since Jeanette's schedules aren't necessarily any more regular than Brian's shift work, what with her own family and husband that seem to require an endless list of chores and trips to the grocers.

'You all right, matey?' he says to Beattie. His brother's towel dressing gown is grubby around the sleeves but still soft, Brian thinks as he gives him a playful punch on the shoulder, then stoops to kiss him on the forehead.

'Me? Fiiine,' he says though he doesn't smile. His fingers grip the wheels of his chair as if he's about to race off. Times like these Brian knows he's itching to get out, even if he can't push himself far.

If Brian had more time he might take him to Woolworths after all, or for a spin around the village green, sparrows swooping from the path as he pushes his brother along the tarmac to the far end of the nature reserve. But the thought of the Fox being out there rankles at him.

'I'll only be an hour or so,' he says at the door. 'Back in time to cook us spaghetti hoops with the sausages Jeanette left in the fridge. Then tomorrow afternoon we'll do whatever you like, I promise.'

Beattie lifts his hands from the wheels to reach for the cassette player.

Outside it's drizzling but Brian doesn't put on his rain mac. A clump of dandelions beside the wood's main pathway bursts into a white cloud as he idly kicks it. *Just keep your eyes and ears open,* he tells himself. *Even your presence is worthwhile.* His mind is soon on Beattie, though, on the trophies untouched on the shelf.

His brother was seventeen when it happened. After the school's rugby coach went on long-term sick leave, their dad offered to fill in. They were all surprised – he worked long hours at the bank, commuting over an hour to London every morning – but he'd decided he should spend more time with his eldest who was regularly in detention for distracting the class. Besides, he'd played for the team at Cambridge University. Why not get back into it?

Realising Beattie could run faster than all the other boys, he spent hours practising with him every week. He upgraded his position to fly half and although Beattie was unsure at first, he was soon won over when his dad bought him the most expensive boots in the sports shop. At home he was let off chores so the two could practise before a big game, leaving Brian to wash the car or take out the bins alone.

Ted will soon get bored, his mum said, but as the team worked its way up the county league their dad only got more involved. Soon late nights were spent poring over applications for sports scholarships at top universities and him helping Beattie stretch his quads, the two of them talking away while Brian – the other side of the wall – tried to sleep. Their mum gradually got excited too – Beattie was hardly much of an academic but this might be his shot. *Just be careful*, she said after watching a scrum one Saturday, wincing to see the adolescent shoulders locking together.

In the end it wasn't a scrum that injured him, or a tackle with the other guys. The final match of the season was the week before the summer term ended.

The morning of the game, Brian's English teacher let the kids take their books outside for class, eyes squinting at bright pages. *Othello* quickly forgotten, everyone began asking Brian about his brother. *Is he going to be famous?* They crowded round, even Mr Matthews who'd heard Beattie had been invited to try out for the junior national team the following week.

Yes, Brian said, suddenly thinking the car washes might've been worth it. *He eats four boiled eggs for breakfast, you know.* By geography, it was five eggs, then six.

An hour before the end of the school day, each class walked out to the school playing field to sit behind the chalk lines of the rugby pitch. Benches were left for some of the parents, mostly mums, who let sandals fall from their feet as they applied tanning oil. Brian's own mum called him over, and to avoid more high-pitched noises he agreed to sit with her. Meanwhile their dad – on his first day off since Christmas – was welcoming the visiting Wendover team who jogged on to the pitch.

Beattie missed a couple of kicks at the beginning. He was distracted, grinning at a girl he was dating. Minutes later the referee penalised him for passing forwards and their dad paced the chalk line until it wore away.

By the end of the first half, though, Beattie was keeping the game in the opposition's half. When he shouted to the wings they followed his instructions and even their dad listened when he suggested a dummy run. The rest of the team rallied around him. Lines of mud striped the grass, pink legs spread across the full stretch of pitch.

In the last six minutes they were awarded a decisive penalty. As his brother lined up the ball and his shirt shone white in the sunshine, Brian imagined he was watching someone at Twickenham. Except this was better. This was his brother.

When the ball soared over the post, the sky blurred as the bench bounced under Brian, a row of feet pounding the ground. Beattie was lost in a mass of boys with grass-stained backs, hands reaching to hug him. Meanwhile their dad patiently waited on the sideline, a smile on his face. Once Beattie was released, he beckoned him over and Beattie ran to him with his feet sliding in the churned ground. As he got closer, he lowered his head for a play-tackle and ploughed into their dad's chest.

The crack made Brian jolt. Suddenly the blurred scene came into focus, his mum's feet stilled. A gap expanded between the two men and with both their shoulders buckling Brian assumed it was his dad who was injured, the forty-five-year-old who never did much exercise. But Beattie's knees hit the ground; it was Beattie lying lifeless in the grass.

*

Partial brain damage, Brian told an aunt over the phone the next day, repeating what the doctor had said. *A severe spinal fracture too, which will impair his ability to walk.*

Neither parent said anything after he hung up and he wondered if he'd explained it wrong. They barely said anything for the rest of the week either. Or at least his dad didn't, poring over the crossword in the newspaper he'd later buy in pocket books from the newsagent.

When Beattie came home from hospital two months later, he lay in bed all day. Visitors came but people didn't know what to say to him. Even Brian and his mum found themselves hovering outside his bedroom door with a plate of sandwiches or a magazine, not sure what to expect inside. Sometimes Beattie's hands gripped the sheets, his tongue struggling to shout the curse words at walls now blank of rugby posters he'd ripped to pieces. Other times he'd pretend to sleep. One afternoon their mum – reasoning that he mustn't forget all his successes – put Beattie's various sports trophies on his shelf and even asked another boy to donate one he'd been awarded as captain. On waking from a morphine-induced nap, Beattie had flushed a deep scarlet to see the boy hand over the bronze figurine.

After a while people stopped visiting. Everyone except Anna. She hadn't spoken much to either of the boys for a while, so they were surprised when she began to turn up on the doorstep after school. Often she brought some sort of flower – a giant daisy or an iris – that she'd carefully position in a cup of water by his bed.

Beattie was having none of it, of course. He didn't want to hear the passages of the Bible she read to him, twisting towards the wall. But still she came. Brian remembers walking past his brother's bedroom one afternoon and seeing her perched on a chair, the Bible neatly spread across her knees. She wasn't reading from it though. In a voice too faint to decipher apart from the odd few words – *her mother's ointments, a bath too hot* – she spoke more than he'd heard from her all year.

It confused the family when, towards the end of September, she stopped turning up. By then they'd all got used to her visits, their mum collecting flower jugs from charity shops. But she didn't come again and never posted a note to explain. When Beattie asked where she was, pulling himself up to stare into the street, no one knew what to say.

Now the rain is falling more heavily. Brian walks along, noticing the bend and flex of his legs. How easy it is for him … Puddles are forming in the road and he resists hopping between them, not wanting to show off in case anyone is watching. *Is someone watching?* The thought makes him slow as he passes the hedgerows. Brian tells himself not to panic, but on nearing his driveway sees the front door is open. His brother sometimes collects the free newspaper from the driveway but never goes out more than a few yards because his legs struggle with the slope.

I must've closed the door when I left. Surely I did?

A chill penetrates. He staggers up the driveway and into the house.

Beattie is lying at the bottoms of the stairs, buckled on his stomach with knees at mismatched angles. From his shaking chest escape giggles – the noise he makes when he's upset but these giggles are higher, like tiny shards through the air.

'Everything OK?' Brian says. He pulls him on to his back and checks him over. On finding no wounds he wants to pull him in for a hug. But Beattie's eyes are fixed on something: the door to the living room. 'Are they still here?' Brian whispers. His brother claws at his own arms.

Waiting by the closed door with truncheon in hand, he attempts to slow his breathing, to plant his feet. He's been trained to arrest a burglar, someone who just wanted valuables, not this silent intruder intent on making them all suffer. Brian whips open the door and lurches through. The room's empty. Is it? He checks behind the sofa, swipes the truncheon through the folds of curtain fabric, then peers through the serving hatch into the kitchen. Nothing but the smell of damp soil.

By the time he's got upstairs his breathing has just about returned to normal. At least his training has served him well as he keeps his back to walls and moves stealthily along the landing. The final room to check is Beattie's. On first glance it seems normal – the duvet fallen on the floor, plate of toast on the side – but walking further in he sees the tape player is open and the cassette taken.

In hospital, Brian stares at his brother's curled sleeping body. He used to be so bulky, indestructible. Brian would compare the width of their thigh muscles as they sat on the school bus.

He now wonders if he did this to him. It's barely two days since they found the hanging rope – how had he left him alone? The question finds a quick answer, though: because he'd double-checked all the window fittings, had bought brand new deadbolts for the doors.

Yet the front door was open when he got there. His brother must have heard someone knock at the door, have looked through the spyhole like he taught him ...

'He has a twisted ankle, but mostly it's the shock. We've put him on some mild painkillers,' the doctor says.

'What happened to him?' Brian asks.

The man puts the clipboard back at the end of the railing. 'It doesn't look like much of a fall. Perhaps a couple of steps, up or down – I couldn't say for sure.'

'Was he running away from someone?' he asks, though mostly to himself.

The doctor is already past the curtain seeing the next patient and all Brian can do is rest his head on the edge of his brother's bed.

Later there's a flurry of voices as Elsie hobbles through the ward, followed by Jim who clutches his car keys.

'Beattie, my boy,' she says with startled eyes. She goes straight to the bed and gives the curled part of Beattie's hip a pat with her shaking hand. 'Whoever did this to you? It's a travesty, a travesty,' she repeats as Beattie's eyes flicker open.

'So you left your brother alone in the house?' Jim asks stiffly from beside the door, positioning himself to make a swift exist. He must've given Elsie a lift.

'Only for a short while,' Brian says. 'He can lower himself on to the toilet. And use his legs for short bursts of time. That's what his occupational therapist says, I have the reports.' The words are sickening with their familiarity, the exact lines he says to his mum. Brian always winces at how she doesn't let Beattie do anything for himself. How she squeezed thirty candles on to his last birthday cake and insisted she wipe his mouth afterwards. Looking at his brother now, he wonders if she was right all along.

'I'll get the boy some chocs,' Elsie says with a determined look. 'And teas for us all.'

'Righty then,' says Brian in a wave of nausea. He wants to take Beattie's hand but it's hidden under the sheets.

In the silence that follows, Brian expects Jim to reprimand him, but instead he lowers himself into the plastic chair by Brian. His neck brace has been removed and pink trails mark the skin, some speckled with faint scabs.

'Should we pray?' Brian asks. He doesn't go to church and isn't sure where the idea came from. Jim stares for a long moment, his eyes not focussing on anything, then says OK. Still slumped in the chair, he clasps his hands together, and they tremble but stay upright, the fingers knotted tightly together. So Brian does the same and whispers his own silent prayer – not to God, but to his brother for forgiveness.

'I shouldn't have left him with his tapes,' Brian says afterwards as if stating this might diffuse something between the two men. Elsie has been gone a while and only the beeps and shuffles of the hospital ward break up the quiet.

Jim raises fingers to his neck. 'The ones by Stephen King?' he says absently. 'I remember Elsie mentioning that. I wonder why he likes horror so much.'

Brian goes to pour his brother some water into a plastic cup from the machine. 'It's only been in the last couple of years, since we got one of those free cassettes that come with the Sunday paper. At school he never read fiction, I don't think. But now he'll spend hours listening and replaying the same bits.'

Jim smiles, finding truth in that. 'We make up horrors to help us cope with the real ones.'

'I guess so.'

'That's a Stephen King quote, I believe. Is that right?'

Brian shakes his head. He's not sure how much of the stories he ever properly listened to. And now the cassette is gone. Why?

196

After phoning his parents, Brian comes back to find his brother awake and sitting leaning against several cushions. Elsie is wrestling with the thick plastic that secures the bags of sweets though Beattie shows no interest. He directs a goofy smile at Brian but it's half-hearted and doesn't reach his eyes.

'Beattie, bro, I was so worried about you.'

His brother nods but says nothing.

'What happened?'

Beattie's smile stretches again but it's even more strained. He nods for something to do.

'Why did you let him in?' asks Elsie, jostling Brian with her elbow. 'The Fox must've forced his way in, I bet?'

Beattie looks away.

Conscious of minutes ticking past, Brian touches his brother's wrist. 'What were you even doing downstairs?'

'I-I can do things,' he says, suddenly angry.

Brian straightens up and sees Elsie shift away with her chocolates. 'I know you can. Please tell us what happened.'

They wait for him to speak but he's brooding. After a minute Beattie opens his mouth, his tongue twisting and rubbing on one side. His eyes focus somewhere beyond them all and slowly grow wet. Eventually he looks up, shakes his head and sighs from a place deep inside him. 'Nooou Bri. No.'

12

'It appears you don't know Anna as well as you think,' Jackson says the next morning. She is at her desk and has poured coffee from her thermos into not one but two cups. Brian gratefully takes the second. It's 7.00 a.m. and he hasn't had much sleep after a night at the hospital.

'I've known her most of my life,' he says, letting the steam dampen his lips. 'We went to primary school together.'

'Before she went to – St David's was it?'

'Yeah, that's some Christian school her mum decided she'd go to when she was eight. Apparently she needed extra discipline, although everyone always said she was so polite. Anyway, there wasn't a bus so Ruth drove her each morning.' As he says it an image appears in his mind: Ruth with her shawl draped across her robust shoulders at the wheel; Anna clutching the crucifix around her neck as she got into the back seat. It must've been when Brian got up early one morning – the Blakes left well before the rest of the families to make the long journey across the county.

'And what about Anna's father?'

'A nice, well-respected man,' Brian says. 'He moved away from the village a while ago.'

Jackson's heavy eyelids lift. 'Why was that?'

He shrugs, not having thought about it all in years. 'His family had a farm in Yorkshire and he went to help out and never came back.'

'So he and Ruth got divorced?'

'Oh no, nothing like that,' he says, shaking his head. 'His family needed an extra pair of hands.' Brian's memories of Robert Blake are foggy, but nevertheless he smiles to think of the man's own easy grin, how he chewed on something whenever he spoke, his jaw going round and round like a cow's. He thinks for a minute. 'I suppose it wasn't long after Anna's little sister Ilene died of cot death, though I'm not sure that had any bearing on it.'

There's a slam as Jackson releases a folder of papers on to the desk. 'Well, you need to do more digging.'

Brian puts down his coffee so he can wipe his eyes. He can't think what to do next.

'All her work sending cushions to churches in Kenya ...' She unfolds one of the newspapers piled on her desk and points to an article by Howard. 'Apparently she almost moved there before her mum became ill.'

'I didn't know about that.'

It occurs to Brian how he never really asked Anna about her charity work. In fact, they didn't speak about much that was really personal to her. In the last few months it'd been just the odd conversation about the miners' strikes or how his brother was getting on. One time she said she was thinking of getting a rescue dog, but he forgot to ask again.

'Spend some more time looking into her past, we need to know why she was targeted,' says Jackson as she drains the last of her coffee. 'There's more to this woman than you first thought.'

Brian drives the Panda out past Aylesbury to the village of Drayton. He has made some phone calls and although he couldn't get hold of Ms Hobbs, the former headmistress at St David's, he has an appointment with Miriam Foster who worked at their primary school. She sounded eager on the phone and insisted it was fine he come right away. Before long Brian finds himself enjoying the trip over in the car. He recalls Mrs Foster quite clearly from school; she was one of his favourite teachers, with soft white hair that tickled his cheek as she leant to look at his work. It comes with a jolt that Brian now realises he's entering the car park of a care home.

'I remember you,' Mrs Foster says as he walks into the living room. Various eyes clock him from behind spectacles, newspapers rustling as they're lowered to see the new arrival. 'Beattie McPherson,' she says with an outstretched hand.

'No, it's Brian,' he says apologetically, taking the hand with its pearl bracelet sliding down the thin wrist.

'Brian?' A small tooth appears over her lip as she thinks. 'Oh! One of my favourites. I remember the lovely pasta shell creations you used to make.'

She continues to grasp his hand so he stands in front of her, trying not to notice how her forehead is mottled pink. The room at least smells nice – like fresh tea made with honey. Spoons chink against china in the room beyond.

'You were always such a well-behaved boy. Almost too much so, if I'm honest,' she says as she gestures to the worn armchair opposite. 'What are you doing these days?'

'I'm a policeman,' he says sheepishly, gesturing to his cap he removed at reception.

Her mouth opens as if to laugh but she thinks better of it. 'Yes, well that does make sense.'

'That's why I'm here, in fact.' He pulls over the chair. 'I'm investigating an abduction.'

'A frightful business. A whole ten days gone, is it?'

'That's right.' The armchair is too low and he stares up at her, past the knees encased in thick nylon.

'Whatever can have happened to her?' Mrs Foster speaks in an unnecessary whisper, since most residents have got up to watch a repeated episode of *Dallas* in the far corner of the room. 'Oh no, don't tell me. The newspapers are full of stories of kidnapping, brutality, fighting in parliament …'

Brian explains how they are making steady progress, but as yet have no single theory. 'You taught Anna at aged eight, is that right?'

'If you say so. My memory isn't what it used to be, like an old pair of shoes gone around the park too many times.'

Brian tries to laugh but the noise comes out strained. 'Anna is blonde, from Heathcote. Her mother was very religious.'

'Ruth Blake, yes!' She slaps her knees. 'What a woman.'

'Oh?'

'The other teachers thought her overly strict, you know,' she says conspiratorially, edging closer to Brian. 'But she taught Anna to be decent and respectful. That's been lost in schooling these days. Children are treated as if they're the centre of a universe around which everything else rotates.'

'So you remember Anna, then?'

'One of the brightest students I ever taught.'

'Oh?' Having flipped open his notebook, Brian now hesitates to put pencil to paper. 'I'm not sure you're recalling the right student.'

'The Blakes? Yes, I believe I am. They had that trouble when Ruth lost the child.'

Brian stays a while longer. The conversation drifts to Mrs Foster's own family and he pulls it round again. 'Is there anything more you can remember about Anna?'

She looks across the room and her eyes settle on the tea trolley slowly making the rounds. 'It was all so long ago,' she says. 'How should I be of any real help?'

'It's hard to say but the past is often important.'

Mrs Foster reluctantly turns back to him, shifting in her seat. 'Anna did grow increasingly insular after her little sister passed on. At lunch she'd stand alone at the edge of the playground. I remember now because I once tried suggesting she join a game of Simon Says but she pretended a wasp stung her finger so she could go inside.'

A few minutes later, Brian thanks her for the time.

'Wouldn't you like to stay for tea?' she says as the trolley finally approaches. 'Thursday is Battenberg day.'

'I need to be getting back.'

As he's leaving she reaches for his hand again. 'You were always such a timid boy.' Her skin is like paper sliding against his and he gently pulls away. 'This could be your chance, couldn't it?'

Brian isn't entirely sure what she means so just fishes in his pocket for the notebook and heads for the car park.

*

On returning to the village he stands by the gate to Anna's front garden, the dark leaves of the rose bush spilling outwards. He has been in her house twice before with Mullins but maybe he didn't really *see* things properly then. Walking up the path he thinks of Mrs Foster saying Anna grew increasingly cut-off and pauses by the front door with its speckled lion knocker that hangs alone in the expanse of peeling paintwork.

In the hallway, he tucks his master key back in his inner jacket pocket and crouches to scoop the post that's accumulated. Some of it is still addressed to Ruth – a Betterware catalogue advertising plastic dishes and a mould to compact old soap nubs together.

The floorboards tilting as he climbs the stairs, he passes Ruth's bedroom with its walls rough with plaster and holes where pictures once hung. On his last visit, he and Mullins pulled up some of the room's floorboards left loose with unscrewed nails but found nothing apart from cobwebs stretched in sticky blankets beneath.

It's Anna's room at the front of the house he wants to see: a nice space with a patchwork runner carefully laid at the end of the single bed, some dried flowers still sweet on the windowsill. He supposes little Ilene might have slept in the room too, like he did with Beattie as boys, even though their house was big enough to sleep separately.

It must have been early December when her sister died. They were getting ready for the nativity play at school and Ruth insisted on overseeing the costumes, *for the sake of authenticity*. Brian's mum complained she already had enough to manage – the shepherds needing matching headscarves and still no plan for the donkey – but agreed to go around, him in tow.

'Tinsel?' Ruth said when she saw what was planned for the

angels' halos. Her colouring books spread across the living room floor, Anna beamed as her mum held a ring of the flimsy silver plastic above her head.

Brian's mum, clutching the rest of the bags in the doorway, pointed out her twelve-shilling budget.

'It's only a bunch of kiddies at school,' Robert called through, winking at Brian in the hallway. He was on his way to the local butcher's, an apron tucked under his arm.

'You would say that!' Ruth called back. 'No respect for the Bible.' But she laughed and waved him off, offering the rest of them tea and shortbread biscuits. Brian sat on the sofa next to Anna while his mum watched Ilene's tiny pink face yawn up at her.

That evening they heard people outside Ruth's house. At first Brian's mum raised her eyebrows, cross at not being invited to some carol singing. *After all the effort I've been to with that woman.* But as they peered out the window they saw an ambulance driver carefully closing the vehicle's doors and Robert surrounded by neighbours with bowed heads.

'What's happening?' he asked his mum.

She only gripped the hood of his jacket.

When Brian turned back the ambulance was already driving away. And Ruth was just a figure at the downstairs window, pulling shut the curtains.

Brian's mum finished the outfits on her own that year, Ruth barely seen around the village except at church where a candle briefly illuminated the deepening creases of her face. As for Anna, she didn't get to wear a halo. Instead she stood at the back of the chorus, disappearing from the stage.

Now Brian looks around Anna's room again: the small bookshelf is filled with texts on Christian tradition, on the lessons of the Lord and the Devil's weakness; the only novels are by C.S. Lewis, Aslan featured on one cover as a glowing saviour. Brian thinks of Anna's last day at school, her silently clutching textbooks as she walked the corridor for the last time, even though they were only part way through the spring term. *Some Christian school*, a teacher whispered, *a good reputation but quite strict with the cane for forgotten homework; although, from the sound of it, Anna might be used to that these days.*

Wandering through the house, he reappraises the list of chores in Ruth's handwriting still stuck to the fridge; the row of polish tins and shoe brushes by the back door, their bristles worn from scrubbing. Where are the family photographs? And what happened to the drawings Anna used to spend so much time on?

At home, he finds his brother lying across the sofa in his dressing gown. Usually he might ask Jeanette to dress him but today he says nothing as he goes into the kitchen where she's cutting his ham sandwich into triangles.

'And how about dessert?' Brian says to her.

'I thought you were watching his ... you know.' She gestures at her own stomach, which presses against her white smock.

'It's OK,' he says and takes a Viennetta from the freezer. 'That hospital food can't have been nice, and the odd treat won't hurt.'

Brian watches his brother scoop up each mouthful of ice cream. He tells himself not to hurry him, that he's been through enough this past twenty-four hours. He can't help lingering in the doorway though. What if, in *all* the hours his brother has spent with a view to the street, he's seen the Fox or at least knows something? And why was he so reluctant to speak last night? As the spoon finally clatters against the bowl, he feels his pulse in his ears, his throat.

He sits down next to his brother on the sofa. It's like Beattie already knows what he wants to ask, squirming sideways with his elbows on the far edge.

'This is important, bro.' The nickname seems disingenuous. As he gives a pretend-punch his knuckles feel wrong against the soft flesh of his brother's arm.

'Nooo,' Beattie shouts, alarmingly loud. Jeanette bustles into the room and automatically pulls him into sitting position.

'Nobody wants to hurt you, Beattie love,' she says.

'Of course I don't.' Brian stands up and looks at the two of them. 'I just need to find out who he let in last night.'

'No!'

'Do you get how important this is?' Brian shouts.

Jeanette turns to him with a stern face. 'It's best if you give him some time.' She says it in such a matter-of-fact way, Brian wants to scream. To collapse on the floor and have someone help *him* up. He can't stop himself. 'All my life it's been about *you*. Even when you're like this, it's *still* about you isn't it?' Desperate for air Brian runs out the house. Gnats swarm as he walks up the high street, their wings sticking to his cheeks that are sweating in the heat. He swipes a hand but they return a second later.

The post office has a wall of newspapers and magazines, then the till and weighing scales towards the back. In the same purple anorak, Deloris stands flicking through some magazine and they exchange an awkward smile as Brian passes. Not letting himself stop, he continues towards Mary who is sitting behind the counter.

'Oi.' Rick steps from the queue and stares, red-faced in his overalls. A scab one side of his bald head gives him the look of having been in a fight although he's probably barely noticed it. 'When are you lot gonna get off your arses and catch this guy?' He gestures at the row of newspapers. 'Bad for all our businesses.'

'We're doing our best,' says Brian as he fingers the edge of the counter. It's rare he's this close to Rick – close enough to see the wisps of hair caught in the drying scab; usually it's across the other side of the pub where the man always sits on the same stool by the fruit machine, occasionally getting up to slam its buttons.

'Why can't you search the bloody houses already?'

'Not without a warrant, we can't.'

A hacking laugh turns into a cough and Rick bangs at his chest. 'What good are you then?'

Mary speaks up. 'I'll have none of this language in my post office.'

Her sharp look causes Rick to pull himself back. 'Still,' he says quietly. 'Pigs are meant to be dirty, not slow.'

'Excuse me?' The magazine still between her fingers, Deloris walks up to Rick and stops just a few inches away. 'As if *you* care. I've heard your caravan park is a dump. All those over-grown weeds and barbed wire.'

It takes Rick a second to regain himself. Then a grin stretches over his ruddy face. 'Hello, Dolly.'

'Don't you call me that,' she says. It's clear he's not backing off. The three people behind turn to stare including Mrs Morgan who clutches a parcel near her face.

Brian tentatively puts out an arm between them, reminding himself to stay calm. He mustn't let things get to him. 'It doesn't matter, Deloris. Let's come back later.'

Rick ignores the elbow that nudges his overalls. 'Harvey told me where he found you.' He speaks down to Deloris, who is several inches shorter than he is. 'Some tacky chip shop, with a hairnet, serving pickled eggs to factory workers.'

'So?'

It's as if Brian isn't there.

'You might've taken off your paintwork, but once a slag, always a slag.'

Deloris's face drains white. She raises a hardened palm but Brian is already striking his elbow into Rick's chest. It doesn't do much, so he shoves Rick hard on each shoulder. People spill out the way behind and he's not sure what to do so grabs at the overall straps and wrenches him over. The man stumbles towards the counter, almost knocking into Mary's stool, and lets out another round of hacking cough-turned-laughter. He doubles over grinning, although – on looking up at Brian – decides to let him have it.

'Until next time, Dolly.' He walks up to her beside the magazines and she stares fixedly at him, her chin raised. As Rick pushes his lips together and lets out a sucking noise, Brian goes after him again. His police training taught him to defend without use of force, which he does, holding his shoulders like before. But as the man gives another wet-lip smacking gesture, Brian throws himself forwards.

In only a moment his forehead has hit bone. Gasps fill the room as Rick's nose runs with blood, first a spot, then a steady trickle that stains his overalls.

'What have you done?' asks Mary, hurrying over. She gives a wide berth to Brian who has a single blood drop on his own uniform. His *police* uniform.

'I'm all right,' says Rick, expanding his chest while the

woman offers a tissue and Deloris goes to fetch more. 'Not sure we can say the same about Brian here. Can we?'

Outside the shop Brian feels woozy and leans against the brickwork. His head is throbbing and, unable to worry about who might be watching, he closes his eyes.

'Here you go.' Deloris pushes a cool bag across his forehead.

When he opens his eyes again she has an amused expression. 'Sorry I couldn't get you better peas,' she says gesturing to the plain white packaging. Although she laughs, she has dark circles under her eyes, which are bare of make-up, lashes in delicate curls.

'They're actually my favourite,' he says and they sit together for a while in the patch of sunshine.

Once the news gets back to Jackson she suspends Brian from police work for the next twenty-four hours. Suddenly everything else falls away as he realises what he's done. 'There's no time,' he pleads. 'This guy's waiting for his next chance.'

The bristles of Jackson's bun escape as she stuffs papers into a file. It's hard to say whether she's angry, but regardless, nothing matters except the case. He babbles on. 'I should never have been so stupid, getting distracted. What if the Fox takes someone else tomorrow?' He wants to say more but the pain is ripping across his forehead again and, as he cradles himself on the carpet, he sees her official police footwear trudge out of the room.

'It's not like you to fight,' his dad says that evening in the Crown.

Two pints of ale wait on the table between them. His dad

suggested the drink – probably cajoled by Brian's mum and the men now perch on worn stools, looking around. On the wall beside the bar, various newspaper clippings document the Great Train Robbery that took place a couple of miles down the road. Its 1960s typeset thick with ink, one headline reads *£2.6 Million Stolen by Daring Bandits* and another shows the gang's leader, Bruce Reynolds, handsome in a black suit. Only a single line mentions the train driver who was never able to work again.

Brian glances at the empty bar stools and glass bowls free from cigarette ash – nobody wants to be out. As he had walked along the main road to the pub he'd himself been reluctant to leave, thinking of Beattie alone in his room, even though Jeanette promised to stay till he got back.

'I've screwed up,' Brian says to his dad. The landlord eyes him from behind the crate of glasses on the bar. 'Just when the village needs me the most.'

'Don't be hard on yourself, son.' His dad meets Brian's eye, then quickly takes a long sip.

Their glasses are soon drained. They mutter about the cricket but sports talk always feels hollow without Beattie.

As they're starting to leave, the back door slams against the wall. 'It's the wind,' the landlord says, though anxiously goes outside to check the yard.

'You're one of the most solid people I know,' his dad says as they walk to his car. Caught unaware, Brian feels his eyes prick and scrapes his shoe over a stone. 'Your mum and I needed to start again somehow, with the move I mean. And you really came through for us with Beattie.'

'Thanks, Dad, it's just …'

'If anyone can catch this guy, I bet it's someone like you.'

The next morning he pulls on his plain clothes, the baggy T-shirt and jeans making him feel young. What's he supposed to do today? Without his uniform a trip up the high street isn't patrolling. Asking questions isn't investigating.

With his brother out on a day trip somewhere with Jeanette, Brian turns on the television. At around ten a tap at the door distracts him from some game show. It's Deloris with her anorak hood pulled up. Brian goes to say hello before hesitating. *What is the point in liking her?* It only lands him in trouble. Before long she drifts off and through the spyhole he sees her shrink to a purple dot.

Back in the living room he kneels on the sofa and wonders what to do. A nicely dressed woman is visiting the neighbour across the road and her two kids are playing on the grass. One, a little girl with a snub nose and freckles, gesticulates towards Anna's house. With Brian's window closed, the scene is near silent: just a little boy's open mouth, eyes screwed up; the mother ushering both of them away, hopefully to a place where skipping ropes still lie on lawns and no one need check under beds at night.

The carpet factory is hot with machines jerking wooden arms upwards, then round again in blurs of blue and yellow. Brian feels self-conscious in his police uniform, which he changed into in the staff toilets to avoid being seen by Gupta on patrol in the village. His bike outside is hidden behind a row of industrial skips.

'I'm here to see Harvey Baker,' he tells the dowdy woman who approaches him with a clipboard.

'He's in the tufting section.'

Brian takes a breath and taps at the badge on his shoulder. It might be an obnoxious gesture – especially as his shirt below is creased – but the rotating machines remind him how quickly time is passing.

The woman shows him to the reception area, a room with an unnecessarily long row of plastic seats. Above the desk is a framed photograph of Michael and several Chinese business-men who seem to be smiling at another camera. Brian plans what to say to Harvey. He's good at slipping out of things but not this time.

Just as he's sitting down, the door opens and Harvey walks in. He must be sweltering in the pinstriped jacket that stretches across his broad shoulders.

Quickly rising, Brian fiddles with the brim of his cap, debating whether to put it on.

Too soon Harvey is up close. His hand slaps him on the back and Brian grits his teeth as the motion reverberates through him.

'Been spending time with my Dolly, I hear.' A set of white teeth flash.

'Well, she's been helping me out.'

Harvey reaches to slap him again, though this time it's softer. 'I'm glad you've been getting along. It's nice for my Dolly to have a friend. She says you're like the brother she never had.'

Brian briefly flushes but then, putting on his police cap after all, asks him to show them somewhere more private.

'What for?' Harvey says.

'I'd like to ask you about Anna.'

'Not this again.'

Brian knows he shouldn't ask questions right here out in

the open, but Harvey is restless. 'What was the nature of your relationship exactly?' he says, putting up a hand to stop him leaving.

Harvey speaks through his teeth. 'That's none of your business.'

'I'm conducting an investigation into her disappearance.'

'Are you? I heard you were suspended.' His mouth twists as he pushes forward. 'One phone call and I could have you in serious trouble.'

Brian is left alone by the reception desk. His head thumps. Black spots spread in front of his eyes. He refuses to go back home but doesn't know what else to do, so stands shaking for a minute. He's about to find Harvey again when a woman taps him on the shoulder. She's petite, with a bow in her hair, pink gloss on wrinkled lips. 'You investigating that girl Anna's disappearance?'

'Yes I am.'

'She worked here you know. Years ago now.' The woman nods. 'Really nice, wasn't she?'

When he can't track down Harvey again, Brian asks to see his dad instead. The same clipboard-wielding woman as before makes a call and, a minute later, Brian is surprised to find Michael strolling towards him. He motions Brian to follow him outside through the car park. At first Brian suspects he's being thrown out but realises they've walked past the entrance gates. 'It's better to be away from the heat and noise,' Michael explains, holding open the door to a mobile building on wheels. Inside the air is cool, as a line of vents whirr. 'Air conditioning made in Taiwan.'

Michael reaches out and Brian makes sure to squeeze tight, just like his dad taught him. Michael seems pleased by this. There isn't much else in the room apart from a desk, two chairs and a silver filing cabinet from the 1970s. A single photograph sits unceremoniously beside a stack of pay slips.

'I was just told Anna worked here.'

At first Michael makes a bemused expression but then taps a biro against his stained teeth. 'Maybe you're right.' He slides open a drawer and finds a folder.

'Surely you must remember your employees?' says Brian. He knows how committed to the factory Michael has always been, the main topic he talks about in the pub when anyone asks how he is.

The man flicks through some papers. 'Ah yes. Answering the phones – although only for two days, it says here.' He prods at a line of text. 'May the fifteenth to sixteenth, 1978.'

'Why for such a short time?'

At this Michael leans back to think. 'Sandra, I bet. She became rather funny about young girls working here. Recruiting a secretary always turned into a nightmare.'

Brian pictures Michael's wife's tight-lipped face, how she often seems so anxious at village fetes. But there is something diligent about her too, like she sees things the rest of us don't.

'Just jealous, most likely,' continues Michael. 'Of course the woman disagrees with me on that point but what else could it be? Late night workings, fumbles under cardigans ...' He gives a scoffing laugh, though loses himself in the idea, stroking his tie while he turns to the window.

'Mr Baker?'

'Anyway, I had to let Anna go. Yes, I remember. Harvey pointed out she had this nice way with the clients. He was fairly young himself at the time, although I threw him straight into a managerial position.' He taps at the photograph. 'Not that there's anything wrong with working your way up, but he was a talented boy. So charming. Especially with Anna. I saw the two of them whispering together and he insisted on helping her in the storeroom.'

'Was Anna upset when you let her go?'

Michael leans back to scratch beneath the bulk of his belly. 'She got over it, I bet. We've got to look out for our wives, haven't we? Even if they can be a tad irrational, going on and on.'

As Michael taps the picture again, it turns a little and Brian sees that, although it's a family studio portrait, the three of them against a screen, Sandra is at the far edge. It's the father and son that occupy the frame, arms over one another in matching blue jumpers.

'Of course the woman was funny with Deloris at first,' says Michael, having warmed up to the topic. 'These past days she can't stop phoning her up and mentioning her at dinner. I don't know what the two of them get up to together. Sandra has always had her obsessions, fixations. You know what women are like.'

Brian gives no reply except to excuse himself.

It's a strangely quiet evening with pollen clotting the air. A field of rapeseed shines yellow as Brian cycles past, a single tree stump in the middle. For a while he lets himself glide and only feels his pulse beat again when he passes the metal sign for Heathcote. Too soon he's thinking about how Sandra insisted that Anna was fired, about her peering up at the CCTV. Was she's involved in Anna disappearance? The break-ins? It seems so unlikely but he remembers what Jackson said: *everyone is a suspect.*

His head pounds as he reaches the main road to the village and speeds jerkily over potholes to his house. It hasn't rained all day and the clouds are pressing down in their darkening clumps.

A man in overalls introduces himself at the door, which is open, a toolbox in the hallway. 'Won't be long,' he says before fiddling with the security alarm in his hands. Brian glares at the kitchen window pushed wide open. 'It was really stuffy,' the man says with a shrug.

Sealing up the house again, Brian reminds himself that he was the one to ask the guy to come. The system was top of the range according to the sales person on the phone.

In the shower the hot water falls over the tightened muscles of his body. Brian doesn't want to face the rest of the evening alone with his thoughts. He stands motionless until the bathroom mirror is covered with steam. Faint lines remain – finger smudges across its glass?

Fastening a towel around himself, he goes to the landing to ask the man if he's used the bathroom, but he's packed up and gone, an invoice on the stairs. It's just fingermarks, Brian tells himself and blinks away more dark spots. Water is dripping from him to the carpet so he ducks into his room for some fresh clothes. Then stops. Across the wall over his bed someone's painted a series of letters in thick, dripping lines. They stretch towards the ceiling and it takes him a second to figure out what they spell:

THIS ISN'T ME

Moving closer, Brian finds they've been hastily applied, with long flecks cast across his pillows. The colour is one he chose to paint the room to make it his own, the pot left in the wardrobe. As he puts his fingertips up to a line, he finds the paint is still wet.

13

Brian scrubs furiously at the paint. It only smears across his hands, along his arms. He scrubs harder till his fingers are raw. How did the Fox get in? His thoughts are a jumble but one keeps returning: maybe it was his brother. All of it. Cooped up in his room so much of the time, maybe Beattie was furious with him? Furious at the village? But no. It doesn't make sense – he'd been the other side of Aylesbury when the paint was applied – and besides, there's no way he'd have the strength in his legs to walk the street let alone break into a home. A second later Brian is disgusted with himself. How could he suspect his own brother?

The back garden is a mass of shadows that move around him as he runs to get a bottle of turps from the shed. Back in his room, he sloshes the liquid across a cloth. Then some more. Its fumes rise up around him, wrap him in their warmth. As he carries on scrubbing, he lets himself sink to the cushion beneath his crouching body. Everything becomes softer.

It's not clear how long he's been there but at some point

the room becomes dim and all he knows is the wall. Nothing seems to matter any more. The thought of just giving up, no more police work, is a tempting idea on which he might hang his hat. His drifting thoughts next find their way to Deloris. Her face. Her laugh. The two could really have something, couldn't they? What if after this was all over they ran away together? Just the two of them. A little house, garden ...

'Bri?' A blur turns into Beattie's outline at the door. Brian puts the turps lid on, then attempts to steer his brother from the room, wondering if he could ever leave him.

That night Brian's dreams are filled with a cry that gets louder and louder, though he can't figure out where it's coming from. Each room of his house is too cluttered to find anything, cardboard boxes overflowing with piles of comics and cassette tapes. At last he realises it's a phone. *His* phone.

Blinking at the alarm clock he sees it's 3.34 a.m. and scrabbles from bed. Downstairs in the sitting room he almost pulls the cord from the phone trying to get it to his ear.

'Yes?'

There's no noise apart from some gentle thuds from above.

'Hello?' he says and twists to the window. A pool of street-light turns the rain into streaks of neon.

The voice is gruff. 'Don't mean to ring so late.' The caller stops to clear her throat.

'Cynthia?'

'But you need to know about him and her. He got her sacked, you know. Lost his temper when she rejected him. And now, that Deloris might carry his child.'

The voice cuts off and is replaced with a mechanical hum.

Brian lets the noise gently pulse as he thinks: so Harvey did have a grudge against Anna?

As he returns the phone another question forms: if Deloris is pregnant does she want to be?

He hates to picture Harvey pressing her to a bed, the face she might pull, so hurries to the front door and out into the rain. At Deloris's house the brass knocker clatters again and again but no lights go on.

'Deloris?' He calls upwards, raindrops falling in his eyes. The landing window remains a blank haze. 'Talk to me,' he shouts hoarsely into the wind.

As he's going to knock again a hand touches his shoulder. It's Gupta in a rain mac zipped up to his chin. 'What is the matter, Constable?'

'I think he might be hurting her,' Brian says.

'You want me to forcibly open the door?'

Brian hesitates and Gupta frowns at his soaking T-shirt, his bloodshot eyes. 'I think you need some sleep.'

'No,' he says and starts to shout again but the man is putting an arm around his shoulders and telling him to come back in the morning.

Light pours through the crack in the curtain. His eyes sting. Having barely slept, Brian has trouble planting his feet on the floor where bed sheets are crumpled. Then he remembers Deloris. Pulling on his uniform he runs down the street through silvery puddles. Harvey's car is parked across the gravel just where it was the night before. Inside the gaudy house the man is smug. God knows what he might have done to Deloris, let alone Anna. Looking around for a rock or a forgotten shovel in the neighbour's garden he vows to break the door down if he has to.

But after a second rap of the knocker the door opens and Deloris stands there in her halter-neck dress, soft folds falling around her knees.

'Oh, hi, Brian.' She gives a weak smile. 'How are you?'

He says nothing as he follows her through to the kitchen.

Sitting at the breakfast counter with a newspaper, Harvey shrugs to see him. 'Allowed to ask your questions again, are you?' Sandra is also there, standing by the hob where she drops an aspirin in water and gives the glass to Deloris.

'I do have several questions, yes,' Brian starts and takes a breath. 'I'm still not sure of the nature of your relationship with Anna.'

'Jesus! You don't think we've got enough on our plates?' Harvey gestures towards Deloris who reddens as she sips the water.

Brian refocuses. 'Who exactly was responsible for Anna getting fired from the factory?'

At this Sandra pipes up. 'That was me.' She then purses her lips while busying around the kitchen scrubbing. The once-gleaming surfaces are dull with marks and stains she sets herself against. 'I was a little scared for her, that's all.'

'Jesus, if Dad was here—'

'Well yes,' says Sandra curtly, stretching out a cloth. Her next words are strained but each placed carefully as if decided on years before. 'Your father has always coddled you. Part of me thinks that's why you're like this.'

The stool screeches. 'Like what?' Harvey asks, now on his feet.

Shrinking from her son's glistening face, Sandra seems fragile in her dress and pinafore.

Brian intervenes. 'What happened with Anna?'

The room is stuck in place as they wait for Harvey to answer, with only the microwave's digital clock ticking over.

After another minute he exhales and lays his hands on the counter. 'Fine. We dated, all right?' His mouth twitches. 'Correction. We went out on one date and well, it was really great.'

Her glass knocking against the counter, Deloris tries to understand. 'You told me you didn't even like her.'

'The next day she wasn't interested,' he continues, ignoring his wife. His voice hardens. 'Her not interested in me? It was humiliating.'

'So your mum was scared for her safety?' asks Brian, glancing between Harvey and Sandra who returns to wiping between tiles, crumbs skittering in all directions. He reaches for his truncheon.

'I only wanted to find out why Anna wouldn't see me again,' Harvey says, throwing some post in a drawer and slamming it shut. 'It's hardly harassment.'

Sandra bustles past Deloris spraying indiscriminately. 'Following her home.' Disinfectant blasts across the cupboards. 'Phoning up late at night, Ruth said.'

'Only because I wanted to know!' Harvey shouts at his mum, exasperated. Fists pound, but it's his own fingers he hurts, the worktop vibrating. 'Why didn't she like me?'

The others look away. A silence holds grip on the room until Sandra lays the cloth on the central island. 'Isn't it obvious?' Harvey dares lift his eyes.

'Ruth didn't let Anna see *any* boys,' she says softly. 'Even as a grown-up it was as if she wasn't allowed from her mother's sight.'

*

Once Brian has taken some notes he goes to leave.

'I'll see you out,' Deloris says.

In the corridor he asks her if she's OK.

'Like I said earlier, I'm really fine.' She smiles and touches his shoulder. 'I'm sorry again about what happened with Rick.'

He doesn't want to talk about the fight. It feels like there are so many more important things to say though he doesn't know what. 'Are you pregnant?' he blurts at the door.

Deloris laughs. 'I'm not, no. Sandra asked me the same thing.'

'Oh?'

'I mentioned to her that I felt ill. Who doesn't, right now? With Anna still gone.' She glances behind into the hallway. 'Plus my dad had an operation yesterday. He's recovering but ...'

Without thinking, Brian takes Deloris's hands. Her head dipped, she stares at their joined fingers.

'Good luck with everything,' she says before pulling away. The gap between them widens as Brian forces himself over the threshold. He wants to ask her to join him but instead puts on his police cap and slowly walks away.

'We're running out of time,' Jackson says later that morning. 'Most missing people don't turn up past two weeks.'

They're standing beside a pinboard attached to the wall. Around them the interview room is strewn with papers and half-drunk coffee cups. Trish's murmurs drift in from reception as she tells someone to *please go home. Or better yet, stay with a friend outside the village.* She's been twitchy all morning and keeps hovering by the door, asking when it will thunder. The sky is hoarding clouds again, an airless quality making them tug at damp collars.

'We have various suspects,' Jackson says, pointing to the display of photographs: Rick grinning outside the pub, the rather sombre headshot of Stan used in the local school booklet about his birdhouse, Sandra at some charity gala, and Harvey handsome in a suit. Ralph is there too, in a blurred black-and-white shot where he looks young, his face in profile so the scar is hidden. Below him is the face he drew with the label: 'Unidentified woman'. Other notes are scrawled around her:

Seen at Anna's house on evening went missing, 18 June
Entry on Anna's wall calendar for same evening:
'a visit from you-know-who' (she was expecting the woman? Why not say her name?)
Has reportedly visited Stan Emmerson on more than one occasion prior to this (though Emmerson denies any knowledge)
No sightings of her arriving in vehicle although unknown Vauxhall Cavalier reported evening of 17 June, parked two doors down
Woman not seen since

Jackson recaps what they know about various villagers in that dispassionate way of hers, eyes barely open as she points to the board with a blunt pencil. They must consider the wider investigation of home intrusion as well as Anna's disappearance, she tells them. Arrows begin to link the faces – Harvey stuck up beside his mum – as she mentions accomplices. It all feels unreal to Brian.

'And what do you know about Stan?' she asks him.

'He's married, but seeing another woman maybe,' he says. 'The same unidentified woman that Anna spoke to the night she went missing.' The table feels insubstantial as he perches on its edge. 'What if Anna found out about the affair and threatened to tell his wife?' He surprises himself to hear the words come falling out. They sound over the top and he can sense Mullins shifting his weight impatiently beside him. 'But if Stan is the Fox, *why* would he go into his neighbours' homes?'

They finish talking and Jackson orders Brian into her office. 'I know you were making enquiries yesterday,' she mutters. 'After I gave you strict instructions not to work.'

He begins to apologise but a stubby finger is pointed at him. 'How do you think that makes me look?' she says and the finger begins to shake. 'I should really suspend you from this investigation altogether.'

'I only wanted to—'

'Just make it count,' she says, her bare face locked on his. 'We need answers before it's too late.'

Brian pores over his notes again: times, dates, names ... It's tempting to go outside to patrol the streets, speak to people, do *anything*. But he forces himself to focus on the information he's already built up. Behind him Mullins is watching CCTV footage from the repaired camera, time compressed as he fast-forwards through the minutes of empty street.

At midday he thinks of Jackson asking about Anna's dad. Several phone calls later he's tracked his number from a friend of Elsie's daughter and rings the Yorkshire number. The voice that answers is rough but friendly, just how he remembers. Brian explains why he's ringing.

'I've been following it all and even spoke to some young lad who turned up at my door with a tape recorder.' Robert clears his voice. 'Course I told him I didn't know anything or else I'd have been on the phone to you lot.'

Brian asks him to confirm that he hasn't seen his daughter the last few weeks. 'Or heard anything.'

A pained snuffling fills the line. 'Not heard since she was a child. I never knew a girl could be so stubborn.'

'Stubborn?'

'We used to be close, her and me. But I must've written two dozen letters over the years and she never replied once.'

Later Jackson is busy making telephone calls in her office – media enquiries, apparently.

It takes Brian hours to transcribe all his notes but by eight o'clock he's entered the final set and taps the return key. His eyes can't adjust to the dim afterwards and he feels his way through the room to reception. Beneath the other door he sees a slip of orange light.

'I thought you'd've gone home by now,' Brian says, walking in without knocking.

Jackson is staring at something on the far wall, which Brian turns to see is blank. 'I still can't work out his motivations. I spoke to this guy from the Met, a psychological profiler for some of the most violent offenders, and he says voyeurism is often the result of an inability to interact in society, that sometimes it can have violent consequences, especially in sexually frustrated men, but it's hard to tell without more to go on.' She pulls at her hairnet, which catches, so she tugs harder and hair spills out. 'He's playing games with us, perhaps. Someone smart. Physically fit and with a fixation on this village.'

'But why Anna?' Brian says.

She smiles tiredly and agrees they are missing this angle.

They chat for a while longer until they recognise they are going round in circles. Jackson picks up her jacket, laying it across her arm. Brian wonders why she brings it every day since it's so muggy.

'You're a hard worker,' she says once they're outside. The night air is cool enough to breathe again. 'That's just what you need to make it in this field. Who knows – maybe one day you might be where I am.'

He must have pulled a face as she smiles tiredly again and taps his arm. 'It's not so bad to be alone, Brian. One is a powerful number.'

Jeanette is at home when Brian comes in the door, but he says he'd like to spend time alone with his brother. After shaving him in the bathroom, he helps to lay out the trophies on the carpet and together they admire them one by one. Brian takes some tissues from the bathroom and polishes the largest until the etched lettering can be seen.

Beattie McPherson
Captain of the Bucks League Champions
1972

He then holds out a cardboard box as his brother puts them inside. Perhaps the shelf can be used for something new, Brian says, smiling at his brother. That night they change into their pyjamas and Beattie sleeps in bed with him, curled into a ball. 'Thanks,' he mouths.

'No need to thank me,' says Brian, stretching out his legs. 'This can be your room from now on. We'll paint it whatever colour you like. There's so much more space for your chair and railings. I don't know why I didn't think of it before.' He turns out the lights and hopes he'll dream of something happy.

Monday morning arrives and more budget has come through for further CCTV cameras. Brian paces up and down the streets to find suitable positions. It's hard to stay positive, but at least he's finished entering all the notes to the computer. A call came in earlier that morning too – Rick saying he didn't want to press charges against him. Apparently all he wanted was to be left alone *so no point in causing a stink*.

Brian skirts the footpath that runs behind Yardley Mews where fungus sprouts in the overgrown grass. The Robinsons have stuck broken glass to the top of their fence and it glints in the sun. So much for peace-loving hippy values, Brian thinks, realising how much people continue to surprise him.

He's about to pass on by when a flash of white makes him pause. He reaches a hand through the leaves and feels something cold coiled in the earth. It's a chain with something dangling down – a handbag. Feeling its sodden leather, Brian recalls the description of the mystery woman's bag as having a chain strap. The feature is quite unusual as far as he knows. So she did visit Stan's? Or at least went behind his house?

Back at the station, Brian returns his thoughts to Stan denying all knowledge of the mystery woman. He phones to check that the London Symphony Orchestra was playing on the night of the eighteenth. 'Yes sir,' the lady reassures him. 'It was a beautiful evening. One of their finest.'

'And a Mr Stan Emmerson had tickets?'

The sound of flicking through paper. 'Yes, indeed he did.'

Brian puts down the phone feeling uneasy and the woman phones back later. 'I double-checked, and actually Mr Emmerson didn't turn up to collect his tickets. It was the same with a few of our clients. A problem with the trains.'

Brian calls the British Rail helpline and is assured by the senior manager that there was a train strike from midday until midnight that day. Stan never made the trip to London.

'I think Stan was covering up an affair,' says Brian, bursting into Jackson's office. She raises her eyebrows. 'And his wife discovered; maybe he thought Anna had found out about it and perhaps told her and he lost his temper. Said it was her fault, and the village's fault too, for not keeping quiet. Maybe if they knew *his* secret, he wanted to know theirs. So he broke into their homes.'

'Why don't you go interview him again?'

'I think he might be at the supermarket,' Brian says, already on his way out. He races to pick up his badge from the other room but stops short: Stan is standing at reception. His supermarket uniform is on, though the collar is undone, his pale chest beneath. Stan patiently waits for Trish to look up from her logbook, then tells her, 'I need to confess.'

PART FOUR

14

Stan waits for the room to react.

'This way, please,' Brian says after a long pause. His face is flushed as he excitedly gestures down the corridor.

'Not right now.'

'No?'

Behind Brian the new policewoman, Jackson, stands with her arms at her sides. Her colleague, Mullins, appears too, a confused expression tugging at his fleshy cheeks.

'It's simpler if you come to my house,' Stan says.

'Why is that?'

On seeing Stan's resolute stance the woman nods. 'Fine. Lead the way.' She then feels at the belt around her middle. A radio is clipped beside her sturdy hip. Mullins heads through the door and re-emerges a minute later; all the while Brian stares gormlessly at Stan.

Outside the light is harsh. Stan dips his eyes and notices the two loose threads where buttons are missing from his super-market shirt. He is supposed to be on his way there now; will already be three minutes late, even if he jogs up the high street and the bus comes straight away. But, he reminds himself, he left a message for Laura which she'll hear when she gets back from her break – *I won't make my shift today, or tomorrow or for the foreseeable future in fact.*

He and Brian leave behind the ugly pebble-dash building and turn for Yardley Mews. The two other officers form a shadow behind a few paces back. Stan can't hear what they might be saying but it hardly matters at this point.

'Stan? What's happening?' Elsie's head pokes up from her geraniums.

'You'll know soon enough,' Stan says and turns to face his house. The ash bench needs another varnish if it isn't to rot in the damp this summer. Even if it does, it can always be used for firewood, which might seem fitting – giant licks of flames engulfing his handiwork while the villagers watch.

He fishes for his keys as they walk up the front garden path. Brian's face has reset – he looks determined with his jaw tightened and hands balled into fists. Stan unlocks the door but before nudging it open turns to the street. Faces are at windows or figures hovered at doorsteps; Elizabeth is the closest, with a textbook dropping Post-it notes over the pavement.

'Requesting backup,' Brian mutters.

'We're right here,' Mullins says. He and Jackson wait beyond the porch, letting Brian follow Stan inside, which he does slowly, glancing around. His breaths grow louder and Stan feels like his every move is analysed. He's no longer just another husband in this village, a supermarket manager with a name badge.

'Shall we go upstairs?' he asks the young man.

Brian's jaw goes slack, exposing a slip of tongue. Outside

someone shouts Anna's name in a crackling voice. Stan peers through the stained-glass window of the hallway to see Deloris in a rumpled summer dress and bare feet. Harvey is beside her with an arm slipped protectively through hers, his suit jacket similarly creased.

'Righty.'

'Would you mind waiting downstairs?' Stan asks the police-woman when she tries to follow. Her black leather shoes pause on the outer doormat.

'I can go alone,' Brian tells her. His determined look has faded but he's poised nonetheless. For a moment Stan feels like a father showing him around – wanting to put an arm over his shoulder – then baulks at the thought of his own son. He takes a long breath and lets a stillness settle inside him.

They slowly walk up the stairs, Brian first, with both hands ready at his sides. More voices call Anna's name from outside and grow louder until it's as if they're beating at the glass windows.

'Into the spare room,' Stan says over the din, indicating down the passage to the left. It's at the back of the house, with a view across the garden, then the tangled mass of brambles that've grown so high this summer. He's enjoyed knowing the gooseberry bush must be bursting out its plump, shiny fruit, even if he does rarely open the blinds, not with the Robinsons next door.

Brian's hand reaches for the doorknob but fumbles. Such nerves, Stan thinks.

'Take a breath,' he says.

The boy does, letting his cheeks swell. Then he swings open the door and lunges in.

The spare bedroom is Stan's favourite – twin beds with lilac eiderdowns that Judy embroidered many years ago. A fresh coat of paint still leaves a tang in the air, the dent above the window frame barely perceptible where he's smoothed it with sandpaper.

Against the far wall the colonial wardrobe stands. The glossed panels reflect streaks of dark blue uniform, Brian's elbows cocked as though he's ready to swing a blow, except he doesn't know where to stand. He edges towards the wardrobe, fingers stretched out.

'You'll need the key,' Stan says as he pauses in the middle of the carpet.

Another gasp of air and Brian turns to him. Stan feels in the pocket of his work trousers and drops the key in the boy's trembling hand.

Back at the wardrobe the lock clinks and Brian peels open the door. It's heavy and takes him two attempts.

Dresses hang on the railing beside a row of three drawers. The wallpaper behind is Laura Ashley's, the oriental print perfectly applied.

Brian moves a clumsy hand between the garments so they sway about. A houndstooth skirt falls in a heap on the floor which Stan resists picking up.

'I don't understand,' Brian says. 'Are these Anna's? Or Ruth's?'

Stan at last rests a hand on his shoulder. 'God, no. All these dresses are mine.'

Back at the station Stan repeats his initial line. The one he practised on the way over the first time around. 'I need to confess.'

The interview room is cool enough with the window left open. Mullins is sent to make teas, which he does with a grunt before leaving them to it. Stan sits opposite Brian and Jackson whose lined face is like a map of contours, her eyelids heavy with skin. He'd like to draw her sometime or, better yet, carve her in wood.

'I lied to Brian here in my earlier interviews for which I am sorry. Really.'

'So the mystery woman seen at Anna's on the eighteenth was actually you, is that what you're saying?'

'Yes, Brian.'

The tape is running but the policeman still takes notes in his large, looping handwriting that's rather messy.

'You dressed up as a woman, have been doing so for the last few weeks?'

'That's it, yes.' He feels energised by the words. As if another part of himself is pushing outwards in insistent throbs, till her edges expand away from his own.

'You're not having an affair?'

'No.'

Brian thinks this over, his pencil spearing the page. He has stopped looking so young recently and has a shiver of hair on his upper lip. 'I'm not sure I understand.'

Since Brian no longer writes, Stan speaks loudly for the recorder. 'I showed Anna my outfit before going to London that evening. She was the only person who knew about the other part of me. But she was so upset. I asked her what was wrong and she didn't tell me. So my mood was dampened and it was something of a relief that the trains were on strike.'

The words don't affect him like they should and the account is overly dry. He continues to explain. 'I promised Judy no one would find out about it all as she thought it would humiliate the family. And to begin with I didn't realise Anna would be gone so long. It was only when I received a phone call from the orchestra admin that I realised how important this so-called mystery woman is.'

He thinks of the first time he heard Jim mention her. It seemed so fitting in a way, like she was taking on a life of her own in people's minds but slipping from their grasp. No one owned her, not even Stan.

'Anna has been gone for almost two weeks.' Brian speaks more angrily now and it catches Stan unaware. He traces fingers down his chin to feel the stubble returning, his old self forever sealing over the new one.

'I never thought it'd come to this,' Stan says and decides he needs to buy a new razor.

Over the next hour Brian grows frustrated. Stan watches as he rubs at his cheeks, which pulls down his eyes so he can see their pink rims. He hasn't been sleeping well, Stan guesses. He has long been aware of the young man. How he pushes his brother around in the park even in the rain. How he takes his dad to the Crown some weekends and tries to persuade him to do the quiz, though the older man always says some other time.

'So you knew Anna was distressed and you walked away?' Brian asks. 'You didn't ask why she was so unhappy?'

Something rattles deep inside, upsetting Stan's voice. 'O-of course I did. It's just she wouldn't tell me.'

'Come on,' says Jackson. 'How could you not even have an inkling? The two of you must've been close for you to show her your outfit.'

'W-we are close, yes.' It's been years since Stan suffered his stammer, something that began at art college and that rankled him for the subsequent decade until he finally saw a speech therapist. 'Sh-she kept mumbling about her mum, about how she didn't deserve her.'

As he squeezes his eyes shut an image appears in his mind: Anna feeling the velvet of his dress sleeve with her moist fingers, her fringe stuck to her forehead. She had gone to fetch something, the stairs banging under her feet, and come back consumed by such a gush of tears that he tried to put an arm around her. *What a wretched creature I am*, she'd said, turning to the stove.

'And how long did you stay?'

'I'm not sure.' Stan thinks of her shoulders heaving as she gulped back tears. 'I wanted to stay and talk but she grew angry, said she wanted to be alone. She pleaded for me to leave. Said she didn't want to be seen like this. In some deranged attempt to soothe her I made us both hot milk but it ended up burning. She was annoyed she'd have to scrub the pan.'

'And was Anna expecting any more visitors that evening?'

'No one she mentioned.'

Brian carries on asking questions, over and over again. Jackson seems impressed and leaves him to it. Wanting to tell them more, Stan describes it all again, trying to feel the pain he's meant to, but it's as if she is sinking deep inside him to a dull, familiar place, then deeper still

'Any idea what might've happened to Anna? Any idea whatsoever?'

Stan speaks into the recorder. 'None at all.'

The villagers are waiting for him to leave the station. Jackson says he might be charged with perverting the course of justice – to expect a letter in the post – but for now he's free to go. They clearly have other things to be getting on with, although as Stan signs the paperwork at reception he notices how Brian stands in a daze. The boy needs arms around him but he isn't the man to do it.

For now Stan doesn't let himself dwell. The crowds surge around him as he walks down the steps but most don't seem angry like he expected. With many of the men gone to work for the day, it's the housewives who stare, toddlers hidden behind their legs, the women's feet stuffed into sandals or trainers hastily put on at the door. Sandra nudges herself forward to ask him, 'Where is she?' When he doesn't reply, carefully side-stepping a pram, she asks again and others join in. They grow more confident in their numbers and form a peculiar chant, asking the question that's been haunting them all for so long.

'Where is Anna?'

The only person not to join in is Deloris who's lingering further along the pavement, the young woman he sees in the supermarket smelling the peaches or sometimes joking with a guy who's stopped to make conversation, all witty comebacks before she sighs and returns to her shopping list. She now watches uncertainly as he goes by.

'Where is Anna?' the rest continue.

The voices follow him home, up his path to the front door. They stand for a few minutes more while he watches from the living room, until the warm, thickening air gets too much and they take their children home.

In the living room he sits upright in his armchair. It's op-posite the half of the blue linen sofa where Anna used to sit when she came round. At first her back would remain rigidly straight and she'd give one-word answers to his and Judy's questions, but after some weeks she relaxed as they got to know each other. It began when Elliot had been in his phase of churchgoing. He liked the hymns, he said, and Judy humoured him, arguing that it'd be nice to take part in more village activities. *Disingenuous*, Stan had pointed out, *none of us believe in God*, but as usual he wasn't listened to.

He had to admit it was nice to see Anna befriend Elliot who wasn't invited to any of the football games or parties Stan heard about at the school gates. Every Tuesday evening Anna taught him Bible study and afterwards walked him back home, then stayed for a cup of Ovaltine. *I just like to listen*, she would say if Judy prompted her to join in more with the conversation. But after helping Anna to sew some cushions for an orphanage in East Africa, Elliot grew tired of the after-school work and said he preferred building his Meccano train set.

Not seeming to mind, Anna continued to turn up on a Tuesday evening so she and Judy could talk about village gossip. Or sometimes Anna babysat while he and Judy went to the Aylesbury cinema, refusing any money even though she was surely living on very little, always in the same tatty dress with the corduroy trim.

For the most part Stan remained in the background while the women talked; when it was just the two of them – Judy upstairs putting Elliot to bed – it unnerved Stan how attentively Anna listened to whatever he said, weeks later bringing up some small comment he'd made. For the first time in years he was reminded what scant attention the rest of his family and friends paid.

It was at the May Ball this year that things changed between them. Anna almost hadn't come to the event on the village green but was dragged along by Elsie who said she needed help getting there. Harvey and the guys by the bar insisted on buying Stan some vintage Scotch. He usually avoided these village events with their endless organisation and women fussing over the exact shade of ribbons, but once there it was nice to clink glasses with the other men. Harvey was dashing in a suit, his arm wrapped around Stan's shoulder so close he could smell fresh sweat under his aftershave.

Later, however, his mind became unpredictable. Having lost count of the Scotches, he stumbled into a table and suddenly needed to get air. Outside, Anna's skirt was blowing about as she collected plastic glasses that'd been carried off by the wind.

'Oh, I like this song,' she said when 'Total Eclipse of the Heart' came on.

He jokily asked her to dance and was surprised that she accepted. A minute later they were swinging in a clumsy offbeat across the lawn while the music crackled and blared from the marquee.

'I'm leading aren't I, Stan?'

'I'm not Stan,' he said. 'I-I'm Corinne.' The name seemed to come from nowhere. Then, as they stepped from side to side, Anna had asked about Corinne: what was she like? When he said she painted, Anna asked what sort of thing? Flowers? Animals?

'No, nothing like that.'

'Then what?'

'Huge slashes of colour, like nothing from this world.'

Then at the end of the ball, as Stan was slumped in a chair waiting for Judy, Anna came to ask when she might see Corinne next.

'Maybe very soon,' he said. 'She likes to explore.'

He started to think of Corinne in the spare moments of the day – how she might react to Judy's celebrity magazines that Stan had always tolerated, what she might say of the rowing boat paintings Judy had found in some marked-down bin in a tourist shop in Cumbria. He started shaving closer too, adding Vaseline to his lips so they became dewy. It wasn't that he wanted to be like the men outside basement bars in Soho, their cigarette ash illuminating only hints of velvet collars and plump mouths. He wanted to be someone wholly different.

The next week Anna came round to see them all for dinner. While Judy and Elliot were going over homework upstairs, Stan suggested that she and Corinne might get on rather well. 'How about a trip to London? We could go to the British Museum?'

'Oh no,' she said from her usual place on the sofa. 'I'm not sure about that.' Stan regretted it instantly and began to retreat to the kitchen until Anna added, 'But maybe Corinne would like to pop over for tea?'

The phone now rings in the kitchen. It's not yet lunch in England, so America won't be awake for another few hours but then Judy might have woken early? Or not been able to sleep, her legs jerking above the sheets like they did when the night was too hot.

'Judy?'

'It's Howard Mills from the *Aylesbury Gazette*.'

Silence.

'Since you were the last person to see Anna, you're likely our best chance to know where she is. Can we arrange a time to speak?'

'I've told the police everything—'

'You said she was upset about something but didn't bother to ask? What aren't you telling us, Mr Emmerson?'

The phone cord stretches as he lets it fall, the receiver tapping on the linoleum. Howard's voice is distant but still there, even as Stan walks back into the living room.

Stan tries to return to his earlier position in the armchair but his knees jostle up and down, like a man with too many hormones, gangly thighs that don't look right in trousers. For years Stan has practised being still, as though if he moves too fast, speaks too fast, someone else might come out. He hits the chair arms with the flat of his hands. Corinne isn't real. Anna knew it as much as he did.

After rescuing the phone from the floor, Stan dials the number that Judy wrote on the back of the address book. It was reassuring she didn't write it inside – an entry next to the other friends and acquaintances – but on the back. The tone lets out several long hums as Stan patiently waits. And waits. Waits and waits for his family to come home.

No reply.

Stan is too wired to sit again in his chair. He needs to sew buttons back on to his uniform; he ripped off the shirt late last night after seven hours of stacking shelves with his knees pressed to the cold supermarket floor. The dull ache of it all, his veins protruding in lines down his wrists in answer to the monotonous lifting of tins of peaches and spam and mushy peas, turning them so the label faces outwards, then again, again. Perhaps he should iron Elliot's shirts too? He left some in the wicker basket and will need them for school in September. So many chores when school restarts and he doesn't want to anger the form tutor any more than he already has. Elliot is a shy boy like he was, a boy who needs his dad. He hurries around to prepare for his family's homecoming, taking out the ironing board from the kitchen cupboard and waiting for the steam to scent the living room with its metallic warmth. His family will be home in less than a month, which really isn't long.

Just as he is pressing into the collar of Elliot's shirt, all his weight leant into the iron's silver point, something flies through the window. The glass turns to several pieces that hurtle towards him, along with white fragments splashed into the air. In the split-second it takes them to reach the carpet, collecting far and wide in a glossy pattern, Corinne has come alive. She shivers through him like the fragments of glass themselves. Judges them beautiful enough for a huge canvas. But after the brick tumbles into the carved table, its rough corner scraping against the fine woodgrain, Stan is back. He peers at the paper tied to the brick, then through the windowpane's angular hole to see Elizabeth glaring back at him on the road. He's not sure what disturbs him more: that she threw a brick into his living room or that she refused to step on to his lawn to do it.

After another moment she walks back to her house and Stan goes to finish the ironing. Three shirts left and one of Judy's aprons too. Press, steam, fold; press, steam, fold ... he's got the knack of ironing since Judy has been gone. It takes just a few minutes before everything is in a warm tower on the sofa arm. Telling himself he has done well, Stan pads around the shards of glass to retrieve the brick. The elastic band has snapped so the paper falls easily into his hand.

It says just one word: LIAR.

Stan judges there isn't much point in fixing the window right now. Everyone can see through it, the breath of wind already wafting in, but maybe it should be that way. He's been hiding for fifteen years.

The shards are more of a problem – he can't work out where to start picking them up.

He's retrieving the dustpan and brush from below the

kitchen sink when a male voice calls to him. 'Stan?' It's strong and deep like a block of mahogany.

Harvey stands the other side of the window of spidery trails. His turquoise polo shirt looks brighter through the hole, as does his tanned face as he bends to see in.

'What a mess, eh?' Harvey says.

'Indeed.'

'Guess you want some help?' He glances at his huge gold watch.

'No thank you. I'll be fine.'

Harvey pushes the front door open anyway – Stan realising he didn't put the catch on – and walks into the living room where he lays a folder of papers on the coffee table, either not noticing the brick or not mentioning it.

'What a pain,' he says, gesturing to the window. 'I know a guy who'll do it cheaper than most.'

In the end it's Stan who picks each piece of glass from the carpet while Harvey watches. *Odd to have him right here*, Stan thinks. Before the May Ball he'd mostly seen the man out and about – buying rounds for friends in the pub or speeding past in his Audi Sport, puddles spluttered under wheels.

He got the impression other men in the village looked up to Harvey for his self-confidence, the way he never had crinkles in his shirts or apologised for being late. A part of Stan might have once been the same. But when Harvey married Deloris, he saw a different side to him, a more competitive side. In a recent pub quiz he'd fallen silent when his wife stood up to answer the world's highest capital city was, in fact, La Paz. It was as if the man considered himself upstaged, humiliated even. And when the twosome left, their linked hands looked too tight, smiles like those on deranged mannequins. Maybe the friction kept their connection alive? Stan knows that's how things are for some married couples.

Harvey now points to something shiny under the sofa that turns out to be a silver ring.

'You've got to buy your wife some nicer stuff,' he says, holding up the ring with its bulbous fake pearl.

Stan takes the ring from him and slips it inside his shirt pocket.

'I'm off to see Pete next door,' Harvey says when Stan has almost finished. 'A business idea.' He taps the side of his nose like it's his secret.

'I see.'

'Don't ask me, cos I can't tell you.'

'I see.'

Harvey leans towards him in a wave of peppery aftershave. 'I might be branching out. Too long with my dad.'

Seeing pores blotched with brown powder on the man's face, Stan pulls back. He's not sure whether it's kindness that Harvey doesn't mention his cross-dressing, or simply self-absorption. 'Why not.'

'You think I can?'

Stan gives an exaggerated smile, suddenly wanting the man gone. 'Why not.'

'Don't laugh at me,' Harvey says but still doesn't go. 'Starting a business takes real guts. And it's hard to live up to what people expect from you.'

Stan considers this for a minute. 'How true.'

That afternoon Stan walks up to the church. The sky is crackling with rolls of clouds that form a dense cover. Stan is relieved to pass no one on the high street except Rick, who he sees at a distance, walking his elderly greyhound on the far path of the village green.

Jim is kneeling at the second pew with his head dipped. Patches of blue and red light fall from the stained-glass window above and saturate the lines on his neck and his interlaced fingers. An hour ago Bobby, the newspaper boy, pushed the week's rag through Stan's letterbox and there on the front page was the headline, *Local Vicar Rapes Girl Four Times*.

'Thank you for coming to see me,' Jim says without turning.

Stan pauses from behind, the click of his last footstep still echoing from the stone floor. 'It's fine.' He sits down next to his friend. It's been years since he even stepped into a church – having lamented the stories of religious wars in Lebanon for so long – and regards the delicate carving of the pew. Recalls Elliot saying he might like the elaborate acorn and partridge by the organ, why didn't they see it together? How stupid that he'd said no.

'I suppose you must be disgusted,' says Jim plainly. He leans back on to the pew.

'Stories can have many different tellers.'

This makes Jim scowl. 'You don't need to sympathise with me. I'm not the victim here. You must have been horrified by that headline.'

Stan isn't sure he was. The man had been so gentle with him, with Elliot. Could an act, years ago, damage the layers of friendship so carefully sculpted?

Odd to think how they had first fallen into conversation. It was over a peony tree, which Judy had planted in their front garden without checking the growing conditions. *Quite difficult,* Jim commented on walking past, *but worth it for all the colours.* This was a few weeks after Jim moved to the village and it took Stan much longer to realise the man had no real garden of his own. By then they'd shared several cups of tea in Stan's kitchen and it felt too late to ask Jim – who spoke of his previous lawns, a lily pond and summer veranda for parties – exactly why he'd moved to a tiny house in Heathcote.

'I should have told you,' Jim says now. 'Admittance would have been something at least.' He rises, making Stan move to let him out. 'I only ever really mentioned my old life to Anna. When she didn't hate me it was such a relief, but I knew she was a rarity.' He scowls before regaining himself. 'So I never spoke of it again to anyone in the village.'

The two of them look at the collection of cushions Anna and Ruth stitched. They are spread across the church in the pews – over two dozen maybe, each one having required hours of patient needlework as rows of colours were added. Only one has a blemish, which Jim readily points out; it's a disciple's face with one eye at a lower angle giving it a wonky, farcical look.

They wind up outside by Ruth's grave. Since Anna went missing, flowers have piled up – some are wilting against the cellophane, others are in plastic pots, which seem sadder still, as if reconciled to last longer than the bouquets. One message – written on a plant pot label – says *Ruth's death was a tragic blow to the community*. The two men frown at each other but don't need to say it aloud: how has Anna's disappearance turned her mother's death into a tragedy?

'What will happen to you?' Stan asks as they head back inside, the clouds beginning to spit rain.

'I have the letter in the vestry,' Jim says. 'But I can't face the answer yet.'

'Can I help?'

The envelope is waiting on the top of the shelves, behind a

candlestick with a blunt top where the wick has been snapped. Jim glares at the rectangular paper until Stan picks it up himself.

'*You* look,' says Jim testily.

'*After some serious consideration, we have judged that it is God's will you continue your work as a lay reader. More than three years of dedication to St Katherine's has proven your commitment and competency in matters of faith. Although we cannot recommend further training to obtain your vicarhood, we hope that—*'

Refusing to believe his ears, Jim whisks the paper from Stan. His eyes move side to side as he scans, muttering to himself over and over.

'It has turned out fine,' Stan says and waits for him to lower the paper.

'I don't know.'

'This is good news, isn't it?'

Jim paces across the vestibule floor as he thinks manically out loud: he's not sure he'll stay in the village after all. He's heard from his daughter who suggested he might come to stay. What if he emigrated to France and learnt the language? Took up French cookery – he could open a restaurant? A small bistro somewhere quiet? Stan watches the paper that flaps from his clenched hand and eventually goes to his friend, putting his arms around him.

'I'm sorry,' says Jim, sinking on to his shoulders. 'It's just all so difficult.'

15

Stan lingers in front of the wardrobe in the spare bedroom. It's dusk, and through the gap in the blinds he sees the last colours of the sunset are quickly fading. The washing line is a dark string across the garden, bare of the dresses he has bought that really need cleaning but remain fusty in the wardrobe. Most are from charity shops in West London that he hasn't even tried on, worried they won't properly fit or, worse, make him look haggard – a freakish combination of features his eyes can't reconcile. It's only the velvet black dress that he's worn. His one splurge from a boutique in Paddington, him mesmerised by the back with its low-hanging folds of fabric. The lady had assumed it was for his wife and packaged it in layers of tissue paper with a ribbon bow, making Stan feel all the less comfortable to know he'd spent a day's wages. Money wasn't particularly tight now he was manager of the supermarket, but there were always things they would like: a weekend away or new trainers for Elliot.

When Judy asked what he was doing in London he said

buying more shingle for the next birdhouse. A stupid lie, he knew, and still she said nothing when he walked in with a shiny bag hooked over his wrist. She was never one for difficult questions.

But what do these clothes mean? He goes through the set of three drawers within the wardrobe. Since Judy and Elliot left he has been filling them with trinkets, again salvaged from charity shops he finds himself in more and more these days, thinking of the women who've left the things behind – the ivory hair clip with the broken clasp, the shell inside a sequinned purse. The handbag was a favourite. Originally from Harrods, the chain strap snapped off when it caught on the doorknob one afternoon. He's sure he laid the bag out on the dresser, meaning to fix the strap's broken links, but couldn't find it again the next day.

He knows these things are mere artifice – being a woman isn't all powders and spinning ballerinas in jewellery boxes – but feels they're important in a way he can't describe. He takes the fake pearl ring from his shirt pocket. Anna had run a finger over its bulbous shape on the anniversary of her mum's death. It was the end of May – almost four weeks after the ball – and, reminded of the date by Judy, Stan offered to light a candle with Anna. The two had grown close. Close in a way he'd never been with Judy who had her galas and her girlfriends, her brisk dismissals if he ever asked after her period pains. Child labour was done without him too. He wasn't allowed in the delivery room – it wasn't a place for men, Judy said.

But Anna was different: vulnerable in a way he found endearing. Stan suggested a small occasion with just the two of them. She could share a story or two about her mum? Or they could look through a photograph album? Although Anna had refused he turned up at her door anyway that evening, with a candle borrowed from their dining-room set.

'I have no matches,' Anna had said, conscious of the blotches around her eyes.

Standing uselessly in her kitchen, Stan grew frustrated that he couldn't make her talk to him. In the time since the ball he liked to imagine himself growing a soft layer of femininity. He had started to read nightly to Elliot, parts of *Pride and Prejudice* and even Angela Carter's *The Bloody Chamber*, which made his son's eyes widen. He had learnt to apply varnish to his woodcarvings and add ornamental features like an ivy border. Now he realises how meaningless these things were. The one person who knew about Corinne was incomprehensible to him. What did that say?

He had brought out the ring from the small bag he'd taken to carrying around with him. Anna said she liked it.

'Even though it's fake?' he asked.

She said it was hard to tell from a distance.

Stan came home feeling jittery, frustrated. He remembered Judy was at choir so went to the wardrobe to look through his new clothes. Until that evening he wasn't sure he ever intended to wear any of the dresses and skirts, finding and bringing them here seemed enough. But then he unzipped the black dress and laid it on one of the single beds before removing his jeans and shirt. The silk lining was cold on his stomach and the dress left his whole arms and upper back exposed.

He was struggling to fasten a catch at the side when the door opened.

Judy's choir book hit the carpet with a horrid thud. Her eyes went from him to the open wardrobe – the wardrobe he'd asked her to keep locked as Ruth's things were inside. Another lie.

'Elliot is downstairs,' was all she said before reaching for the choir book and shutting the door behind her.

Corinne. It'd be easy to say the name came from nowhere but in fact it was borrowed from Corinne Michelle West, the notorious Abstract Expressionist with her unapologetic slashes of black and browns, her refusal to marry. He'd studied her work at the Ruskin School of Art in the late sixties, filling whole canvases with layers of paint, wax and the ends of rolled cigarettes he collected from his acquaintances at the socialist club. The men's tendency to wear the Che Guevara berets and small round glasses grated on him, but he was also excited by the way they spoke of overthrowing governments, of the working man claiming his own power. Sometimes he'd speak during a discussion and a man named Lee would half-heartedly listen before releasing a stream of smoke through which the two men's eyes would meet.

On an evening near the end of the spring term he left his studio late for a drink at the dimly lit pub where they hung out, several streets beyond the university buildings and courtyards. No one he knew was inside yet so he waited by the fire exit where a vent released warm air to the street. Bleary-eyed from staring too long at the layers of paint, he kept blinking as a man approached from the other side of the road. His eyes didn't stop blinking as they struggled to make sense of what then happened: an arm hooked about his waist as he was carried forwards, *hello prince*, denim jacket rough, and them, him and Lee, stumbling down some basement steps. Then it was just the step railing – the wrought iron that thrust forwards, forwards, forwards until it didn't any more. For weeks that same railing was a solid rod across his dreams, across his canvases, that became covered in sludge browns with huge sections burnt away to nothing.

It was the smoke alarm going off that brought Judy to his dormitory room one afternoon a fortnight later. She was a fire marshal, as well as the tennis captain, the girl most likely—

'The girl most likely to do what?' he asked as she stood at his bedroom door.

'I don't know yet,' she said in her American accent. 'But whatever it is, it'll be great.'

When she asked why he was burning canvases in his dorm room and he had no explanation to offer, she said she'd need to contact the warden. It was her duty, she explained. But the next day she turned up again dressed in a cardigan and pink-striped dress and told him she fancied a cup of coffee.

Judy spoke too loudly whenever they went out. She insisted on having the full-price drinks and telling him about each point of her latest tennis match. She berated him for wearing the same flannel shirt that swamped him in its thick wool, for the stutter he'd developed on one particular phone conversation to the dean. But as the weeks passed Stan grew to like the way she was so orderly, so confident in the things she said and did. Even if she was only with him to annoy her parents back home, writing them long letters about his 'odd little communist persuasions', he allowed himself to curl up in the solid shape of her. Neither expected her to fall pregnant after a couple of fumbles – it was all so unaffecting to Stan as she climbed on top of him in his dormitory bed. The act on the basement steps seemed another thing entirely.

Eight months later he had given up his place at college and got a job at a petrol garage on the outskirts of Oxford. Judy attempted to complete her geography degree through distance learning, her scholarship dependent on meeting certain grades, but one day quit without explaining why. They were both too bewildered to talk about any of it and, besides, the rent on their bedsit was overdue. Since Judy was too ashamed to ask her dad for money, in the end Stan's parents let them move into their house an hour down the road. During the bus commute Stan tried not to think of the paintings he'd left beside a skip by the student union and instead concentrated on his new life of being a father. It wasn't all bad. His parents' house had a garage, unused most of the year except in winter when the car would be parked there. Having found a woodwork book in the local library, he taught himself techniques, things like whittling and how to use a coping saw. By the time Elliot was brought home from the hospital he had finished carving a crib and watched Judy lay the baby within its safe walls. Any spare weekends would then be spent modelling things from pine or ash he bought from the workshop in town: building blocks or a rudimentary marble run; a three-layer spice rack for the women's cooking. He liked taking a block of wood and chipping away pieces while his mind went blank, as if the thing was already formed inside and waiting to be revealed.

After finding Stan in the black dress Judy would leave the room if he dared bring it up. 'The neighbours might hear,' was all she hissed one afternoon. Instead they argued over the painting he bought on one of his London trips. It was only a print: Corinne Michelle West's 'Transfiguration'. Judy pointed out the cost wasn't the problem, more that the painting was wilfully difficult on the eye.

'Only because you're not used to it,' Stan said.

'Why should I get used to the ugly blue thing? It's just a painting.'

He paused to remember the line: 'Sometimes the smallest things take up the most room in your heart.'

She was furious at this. 'You and your intellectual snobbery!' she said and ran down the stairs to get Elliot ready for school.

He explained the words were from *Winnie-the-Pooh*, Elliot's favourite book as a little boy, but she was already too far gone to hear.

Now Stan closes the wardrobe doors for another day. The clothes need packing up, he thinks, but he isn't quite ready. Instead he goes downstairs to the living room and stares at the painting. His family is gone and it's still here. Surely that isn't right. A shard of glass catches his eye from the far edge of the carpet – it's so hard to find all the pieces. He retrieves the rowing boat painting from the cupboard under the stairs where it waits with its neat dabs of yellow and pink. A faux Impressionist style but without the sense of movement brought by a fast, skilled hand. This one is like a 'painting by numbers' artwork – his and Judy's life all over, he thinks as he takes down the abstract piece and sets this one in pride of place.

Afterwards he goes to phone Judy. No one picks up so he leaves a message on the machine: he's done some redecorating. Or rather the opposite. Their home has returned to how it was before.

The next morning Stan wakes three minutes before his alarm at seven a.m., like he does every day. Although he told Laura he wouldn't be taking any shifts for a while, the idea strikes him as brash. What else is he supposed to do before his family returns home?

He catches the usual bus from beside the village green and the same driver sticks out his lip to count the coins. Then it's back past his lane and on to the main road flanked by fields either side. Apart from the police car stationed at a lay-by, the scene is the usual: bales of hay, a line of cattle weighed down by udders heavy with milk.

As soon as he gets to the supermarket, however, things change. Under the harsh strip lighting Stan feels exposed. He hasn't put Vaseline on this morning but there could be a trace – a remaining smudge in the corner of his lips.

'I thought you weren't coming in,' Laura says from her desk in the back room. She must've heard what happened as she doesn't ask for any more of an explanation. Following several years of training by Stan she remains a keen employee who regularly works overtime to put her son through a plumbing apprenticeship. Now she lays down the stock report forms to watch Stan open his locker. 'You could do with a break, I expect,' she says uncertainly. 'Why don't you go home to lie down?'

Is that what this is to people? Stan thinks. *A sickness?*

When he doesn't say anything she follows him through the double doors and on to the shop floor. John Lennon's 'Borrowed Time' is playing as he does a check of the bread and rolls section. On a Tuesday morning they are often low after the WI prepares for their evening get-together.

'You don't need to do that,' Laura says more urgently now. 'Dave's just over by dairy.'

'I'd like to.'

Soon enough Stan is left alone to replenish the wholemeal rolls, then the baking aisle with its vast number of icing tubes and pots of sprinkles, all needing to be sorted by colour.

'Hullo, Stan.'

He turns to find Cynthia, her dressing gown wrapped tightly about her small frame. She carries a basket laden with candles, eggs, and icing sugar which she puts down to size him up. Since the Scotts' house was searched and nothing found, the neighbours have seemed ashamed of how they all gawped and expected the worst. Himself prickly to admit he joined them, Stan has since remembered the time Elliot came home with a plaster over his knee. Apparently Cynthia put it on after he came off his bike and said he should be more careful.

'I heard about you. Dressing up 'n' that.'

Stan continues to stack the shelves, turning each pot so the label faces forwards.

'I always liked nice clothing myself,' she says. 'Used to have hair I could sit on.'

He wants to move away but there are several layers of sprinkles left.

'You say you don't know what Anna was thinking that night,' Cynthia goes on in that gruff way of hers. 'Except you weren't *you*.'

Stan turns around.

'You were this ... whatever you call her.'

'C-Corinne?'

'All right, then. Her.'

Stan stares at the woman in her dressing gown. Her eyes are scrunched in focus.

'We're meant to do nice things for them we love, aren't we?' She gestures to the basket of cake ingredients.

'I suppose so.'

'Well, maybe you need to be her again, to remember summat. Even if you find it hard.'

259

Stan is too startled to respond. Seeing she'll get nothing more from him, Cynthia turns to the shelf. 'Right, I need some sugared almonds. They're his favourite.'

He stands paralysed for another second, then finds her a packet from the third shelf. 'I hope Ralph has a nice birthday,' he says.

'It's mine,' she replies. 'When I was a girl my dad would take me to the fairground but there's none of that now.' She gives a limp smile before carrying on with her shopping.

It'll be the last time, Stan tells himself. The silver hook catches the clasp on first attempt and he smooths the black dress over his sides as he goes through to see himself in the full-length bathroom mirror. Both other times he'd been overly aware of the spare velvet where his hips should be, how it puckers inwards for the breasts, but now it feels like his flesh has swollen over the course of the warm, humid day.

Stan feels the skirt glide about his legs as he goes to retrieve the pearl ring from the top drawer of the wardrobe and slides it on over the little finger of his left hand so it sits next to his silver wedding band. He urges himself not to feel guilty – tonight isn't about his marriage to Judy, it's about Anna. The lipstick is a deep red like pooled blood, and he angles it to his lips before deciding against putting some on. It feels like too much. Instead he slips down his left dress strap and begins to write. Curled chest hair tangles amongst the cloying pigment, preventing smooth lines, but the word over his heart is clear enough: Anna.

Sitting on the single bed as he did on the night of the eighteenth before seeing her, Stan tries to remember more. What if he did the same walk round to Anna's house? The same striding past the neighbours with the dark scarf around his head, waiting for Elsie's curtains to close before removing his sandals and running over the scrub land, thistles at his ankles.

But no, not now everyone knows it's him. The clothes are no longer a disguise but themselves the objects of scrutiny. He can't humiliate Judy even more than he already has, Elliot confused about the man who, all his fourteen tender years, he thought of as simply his dad.

Stan is lost for what to do. Still sitting on the bed, he wants to lie back and squeeze his eyes shut. To sleep all night and hope he never wakes. His thighs are starting to jostle though, a piercing sensation overtaking him. It works into his ears, then winds outwards across the room, forming huge circles that make him dizzy. An alarm has gone off, Stan realises, and struggles to the window. It's almost dark and his neighbours are out in the street, Elizabeth shouting something to Pete who follows behind with the pram. Keith from number twelve emerges in tracksuit bottoms, tapping a baseball bat over one palm.

Trying to undo the dress, Stan catches the lining in the zip. He can't find his trousers. And the alarm is screaming in his ears, telling him to get out. Who knows where the Fox might be or what he wants. He pulls up the long skirt so as not to trip on the stairs and in the darkness of his hallway, pauses by the front door. Through the stained glass he sees people are running past, carrying their weapons.

Stan fumbles with the latch before going to throw on the jacket left over the stairs. His fingers tremble. His legs too as he edges back to the door, still in his socks, then steps on to his front path. *I-I'm sorry Judy,* he stutters before taking a gulp and walking out into the night.

The crowds ahead are swarming towards the path beside number seven, across the scrubland to the next street. Stan sees Jim with Elsie and a younger woman dressed in dungarees. He follows them a few yards behind, the dress flowing from underneath the jacket.

The path soon reaches the side of Anna's house, then emerges on to the street. Here people group in huddles with hands clasped over ears. Is it Brian's alarm? The whirring is so loud it's disorienting.

It's with a sick inevitability that everyone turns to look at Stan. Someone tugs at her husband's arm. Although they must be saying things, their words are obliterated. Mouths work but it's all just mime.

Stan stands motionless and lets them look. The air is cold on his ankles, his socks damp under the hemline. He knows if they look hard enough however they'll also see the writing over his chest.

It's Jim who emerges to see him. He doesn't come too close but vaguely smiles, then takes a small glass bottle from his pocket and has a sip.

Then people turn back to the alarm.

'It's number twelve,' Mullins says, motioning to the Watkins' behind. A second later the alarm stops and they rub at their ears. 'Their central heating unit has been prised from the wall,' they hear the police officer tell Brian. 'Trying to get into the house through the utility, I expect. But looks like he was scared off.'

After glancing up and down the row of houses, Brian speaks to the crowd. 'Stay here for the time being, until we know what's what.' He then joins Mullins on his doorstep as the

Indian policeman heads further up the street, shining his torch into windows.

Now it's silent their ears seem hollow. No one says anything for a while as they look about, not knowing where to let their gazes settle. Stan wishes it'd rain, that a downpour would provide a watery layer between each of them, but there are only puddles reflecting exhausted faces.

Elsie is the first to speak. She goes to Beattie who's slumped in his wheelchair on their driveway, a few steps from where Brian talks to Mullins. 'A nice new dressing gown that,' she says in a strained voice, trying to sound cheerful as she taps him on the shoulder. The younger woman follows her and pays a similar compliment.

'This is Jane, my daughter,' Elsie tells Beattie, then – shuffling around – the rest of them too. They raise timid hands to wave although they're all too distracted to make conversation.

'Thought I should visit my mam,' the woman says in the gap that follows. 'I was on the phone to her the first time this man came to her house. All I heard was a bang and my mam disappeared. Thought I'd have a heart attack. Looks like I still might. What the hell does this person want?'

Minutes later the crowd stares at Harvey who's walking towards them in a polo shirt and chinos as if he's dressed for the occasion, though he stumbles down the pavement. Stan hadn't noticed Deloris already in the street a few steps away from the rest of the neighbours, her hair in a wet tangle about her shoulders.

'You could've made sure I was out the house too,' he slurs. 'Don't you give a damn?'

'I'm sorry, Harvey.' She touches him gently on the arm. 'I thought you'd already be out.'

Harvey jerks his face away and catches Stan's eye, then does a double take. 'What in Christ's name ...?'

It feels like Stan's worst imaginings are coming true, or at least those of his wife, as Harvey walks up to him. He's close enough that Stan can see the man's plucked eyebrows.

'Nice breasts,' says Harvey staring at his chest. 'Let's have a feel.'

'E-e-excuse me?'

'I guess I should cover up. Or you'll take me home to bed with you.'

Stan edges backwards.

Deloris weighs in. 'Oh, for God's sake.' She pushes between the two of them, her shoulders knocking into Stan as well as Harvey. 'What does it matter?' She spins round and they realise they're outside Anna's house. The hedge has dropped the last of its rose petals on the grass.

The three of them stand awkwardly before Harvey goes to speak to Pete.

Deloris glances down at Stan's socks, which protrude from the skirt, and frowns. 'Why would you want to be a woman?'

'I don't,' he says. 'Sometimes I just want to feel how another me could've been.' He wants to say more but isn't sure she is listening. Her eyes seem vacant, surrounded by shadows. 'How are you?' he asks her. They've never spoken before. Not a real conversation, anyway.

But she's distracted by a puddle, which she touches with her plimsoll. The ripples seem to disappoint her and she squints up to the roof tops and then higher still, looking for the moon.

Gupta eventually gives them the all-clear. 'Or,' he adds, 'at least as much as possible. If you hear anything, contact the station straight away.' Some people put up a fuss – how can they know for sure the Fox has gone? He says they can't and they walk away uneasily, reappraising each of the houses.

Gupta approaches Stan. 'Your living-room window was damaged earlier today, is that correct?'

'Yes.'

'I'd recommend you stay with a neighbour tonight.'

People give him a wide berth. 'It's fine,' Stan says. 'I have plenty of chipboard.'

He follows the group of neighbours back through the scrubland to Yardley Mews. It has started to rain at last and slashes of water soak his skirt until it sticks to his shivering legs.

Outside the living-room window he stops by the hole in the glass, a deeper cold penetrating as he tries to understand. No reflections obscure his view to the sofa or the coffee table. He steps forward and something cracks: angular sheets of glass have been leant against the wall. Someone has removed them to make the hole larger, large enough – in fact – to be climbed through.

Stan lets himself into the dark hallway. Damp earth scents the air. *Who is in here? And what do they want with him?* Pressing the light switch on he shudders as the walls jump up around him. His plates glow yellow by the kitchen sink and he stares at the speckled crumbs for answers. But he doesn't know what to make of the empty rooms upstairs, wondering if Elliot's sheets were creased before, his wardrobe slats at angles? After checking the final room he tells himself the house must be empty.

Even though he's still shivering in the dress, all Stan can then think to do is pour himself a glass of wine and walk back to the living room. The picture of the two sailing boats is still hanging on the wall but, as Stan leans closer, he sees a long strip has been torn through the middle.

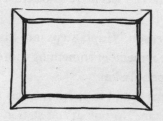

16

Stan sleeps upright in his chair and wakes early the next morning to daylight streaming through the window. Again he considers the rowing boat painting, the person who climbed into his living room to take a piece.

In the shower he watches the last smudge of lipstick come loose and slip down the plughole. Once his body is pale again he changes into jeans and a flannel shirt and hangs the dress back in the wardrobe, though he leaves on the pearl ring. He has to finish what he started the night before.

Gupta is tying up his shoelace when Stan reaches Glebe Crescent. He thanks him for checking all the houses after the alarm went off.

'Of course. It is my job,' the police officer says, standing up. 'Everything in order with your window?'

Stan considers telling him about the enlarged hole and the painting, but now, by Anna's house, is anxious to get inside. The police will not likely understand it anyway – the ripped artwork was specifically for him.

'I need to get into the house,' Stan says as he reaches for Anna's front gate. Orange tape has been plastered across the door but as far as he can see, there's no actual barrier. 'Can you let me inside?'

'What is your reason?' Gupta steps into his path.

'I think I might remember something more.'

'I shall ask for permission.'

As the man turns round to speak into his radio, his patient waiting irritates Stan. No one at the station is answering his call yet he continues to angle his ear to the receiver.

'Almost two weeks have passed since Anna went,' Stan says to him in a sudden burst. 'D-don't you think time might be running out?'

With Gupta following closely behind, Stan walks through the front door into the dingy hallway. He then cups his right hand over the pearl ring as he hesitates before the living room. The low ceiling beams hang as before, and he remembers stooping so the front of his dress fell forwards. He'd been embarrassed by the flapping material but Anna was overflowing with compliments, her voice high and breathy as she admired the velvet. *Is it crushed?*

On noticing the blotches around her eyes, how she breathed too heavily, Stan suggested they have some hot milk. He could always catch the next train to London.

In the galley kitchen Anna took a small pan and poured in milk from a china mug painted with primroses. Stan had been to the house twice before and the same disquieting feeling came over him. It was the bone china cups, each hanging from a thin slip of handle, the framed embroideries reading 'My Angel' meant to be so sweet but jutting from the walls. The smell too – like potpourri but gone stale, covered in dust.

'Please tell me what's wrong,' Stan had said on noticing her trembling hands. 'You've seen every part of me, let me help you.'

Anna shifted towards him, her eyes dipped so he saw just her heavy fringe. 'Your ring is so lovely,' she said.

As he let her feel the fake pearl Stan asked her again. She pulled away and excused herself, saying she needed to fetch something from upstairs. Whatever it was sent her feet clumping hurriedly along the landing. When she returned, however, she was gulping and spluttering, the orange dress crumpled at the hem where she'd wiped her tears. He assumed she'd become too upset to remember what she was getting but maybe she *had* carried something in those damp hands. Something bulky was it? A corner edge of paper between her fingers?

But the milk had gurgled and Stan was distracted by its thick skin as he removed the pan from the hob.

'I've burnt it,' she said, turning away for a minute. 'What a wretched girl I am.'

'It was my fault. Anna?'

There had been a long moment when he felt he was meant to do something, to say something. If only he had asked what she wanted to show him or at least seen where she'd put it. The pan rattled as she dropped it into the sink. 'Please, just leave me,' she'd cried and he shuffled away, consumed by a flurry of thoughts as the dress bunched around his legs.

He now runs a hand behind the china teapot and place mats left out; he pulls open each drawer of the Welsh dresser. Nothing seems unusual – there's only cutlery, cloth napkins, half-used candlesticks ...

Gupta appears in the doorway, 'It's time to leave.'

'Another minute?'

269

'Sorry, orders from above,' he says and motions to the front door.

Stan edges into the hallway, trying to stall for time. So few people would have been able to see inside the house since Anna went missing – only the police, most likely. This is his chance, yet here he is, already by the bannisters. Gupta's footsteps click behind. The table by the front door seems normal – a pile of post is accumulating – but a china bowl catches his eye. Leaning over he sees something cream: a single pearl. His heartbeat quickens. It's resting on top of a brooch which, on closer inspection, Stan finds is shaped like a dog.

'Many missing person cases are dismissed after this long,' Howard says. The reporter had been waiting outside Stan's front window, inspecting the remaining piece of glass that still hung from the frame, when Stan got home from Anna's. Now he stands by the kitchen counter in his grey suit and trainers.

'Anna's case is far from dismissed.' Stan stares through the window at his overgrown garden – the gooseberries will surely split open where not picked.

'Only if people can work out where she might be.'

'There are clues,' Stan says thinking aloud.

'Like what?'

'A dog-shaped brooch.'

Howard gives a fake smile and looks at his watch. 'What about her mother? How well did you know her? A piece on Ruth could help our readers understand and it *could* help us find Anna.'

Stan sighs as he turns from the window. 'I helped to sort out Ruth's possessions. Anna said she found it too hard to have them in the house.'

'And where are they now?'

They go to Stan's attic – Howard relishes each step up the ladder and doesn't mind the dust and cobwebs that stick to his trouser legs as he crouches in the small space, not high enough for either man to fully stand. But he's quickly disappointed to find just two cardboard boxes filled with clothes.

'What did you expect?' Stan asks, pulling tape off the first box. 'You realise I'm not the Fox?'

'Sadly yes.' He flicks behind his ear and catches the biro that flies out. 'Us reporters always expect the worst. Which is actually the best.' The pen waggles as he writes an imaginary headline. 'Too much of the time it's neither.'

A minute later Howard has gone, reassuring Stan he's used to seeing himself out.

Stan takes a handful of Ruth's clothing and lays it on a piece of plastic sheeting. Anna had already made a start on emptying Ruth's bedroom before she asked him. The bed was pulled apart, with marks across the floorboards, and the wallpaper scraped off in sections. She had lingered outside the bedroom door while Stan finished the job, turning every now and then to see her shiny eyes staring through the gap.

'The rug too,' she'd said. Her voice was unusually bossy and Stan only nodded. Then he yanked free the carpet, carried out the bed frame, and finally stripped off the remaining wallpaper.

'Are you sure about all of this?' he said, a fine mist of dust stuck to his sweating arms. It was two days after Judy had left for the airport with Elliot and what seemed like too much luggage for a summer trip. His head full of thoughts of when they'd be home again, Stan had simply followed Anna's orders and borrowed Jim's car to do a run to the skip. The only thing he resisted was getting rid of all of Ruth's things, insisting he parcel up two boxes to keep himself, in case Anna ever wanted them again.

Now he spreads them across the plastic sheet. He's spent so much time thinking of his own clothes this summer that he hasn't been up here to sort through these – some need to be folded in tissue paper to be protected from mildew, others are simply in need of a wash. Stan finds conkers in the pockets of a coat. A cotton handkerchief with 'J' embroidered on the edge, tucked inside the lining of the shawl Ruth always wore. He never knew shawls could have linings but it seems all her clothes have some sort of inner layer. A bulge hangs from a heavy wool cardigan but seems to have no entry point; Stan feels a rectangular shape like a wad of envelopes. There's just a tiny stitch a few inches above, which he scratches at with a nail till it breaks and a cotton end appears. Though at first it feels wrong to tug, the cotton quickly comes away from the seam and soon enough Stan has room to reach a hand down, while the other pushes up the letters so he can grasp a corner.

Stan finds each of the half-dozen envelopes is addressed to Anna. The handwriting is identical and postmarked from North Yorkshire, the first from January 1965.

Dear Anna,

I am all sorts of sorry for not saying goodbye. Christmas can be a tricky time for adults and I had to leave. Luckily there is plenty of work on the farm, my brother says. Too much, most mornings, especially with the frost! Lambs next month by the dozen. You could come play with them if your mother agrees ...

The next was postmarked two weeks later.

Dear Anna,

I understand you not replying to me. All I want to know
is that you are safe and well. The sweetest girl I know —
you can be again! Your mother doesn't mean to be that
way with you. Things got difficult with Ilene's departure
and although I know she is now up in heaven — the lucky
thing! — your mother couldn't overcome her grief. She
knows deep down none of it is your fault. It's no one's
fault Ilene slept too deeply that evening. I know your mum
gets cross and that's scary, but please don't worry.

And by February:

Anna! I still haven't heard from you. Please write me as
soon as you can. Your mum isn't answering phone calls or
letters either. Mary from next door was kind enough to
let me know the house is still in one piece, although she
hasn't seen either of you, not even in church. Why is
that? Please send me even just a single word so I can
get some sleep.

Stan lets the remaining envelopes fall to the floor with a
thud.

A cloud of flies breaks apart as Stan strides up the high street.
Around the corner he sees the stone wall of the church entrance. It's the only place he can think to go.

Jim is walking between headstones in his choir gown, which
he lifts to bend down. As Stan approaches along the pathway

he sees his friend is pulling weeds from various pots and decorative watering cans left beside stone engravings.

'Even when people are dead they still demand our attention,' Jim says, looking around.

Stan's legs jitter as he goes to Ruth's grave in the furthest section. The leaves from silver birches have blown on to her flat headstone and stuck to the polythene wrappings of gerberas and primroses.

His knees press into the wet grass as he leans forward, then begins to remove each bouquet.

'What are you doing?'

'Finding out.'

'Have some respect!'

Underneath a final rotting bunch of gerberas Stan sees the two angel ornaments. One is fine but the other is in two pieces.

'Who did that?' Jim asks, leaning over.

Stan retrieves the broken china from beside the grave and sees lichen has not yet grown across it. The inner surfaces are pure white, as though they've only recently been broken.

Glancing around, Stan wonders when Anna came here – in the last few days? That morning? Voices murmur from the church door. It's Sandra talking with Deloris, a cake stand under her arm. On seeing the two men they hurry over to the graveside.

'What's happened?' Sandra says, looking at the pieces of china in Stan's hand. 'Who did that?'

'I think it might have been Anna.'

'Excuse me?'

Three faces stare at him but Stan doesn't have time to explain. He needs room to think so walks along the pathway that runs towards the easterly part of the woods. Jim calls from behind – 'we'll alert the police' – and it's just Deloris who trails after him.

She says nothing as they reach the opening of the woods. The trees seem denser than usual, blocking out light so the shadowy floor obscures roots.

'Anna must be here somewhere,' he says, his eyes searching the layers of moss, the ivy twisting around branches.

Walking past him Deloris begins to call Anna's name. He joins in too, shouting loud enough that birds flap above. They holler in all directions like the trees themselves might answer. A minute later though it's obvious they need a plan so Stan catches his breath in a small clearing.

'A greyhound-shaped brooch,' he mutters to himself.

'Sorry?' The bracken stills as Deloris pauses, already yards beyond. 'You mean she's with Rick?'

Stan frowns before remembering the man's dog, the one he always walks around the village green. Anna had once told him it was such a nice animal, that she wished she could have one like that of her own.

Now Stan and Deloris are running towards the caravan site. They charge through the nettles, through bindweed, which sticks to their thighs but doesn't slow them down. Although Stan leads for a few minutes, Deloris soon overtakes again. As the sky rumbles and she tugs up her anorak hood, it's as though she's been waiting for this moment all her life. Stan struggles to keep up as she makes her way past banks of mud, plimsolls leaping over puddles and through brambles.

'Why would she be with Rick, though?' she calls back to him.

'Maybe he's the Fox,' Stan breathes. 'I honestly don't know.'

The thought of Anna with Rick spurs her on and she attacks the ground even faster than before. Stan follows the swishing sound of her arms in the anorak but several times looks around to see just dark green in vast layers of moss and tree branches merging together as they shake in the wind. The rain is picking up and everything is colliding, the ground slipping away from his feet. His breaths become ragged and by the time he reaches the caravan site he's soaked through.

He finds Deloris waiting by the side entrance where a rusted metal sign reads: *Rick's Caravan Park. Beware of the Dog.* A beech hedge has grown around a line of barbed wire. On the other side the ground levels out and trees give way to bushy grass. The sound of cars can be heard beyond, but not for another quarter of a mile. Even as Stan squints he can't see much ahead apart from more blurred green in the driving rain.

The two of them pass a mud track leading to the site but take the more direct route over banks of grass and ragwort.

Turning a corner they see a line of six or seven caravans either side of a field, then a mobile building at the end next to a wooden structure. A solitary picnic table is covered with two sodden paper cups. The rest of the land is deserted.

'Anna!' Deloris shouts and throws her fists against the first caravan door. It rattles but doesn't open, the windows remain dark.

Stan heads for the mobile building at the end. His only real interaction with Rick has been him whistling at Judy in the Crown a couple of times. A leering smile full of chipped teeth and fillings. He hadn't said anything to the large man who towered over the other punters at the bar. Now Stan strides forwards, using his fists to wipe rain from his eyes. Outside the rectangular building is a yellow Walls' ice cream sign, dented in the middle, and another old picnic table.

'R-r-ick?' Stan says. The door's window is cloudy, a faint

crackle of radio behind. Stan fills his lungs. 'RICK!'

A thud is followed by the sound of unlocking. The door opens and Rick stands in his oil-smeared overalls.

'What do you want?'

'We're looking for Anna.'

'Who's "we"?' Rick looks behind him. 'Jesus, it's Dolly for a wet anorak competition.'

'Just tell us where she is,' Deloris says, glowering.

A purple bruise mottles his nose. 'And why should I do that?'

As Deloris starts to shout, Stan knows the noise should be coming from him too. He should be fuming, waving arms around. Except he's not. He's shrinking further into himself, just like that evening on the basement steps. It's easier to focus on material objects. The picnic table has been skilfully put together. These cheap woodworks never get much respect yet require the same careful joinery, the precise shaving.

'Not my fault she's got emotional problems,' he hears Rick say. At this something vibrates deep in Stan. His eyes still on the wood, he grips the seat with both hands and yanks the table into the air. Brown rushes up above him, the damp wood spongy at his fingers, and he throws it to the floor where its legs come apart.

'What are you doing?' Rick shouts, eyes bulging.

'Tell us when you last saw Anna,' Stan says.

'Last week maybe.' Rick gives an awkward shrug. 'I was just giving her space to get her head together.'

Stan and Deloris turn to the caravans. The rain is still falling heavily, so even if they had occupants, no one would be out.

'You can't search my place,' Rick yells from behind.

'Are you serious?' Deloris whips round and her anorak flaps. 'I'll ring the police.'

As he says it, they see movement to the right through the beech hedge. A minute later Brian emerges in his police uniform. He holds something up as he walks towards Rick.

'I have a warrant to search this entire site,' he says.

Rick follows a distance behind while the three of them head towards another caravan. Brian gives a sharp knock and then, when silence follows, opens the door: nothing but a fold-up table and the smell of rot.

'Why did you come here?' Stan asks as they walk to the next one.

'I knew Anna worked in the carpet factory to save money but she didn't make much. So I traced her bank records to May 1978 and saw she took out four pounds. The next week Rick added four pounds to his account.'

'But no one knew she had a caravan?' Deloris says, following.

'I guess not.'

Rick ambles up behind. 'Like I said, she's not here.'

Deloris runs to the next caravan. The door opens a crack.

'Have you seen a blonde woman pass by here?' Deloris asks the occupant.

'Huh?'

'Or heard a scream? Any unusual sounds?'

The door opens further and the rest of them see a middle-aged woman with a plastic rain cap over her head. 'No, I ain't. But it's too overgrown to see much over that way.' She gestures beyond the mobile building where the hedge competes with high-growing brambles. 'Too much rain.'

'What's back there?'

'The owner said it's full of barbed wire. We've stuck inside mostly.' The woman peers over Deloris's head to see Rick. 'Found your dog yet?'

Stan is the first to run past the mobile container. There's no obvious opening to the coarse thicket of brambles and thorns that spear the sides of his shirt. A thrashing behind starts as Brian uses his truncheon to clear a path. Past the initial hedgerow the shrubs are less dense before the land dips low and becomes wet. Stan slips on an upturned root and is propelled forwards, landing with a dull thump on his shoulder.

'Are you all right?' asks Deloris.

He pushes himself up and tries to blink away the spots. The hill continues down to a boggy expanse of pooled mud.

'Where to?' Brian puffs out his cheeks.

The only sound is them taking ragged breaths. Then animal yelps. A greyhound? To reach it they have to run down into the thick bog and up the other side, around a rotten bark.

'Is this even part of the woods?' asks Deloris.

'It must be Rick's land but I didn't realise it went back this far.' Brian overtakes and leads them doggedly another couple of minutes. Eventually a shape emerges through the rain: a boxed caravan. It's not like the others with their curved edges but one from the 1970s, rust browning each corner. Branches enclose it from all three sides and hang over the far end.

Once within a few feet they see a china bowl is in front of one of its flat wheels. A dog bowl, Stan thinks, seeing the water inside is free of leaves, recently changed.

'You go first,' Deloris says as she stops in the mud. Brian passes several sets of footprints that line the edges of a cloudy pool and stops in front of the caravan door. A set of navy-blue curtains is drawn over the window.

Stan waits next to Deloris, trying to quell his nausea. He watches Brian go to speak into his radio then decide against it and slowly pull on the handle. After a metallic creak, the door opens and Stan can only see darkness beyond. Brian hovers in front, saying nothing.

'Is she there?' asks Deloris.

Brian's head falls. 'Oh.'

'What?'

Stan follows Deloris to the door and they peer inside at the single bed, the tiny sink with a pipe unconnected at the bottom, then the set of shelves at the other end. 'It's empty,' she says, stepping in to yank open a cupboard beneath the bed. Nothing is in there except a tin of petrol and a local *Gazette* from two days ago.

Brian takes a few paces back and begins to scream at himself in frustration, a boyish sound that Elliot might make. Seeing Deloris go after him, Stan steps inside the caravan.

A blue light is cast on everything from the curtains. The single bed is uncovered so he can see the 1970s floral print, now faded with patches missing from the foam. A patchwork quilt has been folded at the end.

Stan is conscious of the rainwater dripping from him. Although the caravan has a strong smell of mildew, there's something careful about how the mat is placed on the floor, how the chain is wrapped around the tap that gave its last drop long ago.

On the set of shelves there's an almost-finished bag of peanuts, three cans without labels and a tin opener. A plastic bottle is filled with water. The only thing of value is the pocket Bible that rests on top of a red square tin decorated with pictures of shortbread biscuits. Stan opens the Bible to see 'A. Blake' written neatly in the front cover. Many passages are underlined, some with notes in the margin, but Stan is instead drawn to the tin. Gently picking it up he feels its weight for a second. He then slowly draws off the lid to see the contents: a glass stopper that looks like it belongs to a perfume bottle; a baby's rattle; something balled which he realises is a single lace glove.

Stan brings the box closer to the light, though not too close so rain falls on it. He can tell these things have been well cared for. A cassette of *Salem's Lot* still has its tape tightly wound. The postcard still has neat corners. *Dear Mum, happy times in Cornwall. I found you some unusual geranium seeds. How's the new vicar? Best, Jane.*

There's also a key, the crinkled foil of a milk bottle top, a teabag that smells like ginger, and a pot of medical skin cream. And – curled around the outer edge – a strip of the rowing boat painting.

But it's the small, framed embroidery at the bottom of the box that Stan is most surprised by.

My Angel is written in yellow cross-stitch, then:

Ilene Blake

2 September–6 December, 1964

Thinking of the other embroideries he saw at the Blakes', Stan knows he assumed the same thing most neighbours would: that the needlework was for Anna. Instead they served as constant reminders of her little sister.

'I'm going higher to get a signal,' Brian says outside.

His breathing slows as Stan makes sense of it all. He remembers the funeral for Ilene – Ruth hunched over the tiny coffin that was almost covered by the white roses with leaves curling across its edges. Seven-year-old Anna wasn't allowed in the front pew and afterwards her mother had shouted when she asked for a shortbread biscuit. A month later Robert left and the house's curtains were drawn. The years passed and Anna was always a figure at her mother's side, carrying the shopping bags or picking up a prescription. Stan heard villagers say such nice things about the cushions they made for church, *the two must spend hours on each one; they must barely leave the house!* Like others, he hardly spoke to Ruth apart from the odd conversation on the pavement. She wasn't a rude woman, only terse, as though she had somewhere else to be. Even towards the end, as she became ill, no one knew what was wrong with her. Everything was left to Anna.

Once more Stan thinks back to the last evening he saw her: Anna in the kitchen with arms hugged to her chest. A slip of paper between her fingers? At last he remembers what was in her hands: an envelope. The handwriting was the same as he'd seen in her dad's letters – she must have uncovered another stash not long before he'd arrived, must have wanted to tell him but not been able to find the words. Over twenty years of thinking her dad had left without an explanation, not wanting to ever see her again. Anna must've been so confused, so angry ...

The caravan tilts as Deloris steps inside, water dribbling from her mac to the floor. She picks up the quilt to hug it to her. A pillow lies beneath. It's covered in many stitches, like the other tapestries, though these are even finer to allow for the delicate fabric.

'How did Ruth die?' Deloris asks.

'She stopped breathing.'

Her face goes pale. 'Do you think ...'

Stan nods. 'I think Anna couldn't take it any more.'

A noise starts up close by and they freeze. Deloris lowers the cushion, her mouth dropping open.

The noise comes again: a slow squelch.

'Anna?' Stan whispers. *Squelch, squelch.* He leans forward to open the door, but it's just the dog pawing in the wet ground. Its rib cage shows against wet fur.

Deloris steps to the door to look out with him. 'So where is she?'

17

Deloris steps out of the caravan. She doesn't know where to go, only turns her hands upwards as if trying to catch the rain. The water slides from her palms, joining the lashes that beat at the wet ground to form brown spikes. Then Stan stoops under the door and closes it behind him. He speaks with pointed elbows. The velvet dress is gone and his usual plaid shirt sticks to his chest, smeared with soil. He is explaining something to Deloris.

The most southeastern edge of the woods can be surprisingly noisy. People might think that away from the village it'll be all breezes blowing silently through the grass, the odd bird call at sunrise. But there are sounds throughout the night, crows screeching among the branches, thistles that rise up in tangles around the barbed wire. More than once she has become disoriented on her way back, everything dark till a pair of eyes shine through the mist. It's the forgotten part of the woods – technically part of Rick's caravan park – though even before that it was given up on. A shame, really. All land is God's, as her mother wrote in a letter to the Ordnance Survey office after seeing the patch left without markings on a map.

A thorn presses into Anna's thigh as she peers down again. Deloris is pacing about – or at least trying to in her plimsolls weighed with mud. She throws her head up to the sky, eyes tightly shut amid her pale face. Too pale, her sunbathing days over. As Stan walks to her, Deloris's eyes open again. Anna falls to the bracken, which cracks and splinters around her. Enough, she thinks. She promised herself no more watching.

So she crawls backwards and, staying low, heads for the thicker vegetation where the mushrooms wait in their light and spongy huddles. Her appetite gone with the thought of what she must do, she continues round the corner to where the stream endlessly chugs its brown water.

Anna lets her skirt catch on the thorns as she passes. It doesn't matter any more and it even makes her smile to think small parts of her will be left throughout the woods.

As the ground becomes firmer underfoot, she stops to look around at the silver birch trees, their trunks pale as bone in the evening gloom. Maybe there's still a way to escape this person she's become?

For weeks she has tried to resist, even moving to the caravan to stop herself slipping into houses. Still she was drawn back.

Her mother was right: she is a wretched creature. Even at seven years old she was causing pain.

Over the years she has tried to pinpoint what she might have done wrong. That December evening she was hanging glass bells on the Christmas tree her dad had brought home, the smell of shortbread still in the air. Was it when an ornament slipped from her fingers and smashed against the floor? Was that the moment Ilene stopped breathing? Or maybe it was a minute *later when her mother couldn't find the dustpan and brush, looking in the various cupboards while her baby sister twisted on to her belly.*

There was no way of knowing for sure. All her mother said was she was a spoilt devil of a child. Then only the weakest light fell through cracks in the curtains, Christmas was nothing more than a prayer at the dinner table. In January, with a fresh scattering of snow, Anna and her mother sang hymns together for the first time in weeks but came home to find her dad's suitcase by the door. He can't forgive you, her mother later sobbed.

Years passed and no amount of church sermons or cooked dinners or cross-stitched cushions could make up for what Anna did. She learnt to pass silently around the house lest her mother complain. To ignore the looks from Brian who surely couldn't actually like her, not if he came close and sensed her poison that curdled deep within.

The same with Harvey. An evening of smiling across at the boy who acted so tough but drank lemonade with her, who was surprised when she kissed him and later asked if they could go out again. Her mother was watching from the doorway. He's in it for a dare, she said, didn't you see him flinch?

Of course there were nice moments too. Needlework cushions piled up in their hallway and her mother saying she was proud of her. Saying yes, she should go to Kenya to continue the project, although – weeks later – tearing up Anna's passport application. 'We need each other,' she said.

For a time Anna agreed the two of them must stick together. It became too difficult though. The thrown plates, the grasp that left marks around her arms and never anyone she could tell.

Although she tried for most of her life, in the end it was over so quickly. A cushion was all it took.

Afterwards Anna picked up the rest of her dad's letters from below the floorboards and went to call for a neighbour. The next day she found herself removing the paintings in her mother's room, emptying drawers, then stripping away the wallpaper ... Ridding herself of the woman who claimed so much of her life and soul. At least it was over, she thought.

But at the funeral a blockage remained between her and everyone else. She tried to talk but the words sounded wrong. People were uncomfortable and turned away, or else she did, struck by the look on their face. Let them go back to their homes, she thought, to their families and children with podgy limbs side by side in the bath, the smell of roast chicken, matching dents left in the sofa.

The first time was a mistake. A trip to thank Elsie for letting her help with the jumble sale; she'd heard the cheery voice she used only to speak to her daughter. Then, through a slip of open door, Anna saw her crockery mixing bowl and fridge covered in postcards.

It went on, though.

Sometimes she would lie on the floorboards to feel the vibrations of a television below, would pore over entire photograph albums while neighbours were at work.

Of course it was wrong to take their things. She only wanted to hold them close to her. Stan's rowing boat painting that he decided not to hang as if that might help mend his marriage; the home videotape Jim tried desperately to forget; Beattie's trophies that haunted him more than horror stories ever would. As for Deloris, her friend never quite grasped how important a family could be. She only wanted them to open their eyes. Some of the people she loved best, even if they never really knew who she was.

But her dropped glove became a crime scene. And now

newspapers talk of a sexual deviant, camping trips cancelled, children too frightened to ride their bikes in the street. She hears the villagers' words: like an animal, they say, but with hands to pick your locks. And shallow breaths to hide beneath your bed then wait for the first creak of mattress.

They're not really describing her, are they? A sweet girl, people always said. The kind that wouldn't say boo to a goose. But she knows people can be many different things: a sweet girl, a home intruder; a churchgoer, a scrawler of paint on bedroom walls; someone who leaves clues, too – a brooch carved like a greyhound, even if no one understood that it meant deep behind the caravan park where only animals belong.

Despite herself, she begins to run. The path is narrowing and brambles catch at her skirt, her skin. Rain pricks at pools of water in the potted earth, sliding under her ankles. Is that a face reflected in the dark surfaces? A snuffle in the bracken?

She lets out a scream but muffles it with her hand. Hot breath on her palm.

It's too late. Now everyone knows.

The oak is waiting, the rope covered by bracken around the tree roots. Anna scrabbles to untangle it from the wet layers.

Voices are speaking close by, a radio crackles somewhere amid the bushes.

She throws the rope over the branch and it slides off. So she goes again, fumbling, so tired.

Another voice comes from around the corner.

Surely they hear the snapping of twigs as she scrambles up the trunk and twists around to lower herself on to the thick branch, staying close to the base to retie the knot?

They must hear her muffled breaths as she pulls the rope over her head.

A calm sinks through her, enough to sit for a moment, to look out towards the village and the people coming for her.

All she can think is 'sorry', but maybe they'll be sorry too?

A face appears on the pathway as she pushes from the branch, as the air whips through her dress ...

Harvey sees something move ahead. He's been out looking for Deloris who the Braithwaites saw head in this direction. He was going to ask if she wants to go to his parents' for dinner. Pork chops, he tells himself as the orange shape ahead slowly gains detail: floral print ground with mud beside a limp arm, two shoes with their soles coming away. The body twists, the rope creaking, and he sees Anna's face. Her neck is at an odd angle, her eyes open and unblinking. Staring right at him.

'Jesus!' He runs to her and grabs her legs. He pushes his shoulders beneath her knees as if they're children again, playing a game. Her skin is still warm, the mud on her dress not yet dried to flakes.

'Help!' he screams from a rough throat. 'Help us, somebody!'

A radio crackles, nimble footsteps sound, and Brian's police boots are soon on the path in front.

'Here,' he breathes. Some of the weight is relieved from Harvey's shoulders as the two men crouch side by side, Anna's limp body on top.

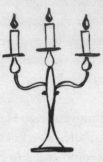

18

After Gupta arrives with Jackson, they lay Anna on the ground. Her usually large cheeks now sink inwards. Harvey kneels over her and brushes away the overgrown fringe that's matted with dirt. Anna's eyes have closed on their own – or had they already been that way when he found her?

'Careful,' Jackson tells him.

'Of course I am.'

'We still need to examine the body.'

The words are like punches at his gut. *The body.* He presses two fingers under her jaw like they do in the films. No pulse. The warmth is draining too.

He takes off his leather jacket to drape over her, though it doesn't go with her dress. It's all he can think to do as the police shuffle around behind with their radio reports. 'Time of death: six forty-five on the evening of Tuesday the third of July. Cause of death … pending inquiry.'

Harvey clamps his teeth. How could she have done this, the girl who once shared his lemonade, who kissed him on the lips with a fierceness that left him stunned?

The ambulance men turn up some minutes later. After their routine checks, they strap Anna on a stretcher and prepare the van. Harvey holds the door for them even though it's unnecessary. He's merely in the way.

A few steps into the undergrowth Brian turns his back to them all, the heel of his hands pressed to his face. Jackson trudges up to him.

'It isn't your fault, McPherson. You did everything you were supposed to.'

Through the trees Deloris sees the badge of Brian's cap shine. The weak sunshine doesn't seem right on him or anyone. She runs past to where Anna is being loaded into the ambulance.

'Some space, miss, please,' the man tells her.

'I just want to see my friend.' They pause and Deloris steps from the path of sunlight to let its rays fall on Anna's hair. For a second it's golden.

Jim prepares the church for an impromptu service. He has heard the news from Michael who, after walking around in a daze, now sits on the front pew, flicking through a prayer book. 'The binding is pathetic,' he mutters.

Dressed in a freshly ironed gown that falls around him, Jim lights the candles along the table, then those on the sill beneath the stained-glass window. There should be more – hundreds, even – but all he has are the two boxes from the vestry.

Villagers are starting to arrive. He only told Sandra, but now all sorts of people are taking seats in the pews, some commenting on how they should go to service more often. Harvey arrives arm in arm with Deloris, followed by Stan and another dozen people. Soon the pew is filled up around Michael who puts the prayer book on his knee to speak to the Morgans who have the same dull-eyed expression as always. Some men have come straight from the office and have briefcases tucked beside their feet. Elizabeth arrives with mascara smudged around her eyes, Pete behind, pushing the pram. 'It's almost dinner time, but we can feed Anna later,' he says. 'This is more important.'

'Anna?' Elsie says from her place squashed in the middle of the third aisle.

'We hadn't managed to agree on a name,' explains Pete, 'so we thought this might be nice.'

Once everyone is settled Jim begins. Rather than stand in the shadow of the pulpit he remains on the carpet between the aisles.

'Let's take this time to remember the woman who lived among us for so many years. Who listened so attentively to many of us, yet whose own words often remained unsaid – maybe because Anna couldn't find them within herself; maybe because we didn't take enough time to hear them.'

Stan sits near the back, beside the organ. His stutter was too bad to speak to Mary on the way into church. Hearing Jim speak of Anna's short twenty-seven years, he lets himself buckle forwards, his teeth scraping against the trouser fabric over his knees ...

Even after Jim finishes with a solemn prayer, people still don't want to leave. Jim sits on the step leading to the altar.

'It'd be like accepting she's gone,' someone says.

In the gap that follows Mary begins, 'I remember Ruth's funeral, so I do.'

People murmur they do too.

'It was a nice occasion, wasn't it? A saintly woman.'

Again a murmuring assent but Stan pipes up. 'No,' he says, finding his voice. 'Sh-she was many things but she wasn't saintly.'

Heads turn as they wait for him to say more but he falls silent again.

Instead people tell stories about Anna.

'She played in the road outside my house,' says an old woman. 'And she was so sweet with her baby sister, always tying ribbons around her pram. Such a shame what happened.'

'Then she were parcelled off to religious school. Do you remember Ruth behind the wheel?'

'I'd be scared to take the bins in, the look of menace in her face.'

Not all the stories fit and people quibble over details but it doesn't seem to matter.

'We can all agree she tended to her mum for that many years; she listened to us; she helped our church. Surely that can't be cancelled out by any upset she's caused the village these past weeks?'

Most shake their heads – no it can't.

Sandra tears some wafers into a basket. 'On this church camping trip,' she says, passing the basket around for them all to have a piece, 'Anna said she'd go on holiday in those woods one day and we laughed, said she wasn't much of a traveller. Yet she almost went to Africa, didn't she? Only she didn't want to leave her mother ...'

Not content with the dry bread, people drift home, mumbling about dinner. Harvey gets up and tells Deloris to stay if she wants. She looks at him blankly and they say nothing more.

Then just a few of them are left: Stan, Jim, Brian and Deloris. Brian shakes his head as he rises and walks to the stained-glass window. 'She was just lonely, wasn't she?' he says. 'All she wanted was the intimacy of being part of a family.'

'And some attention.' Jim goes to put out the candles and they realise how dark it's got outside. 'To go into people's houses like that ... She must've known we all thought she'd been abducted. She let us think that.' He cups the final flame and blows away the smoke.

Stan isn't sure. To him Anna seemed frustrated at how blind they were to her, and to themselves as well. For years she observed them all, even before slipping into their homes. He doesn't say this out loud, though. It's something people need to figure out for themselves.

Instead he helps Jim to collect up the prayer books. As he passes Deloris he puts a hand on her shoulder but she doesn't move.

It's only as they're all leaving that she speaks. Stan is wondering aloud what to bury Anna in. Surely some different clothes? Her orange dress was damaged and, besides, her mother made it.

'That doesn't mean she wouldn't want it,' Deloris says, walking out past the men. 'Family relationships can be tough, but it doesn't mean everything is lost.'

19

Two weeks later school has broken up for the summer. Bikes once again rattle past windows and deckchairs dent lawns. It's still wet but slowly drying out. The weatherman says August might even have some proper sunshine.

On the Saturday afternoon the cake fair fills half a dozen stands across the village green. Sandra spreads doilies over her own table, which she's positioned right at the entrance. 'This event *was* my idea,' she tells Elsie who sniffs at the courgette loaf wrapped in cling film. 'All proceeds go to the church on Anna's behalf.'

Elsie picks up a paper plate, heavy with carrot cake.

'Anna's favourite,' Sandra tells her.

'Was it?'

'Possibly. I'm not altogether sure.'

The afternoon is slow to attract visitors who hover by the playground while children queue for the slide. Once the tombola starts, though, a crowd gathers as Michael calls out the numbers. Sandra has insisted he sell the tickets and, while elderly women and kids each come to collect their prize, he keeps glancing at his wife. The last week has seen them argue more than in their whole marriage: mostly it's over Harvey's childhood – Sandra insisting he was spoilt, Michael saying that's hardly his fault, he only wanted the boy to have all the opportunities in life he never had. By the Wednesday he was sleep deprived and had his first sick day from the factory in fifteen years. The two of them spent most of the afternoon drinking wine and watching a soap about some American family of sisters. Neither of them can wait for the next episode.

After the last tombola prize is collected, Harvey ambles up to his dad.

'I need Mum too.'

Hearing her name Sandra cocks a head and gestures them over to her stall.

Harvey swigs from his bottle of beer before telling them he plans to start his own business in importing liquors.

'Liquors?' says Michael. 'You don't know the first thing. It's not just about drinking them.'

'Let him speak,' says Sandra.

Harvey explains how it's time to go it alone, and Pete might be interested in helping him. Since he was eighteen his dad has given him everything, stuck up for him when employees called him overpaid, shown him how much can be achieved in life. 'But it's time to make you properly proud, Dad.'

Michael scratches above his belt. 'I bet you'll be needing to borrow a lump sum?'

'No, I've saved myself.'

At this Michael is perturbed. 'You have? Clearly I pay you too much.'

'Good for you, Harvey,' Sandra says with a smile for her son.

'I think that's a wonderful decision.' The two men continue to bicker and so she folds a napkin around a biscuit to go enjoy on her own.

No one mentions that Deloris isn't at the cake fair. She left Harvey's house a couple of days earlier with her old duffel bag slung over one shoulder. He didn't ask where she was going; the football match had just started and, besides, he has her letter on the kitchen worktop. Men don't read love letters he'd told himself as he carried the envelope to the dustbin, then put it back where it was. Maybe later, in bed, when he knows the doorbell won't ring.

Now, further down the high street, Deloris is sprawled out on Brian's sofa. His old T-shirt has the A-Team on it, emblazoned across her chest. Brian is upstairs talking with Beattie about some shopping trip they'll take. She might go with them to Aylesbury – the weather isn't bad and she could use some fresh air. The last days have been spent walking in the woods or with Brian, curled up together on his sofa. She went to see Sandra the day before she left Harvey's and thanked her for worrying.

'Of course I did. I still do,' Sandra said in her frilled rubber gloves. 'If you ever want to come back and see me ...'

'You guessed that I'm leaving:'

'This village was never really your home, was it?'

A headache still throbs in Deloris's head from crying; it's like the tears just won't stop. It's not just Anna, though. It's something else she has to do.

'It's time for me to go,' Deloris now tells Brian as he walks into the living room.

'No.' His chest sinks beneath his dressing gown. 'Really?'

Without letting herself begin to cry again, she goes upstairs to pack together her few things. 'Don't you need me to get more of your stuff from Harvey's?' asks Brian.

The duffel bag is one she used for school. Since the zip is broken, she ties the arms together with her silk scarf.

'No thanks. I don't need all those dresses.' Inside the bag the perfume bottle clinks against a book. Tucked inside its cover is the photograph of Deloris by the swimming pool with her dad, unfolded so he is next to her. She took a picture of her and Harvey too; not from their wedding day, but when they first met, them both looking so young at a discotheque in Soho.

At the door Brian pulls her to him. 'Sure you won't stay with me?' Her hair catches between their lips as he goes in for a kiss. 'The last two days have been the best of my life.'

'I'm glad.'

'Where did you say you were going again?'

Deloris shrugs. 'I'm not exactly sure, but first I need to visit my dad.'

Smiling to himself, Brian undoes the scarf from her bag and goes to tie it around her head.

'No, that's dumb,' she says.

'Oh, go on.'

'OK.' She laughs that same wry chuckle and he beams back at her.

Deloris calls goodbye to Beattie upstairs and hears him switch off a tape. Then she gives Brian a final kiss on the forehead and, before changing her mind, walks outside and up the street. The day is clearing and a lawnmower hums in the distance. At Anna's house she pauses at the front gate. A for sale sign is already up.

'You were right,' she says out loud, thinking of Anna staring at her gleaming kitchen with the Magimix and gadgets. Then the photo left out in the kitchen – not about her bikini at all, but her dad folded over; and her grandma's old-fashioned lavender scent. 'I should have got to know you better.'

She takes a last glance before hurrying to catch her train. Sharon has promised to meet her at the Croydon grocers so they can buy ingredients for a special home-cooked dinner: fish, chips and mushy peas.

Dropping into the station, Brian shyly thanks Jackson for her work. An untouched Victoria sponge waits on the side. Mullins is there too, sitting at the computer, but Gupta has already left.

'His next job,' Jackson says, seeing Brian stare at the empty coat peg.

'Do the honours, won't you?' She gestures at the cake. 'We've got some time before we need to get back to Eddlesborough.'

The three of them each enjoy a slice and look over a collection of drawings found under Anna's mattress when the house was cleared out: a colourful rendering of a home with a pink roof and striped door; two stick figures titled 'Me' and 'Mum' with their arms linked.

Afterwards Brian is careful not to smudge icing sugar on their corners. He asks Mullins to open a plastic folder for him to slide them inside, then goes home to see his brother.

Across the scrubland at Yardley Mews, Jim is packing up boxes before he returns to Guildford later that afternoon. Even if he goes back to work in insurance, he won't be able to afford much on his own but then his years in Heathcote have proved he doesn't need a lot. Since leaving he hasn't returned to the village of Ripley – a few miles from where Sarah's parents live – but the years have passed and wounds healed, he hopes. Either way he needs to face up to his past, to forgive himself. Isn't that what Anna was telling him when she played his tape? He takes a crucifix off the wall and adds it to his final box.

He considers going to say goodbye to the vicarage but decides against it. A new young man has shown interest in the position and has been given an initial interview that the DDO said went rather well. Whether that happened before or after Jim said he was leaving, he doesn't like to think. At least he's been asked to give Anna's funeral, a request he suspects Elsie was behind.

He goes to say goodbye to Stan but no one answers the door. Sitting on the bench for a moment he toys with the idea of putting a note through the letterbox but eventually gets up and walks away, already thinking of the days ahead. He has heard again from his daughter, who has invited him to stay. He really must go buy a French phrase book, plus a present for his granddaughter. Perhaps a pocket Bible.

Inside, Stan waits for Jim to leave then returns to the living room. Goodbyes are always hard and he senses another significant one approaching.

The abstract blue painting does look impressive on the wall. For a week he's been gazing at it, taking it down, putting it up again. The rowing boat artwork is back in the cupboard under the stairs. Before hiding it away Stan had felt the rough strip where Anna tore the piece off. It's an ugly, gauche artwork and – he agrees – he doesn't need to live with it any more. As for the clothes in the wardrobe upstairs, he has no clue what to do with them. One thing is for certain – he will not apologise to

Judy or beg her to return. He can't regret their fifteen years – they brought him his son – but like he said during their various phone calls, whether she stays is up to her.

'Your stutter is back,' she'd said.

'Y-yes.'

'It suits you in a funny way.'

Their flight returns to Gatwick the following Tuesday. In the meantime he has some painting to do. A canvas requiring layers of paint applied by a thick brush or even by hand.

Later Stan walks up the high street. Village life is already returning to normal – the Robinsons have opened all their windows; lawnmowers hum and fill the air with the scent of fresh grass. He waves to Elsie who's crouched over her geraniums before he turns on to the high street. Kids' screams catch at him but they're just excited, zigzagging across their playground towards their mums who share the latest gossip: another husband is home from the Falklands. 'He's not quite right in the you-know-what,' one woman says, tapping her forehead.

Stan continues towards the church and graveyard. A man is ahead, skittishly crossing the street in front of a car. It's Ralph, out for a walk despite it still being light. He bends to retrieve a milk bottle from beside someone's bin.

Stan is surprised to see him carry on to the graveyard. They both wind up standing in front of Ruth's grave. The mound of grass next to it will soon be prepared, Stan thinks.

'I often come here to stretch my legs,' Ralph says without being asked.

Stan doesn't reply but crouches down to gather up the wilting flowers. He creates a pile to one side, then reaches for the angel and its broken wing. A layer of super glue and they might just fit together again.

'A sorry affair.' Ralph watches from above, still clutching his milk bottle.

'Were you close to Ruth and Anna?' Stan asks to fill the time.

'Oh yes,' he says indignantly. 'I lived across from them for twelve years. Saw curtains closing, opening, all of their routines. It was important to watch Anna ...' He drifts off before speaking again. 'I just wished I had that night she ran away. I was too busy with these damn milk bottles.'

He snatches up a bunch of browning heather. 'Silly that people put these here without any water.' Stan waits as the man heads off towards the tap on the stone wall by the church. A minute later he returns with his milk bottle filled with water. The heather fits nicely inside the glass container that he leaves beside the headstone.

'We all played our part – I certainly did,' Stan says to the man. 'Hopefully we can learn from Anna too.'

Ralph seems unconvinced, but then takes a final look at the milk bottle before turning for the pathway. 'Anyway, I must get home. Cynthia and I have made plans, you see. I'm going to take her out for a birthday dinner. And I'm already an hour late.'

About the Real Fox

Growing up, I heard stories from my parents about the real-life Fox who terrorised the local village and surrounding areas during the summer of 1984. I was born in July that year, in fact, so was just a baby at the time. My sister and I had trouble believing our mum and dad when they talked about borrowing a neighbour's Samurai sword or hiding a pickaxe in their bedroom cupboard. It seemed too bizarre, like the stuff of horror films.

Vigilante groups were set up and word had it that if they caught the Fox he was 'a dead man'. Bars were installed across windows and DIY shops sold out of locks, such was the escalating demand.

> 'On the Saturdays, the gunsmith in Dunstable would sit with his wife explaining to the enormous queue outside the shop that you couldn't just buy a shotgun, that blank-firers don't have much terminal effect, and that an air-rifle might hurt him only badly enough to piss him off and make him retaliate.'

Yet the Fox still managed to get into homes. One family found a hole in their outer wall where an unused central heating outlet had been prised away. Somehow, the bars, traps and patrol groups weren't enough.

It was only later that people found out that the Fox had, in fact, sexually assaulted several men and women. He also stole and fired a shotgun, injuring someone's hand. Before this it hadn't been clear what happened where. In the era before mobile technology, people relied on gossip from neighbours and the weekly local newspaper.

With DNA profiling in its infancy, the police working on the case mostly depended on eyewitness accounts and patrol work. Officers hid in houses and barns trying to catch the Fox. They patrolled local streets at night and stopped people to ask them questions (at the time you could search anyone judged to be acting suspiciously).

The operations room was set up in Dunstable police station where a new computer was brought in to compile databases. At a time when paper log cards were commonly used, this was a novel way to catch a criminal. The computer was in part manned by officers from West Yorkshire who had valuable experience after hunting the Yorkshire Ripper during the late 70s.

Based on reports, the Fox was believed to be between twenty and thirty years old, of slight build and with long, smooth fingers. He was usually masked and said to have a northern accent, possibly Geordie.

During the same period a masked man had broken into houses in the town of Brampton, Yorkshire. It seemed likely that he and the Fox were the same person.

The police traced his tracks across the fields to the M18 motorway and the place where the Fox had left his mask, gloves and gun – all found covered with leaves. There were tyre marks, too, as well as other evidence linking the crime in Yorkshire to those down south.

Next the police had a breakthrough when fragments of paint were discovered on a broken branch, deposited there when the Fox had reversed his car. After being forensically examined, these were found to belong to a British Leyland car, 'Harvest Yellow' in colour. It was simply a matter of finding it among the thousands registered in Britain.

On visiting an address in Kentish Town, London, two officers discovered a man cleaning his yellow Leyland. They saw the scratched paintwork, and in the boot of another car belonging to this man, Malcolm Fairley, they found a pair of overalls with a leg missing – the leg that had been cut up to make a mask, used on some of the offences.

The police 'Foxhunt' was not cheap, costing at least £200,000, for which Bedfordshire was asked to foot the entire bill. (The cost to that county of policing the miners' strike was £800,000.)

'I never wanted to hurt anybody,' Fairley told St Alban's Crown Court at his trial in February 1985. According to his defence barrister he 'had no clear idea of right and wrong'. Fairley reportedly said, 'I wanted to stop it but I couldn't. When I got the gun I felt I could get what I wanted.'

He was given six life sentences for his crimes and was released from prison in 2012 under a new identity. His current whereabouts is unknown.

For many years Fairley lived in my imagination as a strange, lone figure who wanted to be close to people and their everyday lives. (I didn't realise until more recently that he had committed these very serious crimes.) Arguably, he was motivated by more than sexual gratification – often spending long periods in homes without attempting an attack – and it's this question of his psychological complexities that makes him such an unforgettable figure and the inspiration behind this novel.

Police step up hunt for 'Fox' after assaults on three young people

By Stewart Tendler, Crime Reporter

As police patrols searched property and watched the roads of a Chilterns village yesterday the armed man wanted for sexual attacks and burglary, nicknamed "The Fox", evaded their hunt, broke into a house and assaulted three young people. The police had been called to the village of Edlesborough on the Buckinghamshire/Bedfordshire border after a man reported an intruder escaping from his home.

Dozens of armed officers were brought into the area, some with dogs, but three hours later the man broke into a second house 500 yards away.

A girl aged 18 was raped twice and her brother, aged 17, and her boyfriend, aged 21, were also sexually assaulted. They were in the same room when the girl was assaulted by the man, who was armed with a shotgun. All three were also beaten.

The man had become the target of a large police hunt in the Leighton Buzzard area after 25 burglaries in the past four months. During the past eight weeks, however, the search has intensified because the burglaries have become linked with increasing violence.

Earlier this week the man raped a woman aged 35 after her husband had been tied up in their home. Last week he attacked another couple in their house, but fled when the woman removed a gag and screamed.

On Thursday night Det Chief Supt Brian Prickett, head of Bedfordshire CID, appeared on BBC Television's *Crime Watch* programme to appeal for public help.

Yesterday, the police officer said that he did not know whether his appearance had provoked the man into fresh attacks. The police are now being advised by a team of psychiatrists and Mr Prickett said: "I am fearful that the man will commit a murder."

Police advice to potential victims is to obey the man's demands – he never makes any conversation apart from giving orders in a soft northern accent – because of the risk of violence.

The man, about 5ft 9in tall, medium to stocky build, with brown curly hair, pullover and a balaclava helmet, made his first appearance in Earlesborough just after 11pm on Thursday.

Mr and Mrs Michael Jansen were asleep in their home when their pet cocker spaniel barked from downstairs. Mr Jansen, whose two children, a girl and a boy, were also asleep, went downstairs and reached the kitchen just as the man fled through the kitchen door, taking with him a small amount of money.

Mr Jansen later heard a disturbance among horses in a field behind his home. The field leads on to the lane where the attacker struck again at about 2am yesterday.

Mr Prickett said that the second alert was checked out thoroughly and police units were still in the village well after 2am.

They discovered the second attack when the three young people managed to free themselves, after being bound with electrical flex, and raised the alarm. Before leaving their house the man had watched some video films and is thought to have made himself a meal.

In similar attacks on other homes he has also made himself meals and cups f tea, and watched television. But police do not believe he is living rough.

Yesterday, as a police helicopter and light aircraft surveyed the countryside, Mr Prickett said that it was clear the man had good local knowledge. He is believe to be in his early to mid-twenties and may be someone whose family believes he goes to bed each night, when in fact he is out prowling.

Mr Prickett said that further offences were likely. The police have already urged the public to take care, and he acknowledged that local people were growing increasingly upset by the attacks.

The police operation is now a joint one between the Bedfordshire and Thames Valley forces and Bedfordshire police had withdrawn their officers from miners' picket line duty in Nottinghamshire.

Villagers were yesterday angry about the attacks on the three young people.

One, Mrs Edna Grant, aged 73, who lives alone, said: "I am so terrified that I just cannot sleep. Every noise you hear at night is terrifying. He seems to know his way round the village. That is what is worrying us."

One near neighbour, who did not want to be named, said: "We heard nothing until about 3am, when all hell seemed to break loose. There were police everywhere, knocking on doors and searching buildings. The whole idea of what happened is absolutely petrifying."

Manhunt: Police officers, some armed and wearing flak jackets, searching the village of Edlesborough yesterday for a man who has carried out sexual assaults and burglaries

306